O. HENRY is one of the most widely published of modern authors. His works—more than six hundred stories—have been translated into nearly every language. He has often been called "the American De Maupassant" and ranked among the world's outstanding short-story tellers.

Perhaps the best description of O. Henry was given by Bob Davis, editor of *Munsey's Magazine* and one of his closest friends: "I don't believe anyone enjoyed absolute intimacy with him. He was not especially communicative in conversation, although to his readers he gave himself utterly. His shoulders were wide, his carriage erect. His head was massive, the brow broad, and the eyes open. When he laughed his whole face lit up. He spoke with a pronounced Southern accent, combining deliberate gestures with his speech. A better listener than a talker, but a marvelous audience under all circumstances. Where did he learn so much of life? By living it, I suppose. He had considerable of that thing called experience."

THE POCKET BOOK OF

O. HENRY

STORIES

EDITED AND WITH AN INTRODUCTION BY

HARRY HANSEN

WASHINGTON SQUARE PRESS, INC. • NEW YORK

THE POCKET BOOK
of
O. HENRY STORIES

A *Washington Square Press* edition

1st printing......................October, 1948
18th printing....................October, 1967

A new edition of a distinguished literary work now made available in an inexpensive, well-designed format

L

Published by
Washington Square Press, Inc., 630 Fifth Avenue, New York, N.Y.

WASHINGTON SQUARE PRESS editions are distributed in the U.S. by Simon & Schuster, Inc., 630 Fifth Avenue, New York, N.Y. 10020 and in Canada by Simon & Schuster of Canada, Ltd., Richmond Hill, Ontario, Canada.

CONTENTS

A Word About O. Henry

By HARRY HANSEN

FOR nearly fifty years thousands of Americans have found in O. Henry's stories the magic key to their own brand of Arabian Nights Entertainment. In the ten years of his greatest activity, from 1900 to 1910, he wrote nearly 300 stories filled with good-humored comment on the fortunes of men and women, and touched the drab routine of city life with the brush of romance. He wrote when George Ade was creating merriment with his *Fables in Slang*, and Finley Peter Dunne was turning the laugh on politicians with "Mr. Dooley." His popularity has outlasted both. "When I get low-spirited I read O. Henry," said Robert H. Davis, his biographer. Today the desire to read him is as persistent as ever.

O. Henry was the pen name of William Sidney Porter, who was born in Greensboro, N. C., Sept. 11, 1862, and died in New York, June 5, 1910. In later years he spelled his middle name Sydney. His schooling stopped at 15, but not his reading and his eagerness to write. As a lad he worked in a Greensboro drug store, which today celebrates his name. At 19 he went to Texas to live on a sheep ranch and build up his health. He became a good horseman and even a broncho buster before he went to Austin, where for some time he worked in the general land office.

Everything that happened to Porter after he grew aware of the picturesque life around him has filtered into his stories. That is why they are located in the cattle country, Central America and New York. But the stories of city life, for which he is most famous, have in them an acceptance of life's ironies that may reflect his own bitter experiences. In his fifteen years in Texas, during which he married and became the father of a daughter, somber events cast a shadow on his friendly spirit. He had become a teller in a bank and lost his job when his accounts showed irregularities that ran slightly over $1,000. His Austin employers seem to have been reluctant to prosecute him; for nearly a year he worked on a newspaper in Houston unmolested. Then, apparently to avoid arrest by federal authorities, he went to New Orleans and soon after took passage for Trujillo, Honduras, which became the locale for the connected adventures in his first book, *Cabbages and Kings*. He was called back to Austin by the serious illness of his wife, who died soon after his return. He was then tried on a federal charge of embezzlement and convicted.

For three years and three months Will Porter served in an Ohio prison, a helpful prisoner who took his punishment gamely, although ever after it cast a shadow on his life. Out of it came his compassion for under-dogs and some of his best stories, notably "A Retrieved Reformation," which made a national hit as a play called "Alias Jimmy Valentine." His pen name has been traced to the captain of the prison guard, Orrin Henry. Porter thought "O. Henry" sufficient as a signature. When he began writing he asked editors to keep his identity secret.

In New York, O. Henry lived in rooms near Madison Square and in Irving Place and carried on a feverish struggle to pay his bills with money earned by his stories. His friends, Robert H. Davis, Arthur Bartlett Maurice, Irvin S. Cobb and other editors and writers have described his quarters in Irving Place, where he had a front room with windows reaching to the floor; here he would sit and stare at the passers-by, while he wove little nets of adventure around them. He began to put the lonely and hopeful little people into his stories—girls who, he imagined, drifted to the big city eager for love and a career, and became the playthings of fate; young men who looked eagerly for advantages; bums and misfits who accepted adversity with a boastful air and sometimes displayed a sentimental, story-book attitude.

If the plot was tragic, O. Henry spiced the action with a bit of dialect, and nothing was ever so drab that he could not supply a touch of tinsel. It was at this point that he invented the snapper or twist, which gives an unexpected ending to many of his stories. This is best exemplified in the shorter tales, such as "The Furnished Room," "The Skylight Room," and "Springtime à la Carte," but it occurs also in some of the longer ones. It will be recognized as an elaboration of the conventional anecdote that has amused American listeners since the days of the group around the cracker-barrel at the country store. O. Henry was an inventor of plots, fantastic situations in which characters capered rather than lived. His aim was entertainment, and to hold the reader he made his characters perform. He often thought of them as yearning for romance, and so he made them put on a brave front when their fortunes were low, aping the well-to-do and living a sort of modern Arabian Nights atmosphere. And although he rarely described a full-length character or dug deeply into his motives, he visualized him as an individual, part of the vast currents of the city's life. When he was protesting that it would be wrong to call Nancy, of "The Trimmed Lamp," a shopgirl because she worked in a store, he wrote: "There is no type, but a perverse generation is always seeking a type." He rarely made a man so bad that the culprit did not apologize for his shortcomings. Underlying all of O. Henry's stories is this attitude of friendly understanding, a willingness to accept all the waifs and strays as members of the human family. Sometimes O. Henry is amused by them, sometimes ironical, and at times he leans toward the sentimental, but he accepts what fate deals out, and he would rather make a crook ridiculous than vicious.

O. Henry hit his stride in his second book, *The Four Million* (1906), which became widely popular. Forty years after its first publication, "The Gift of the Magi" was produced as a motion picture. Other stories appear in *The Trimmed Lamp* (1907), *Heart of the West* (1907), *The Voice of the City* (1908), *Roads of Destiny* (1909), *Options* (1909), *Strictly Business* (1910), *Whirligigs* (1910), and in *The*

Gentle Grafter, Rolling Stones and *Waifs and Strays,* published after his death.

No formula for storytelling remains unchanged, if the author has vitality and ambition. O. Henry's stories were immensely popular in his lifetime, but there is evidence, both in the final work and in his expressed intentions, that he was dissatisfied with glibness and wanted to dig deeper into human behavior. He wanted to strip a man of his conventional manners and attitudes, for "about the only chance for the truth to be told is in fiction." In reaching this conclusion from his own experience, O. Henry was reiterating the conviction of scholars that the myth reveals more than the historical record. Moreover change was already taking place in storytelling, even among the professed entertainers. Underlying motives of human conduct were being traced to mental and physical vagaries, and the effect of social and economic influences on the individual's course in life was being weighed. What O. Henry might have accomplished cannot be guessed, but it would have been substantial.

Today O. Henry's stories take on the character of period pieces. Just as Bret Harte's stories revive the pioneer West of miners, gamblers and road agents, so O. Henry's tales revive the ways of the early 1900's. When he poked fun at the Gentle Riders, the Rough Riders of the Spanish-American War were fresh in everybody's memory. To Americans the little republics of Central America seemed just as absurd as he described Anchuria; Richard Harding Davis had romanticized their revolutionaries and adventurers. The talk about "tainted money" expressed the growing resentment of the public against immoderate gains by unfair business methods. Perhaps the modern reader will get his biggest kick from the fabulous buying power of money in O. Henry's day. According to one of his stories a dinner of steak with mushrooms cost 50 cents and the more fashionable 60-cent table d'hôte included wine. O. Henry wrote Al Jennings about his first year in New York in 1902 in pleased terms: "I have all the work I can do. Have averaged about $150 per month since Aug. 1."

He was a shy, retiring man who enjoyed a drink and the company of a few intimates, chiefly editors. He was always pressed for time, because the stories he wrote were short and his funds easily exhausted. Editors who clamored for more stories kept him grinding away. To him life was a haphazard business, in which rewards were bestowed erratically, but he looked on its vagaries with a tolerant smile. Luck and chance play a big part in his stories, tragedy enters, but bitterness stays outside. When his career ended with a stroke at 47 some of his best work was still to come, but he had made an indelible impression on the short story and many of his tales will last.

THE POCKET BOOK OF

O. HENRY
STORIES

The Gift of the Magi

ONE dollar and eighty-seven cents. That was all. And sixty cents of it was in pennies. Pennies saved one and two at a time by bulldozing the grocer and the vegetable man and the butcher until one's cheeks burned with the silent imputation of parsimony that such close dealing implied. Three times Della counted it. One dollar and eighty-seven cents. And the next day would be Christmas.

There was clearly nothing to do but flop down on the shabby little couch and howl. So Della did it. Which instigates the moral reflection that life is made up of sobs, sniffles, and smiles, with sniffles predominating.

While the mistress of the home is gradually subsiding from the first stage to the second, take a look at the home. A furnished flat at $8 per week. It did not exactly beggar description, but it certainly had that word on the lookout for the mendicancy squad.

In the vestibule below was a letter-box into which no letter would go, and an electric button from which no mortal finger could coax a ring. Also appertaining thereunto was a card bearing the name "Mr. James Dillingham Young."

The "Dillingham" had been flung to the breeze during a former period of prosperity when its possessor was being paid $30 per week. Now, when the income was shrunk to $20, the letters of "Dillingham" looked blurred, as though they were thinking seriously of contracting to a modest and unassuming D. But whenever Mr. James Dillingham Young came home and reached his flat above he was called "Jim" and greatly hugged by Mrs. James Dillingham Young, already introduced to you as Della. Which is all very good.

Della finished her cry and attended to her cheeks with the powder rag. She stood by the window and looked out dully at a gray cat walking a gray fence in a gray backyard. Tomorrow would be Christmas Day, and she had only $1.87 with which to buy Jim a present. She had been saving every penny she could for months, with this result. Twenty dollars a week doesn't go far. Expenses had been greater than she had calculated. They always are. Only $1.87 to buy a present for Jim. Her Jim. Many a happy hour she had spent planning for something nice for him. Something fine and rare and sterling—something just a little bit near to being worthy of the honor of being owned by Jim.

There was a pier-glass between the windows of the room. Perhaps you have seen a pier-glass in an $8 flat. A very thin and very agile person may, by observing his reflection in a rapid sequence of longitudinal strips, obtain a fairly accurate conception of his looks. Della, being slender, had mastered the art.

Suddenly she whirled from the window and stood before the glass. Her eyes were shining brilliantly, but her face had lost its color within twenty seconds. Rapidly she pulled down her hair and let it fall to its full length.

Now, there were two possessions of the James Dillingham Youngs in which they both took a mighty pride. One was Jim's gold watch that had been his father's and his grandfather's. The other was Della's hair. Had the Queen of Sheba lived in the flat across the airshaft, Della would have let her hair hang out the window some day to dry just to depreciate Her Majesty's jewels and gifts. Had King Solomon been the janitor, with all his treasures piled up in the basement, Jim would have pulled out his watch every time he passed, just to see him pluck at his beard from envy.

So now Della's beautiful hair fell about her rippling and shining like a cascade of brown waters. It reached below her knee and made itself almost a garment for her. And then she did it up again nervously and quickly. Once she faltered for a minute and stood still while a tear or two splashed on the worn red carpet.

On went her old brown jacket; on went her old brown hat. With a whirl of skirts and with the brilliant sparkle still in her eyes, she fluttered out the door and down the stairs to the street.

Where she stopped the sign read: "Mme. Sofronie. Hair Goods of All Kinds." One flight up Della ran, and collected herself, panting. Madame, large, too white, chilly, hardly looked the "Sofronie."

"Will you buy my hair?" asked Della.

"I buy hair," said Madame. "Take yer hat off and let's have a sight at the looks of it."

Down rippled the brown cascade.

"Twenty dollars," said Madame, lifting the mass with a practised hand.

"Give it to me quick," said Della.

Oh, and the next two hours tripped by on rosy wings. Forget the hashed metaphor. She was ransacking the stores for Jim's present.

She found it at last. It surely had been made for Jim and no one else. There was no other like it in any of the stores, and she had turned all of them inside out. It was a platinum fob chain simple and chaste in design, properly proclaiming its value by substance alone and not by meretricious ornamentation—as all good things should do. It was even worthy of The Watch. As soon as she saw it she knew that it must be Jim's. It was like him. Quietness and value—the description applied to both. Twenty-one dollars they took from her for it, and she hurried home with the 87 cents. With that chain on his watch Jim might be properly anxious about the time in any company. Grand as the watch was, he sometimes looked at it on the sly on account of the old leather strap that he used in place of a chain.

When Della reached home her intoxication gave way a little to prudence and reason. She got out her curling irons and lighted the gas and went to work repairing the ravages made by generosity added to love. Which is always a tremendous task, dear friends—a mammoth task.

Within forty minutes her head was covered with tiny,

close-lying curls that made her look wonderfully like a truant schoolboy. She looked at her reflection in the mirror long, carefully, and critically.

"If Jim doesn't kill me," she said to herself, "before he takes a second look at me, he'll say I look like a Coney Island chorus girl. But what could I do—oh! what could I do with a dollar and eighty-seven cents?"

At 7 o'clock the coffee was made and the frying-pan was on the back of the stove hot and ready to cook the chops.

Jim was never late. Della doubled the fob chain in her hand and sat on the corner of the table near the door that he always entered. Then she heard his step on the stair way down on the first flight, and she turned white for just a moment. She had a habit of saying little silent prayers about the simplest everyday things, and now she whispered: "Please God, make him think I am still pretty."

The door opened and Jim stepped in and closed it. He looked thin and very serious. Poor fellow, he was only twenty-two—and to be burdened with a family! He needed a new overcoat and he was without gloves.

Jim stopped inside the door, as immovable as a setter at the scent of quail. His eyes were fixed upon Della, and there was an expression in them that she could not read, and it terrified her. It was not anger, nor surprise, nor disapproval, nor horror, nor any of the sentiments that she had been prepared for. He simply stared at her fixedly with that peculiar expression on his face.

Della wriggled off the table and went for him.

"Jim, darling," she cried, "don't look at me that way. I had my hair cut off and sold it because I couldn't have lived through Christmas without giving you a present. It'll grow out again—you won't mind, will you? I just had to do it. My hair grows awfully fast. Say 'Merry Christmas!' Jim, and let's be happy. You don't know what a nice—what a beautiful, nice gift I've got for you."

"You've cut off your hair?" asked Jim, laboriously, as if he had not arrived at that patent fact yet even after the hardest mental labor.

"Cut it off and sold it," said Della. "Don't you like me just as well, anyhow? I'm me without my hair, ain't I?"

Jim looked about the room curiously.

"You say your hair is gone?" he said, with an air almost of idiocy.

"You needn't look for it," said Della. "It's sold, I tell you—sold and gone, too. It's Christmas Eve, boy. Be good to me, for it went for you. Maybe the hairs of my head were numbered," she went on with a sudden serious sweetness, "but nobody could ever count my love for you. Shall I put the chops on, Jim?"

Out of his trance Jim seemed quickly to wake. He enfolded his Della. For ten seconds let us regard with discreet scrutiny some inconsequential object in the other direction. Eight dollars a week or a million a year—what is the difference? A mathematician or a wit would give you the wrong answer. The magi brought valuable gifts, but that was not among them. This dark assertion will be illuminated later on.

Jim drew a package from his overcoat pocket and threw it upon the table.

"Don't make any mistake, Dell," he said, "about me. I don't think there's anything in the way of a haircut or a shave or a shampoo that could make me like my girl any less. But if you'll unwrap that package you may see why you had me going a while at first."

White fingers and nimble tore at the string and paper. And then an ecstatic scream of joy; and then, alas! a quick feminine change to hysterical tears and wails, necessitating the immediate employment of all the comforting powers of the lord of the flat.

For there lay The Combs—the set of combs, side and back, that Della had worshipped for long in a Broadway window. Beautiful combs, pure tortoise shell, with jewelled rims—just the shade to wear in the beautiful vanished hair. They were expensive combs, she knew, and her heart had simply craved and yearned over them without the least hope of possession. And now, they were hers, but the tresses that should have adorned the coveted adornments were gone.

But she hugged them to her bosom, and at length she was able to look up with dim eyes and a smile and say: "My hair grows so fast, Jim!"

And then Della leaped up like a little singed cat and cried, "Oh, oh!"

Jim had not yet seen his beautiful present. She held it out to him eagerly upon her open palm. The dull precious metal seemed to flash with a reflection of her bright and ardent spirit.

"Isn't it a dandy, Jim? I hunted all over town to find it. You'll have to look at the time a hundred times a day now. Give me your watch. I want to see how it looks on it."

Instead of obeying, Jim tumbled down on the couch and put his hands under the back of his head and smiled.

"Dell," said he, "let's put our Christmas presents away and keep 'em a while. They're too nice to use just at present. I sold the watch to get the money to buy your combs. And now suppose you put the chops on."

The magi, as you know, were wise men—wonderfully wise men—who brought gifts to the Babe in the manger. They invented the art of giving Christmas presents. Being wise, their gifts were no doubt wise ones, possibly bearing the privilege of exchange in case of duplication. And here I have lamely related to you the uneventful chronicle of two foolish children in a flat who most unwisely sacrificed for each other the greatest treasures of their house. But in a last word to the wise of these days let it be said that of all who give gifts these two were the wisest. Of all who give and receive gifts, such as they are wisest. Everywhere they are wisest. They are the magi.

The Skylight Room

FIRST Mrs. Parker would show you the double parlors. You would not dare to interrupt her description of their advantages and of the merits of the gentleman who had occupied them for eight years. Then you would manage to stammer forth the confession that you were neither a doctor nor a dentist. Mrs. Parker's manner of receiving the admission was such that you could never afterward entertain the same feeling toward your parents, who had neglected to train you up in one of the professions that fitted Mrs. Parker's parlors.

Next you ascended one flight of stairs and looked at the second-floor-back at $8. Convinced by her second-floor manner that it was worth the $12 that Mr. Toosenberry always paid for it until he left to take charge of his brother's orange plantation in Florida near Palm Beach, where Mrs. McIntyre always spent the winters that had the double front room with private bath, you managed to babble that you wanted something still cheaper.

If you survived Mrs. Parker's scorn, you were taken to look at Mr. Skidder's large hall room on the third floor. Mr. Skidder's room was not vacant. He wrote plays and smoked cigarettes in it all day long. But every room-hunter was made to visit his room to admire the lambrequins. After each visit, Mr. Skidder, from the fright caused by possible eviction, would pay something on his rent.

Then—oh, then—if you still stood on one foot, with your hot hand clutching the three moist dollars in your pocket, and hoarsely proclaimed your hideous and culpable poverty,

7

nevermore would Mrs. Parker be cicerone of yours. She would honk loudly the word "Clara," she would show you her back, and march downstairs. Then Clara, the colored maid, would escort you up the carpeted ladder that served for the fourth flight, and show you the Skylight Room. It occupied 7 x 8 feet of floor space in the middle of the hall. On each side of it was a dark lumber closet or storeroom.

In it was an iron cot, a washstand and a chair. A shelf was the dresser. Its four bare walls seemed to close in upon you like the sides of a coffin. Your hand crept to your throat, you gasped, you looked up as from a well—and breathed once more. Through the glass of the little skylight you saw a square of blue infinity.

"Two dollars, suh," Clara would say in her half-contemptuous, half-Tuskegeenial tones.

One day Miss Leeson came hunting for a room. She carried a typewriter made to be lugged around by a much larger lady. She was a very little girl, with eyes and hair that had kept on growing after she had stopped and that always looked as if they were saying: "Goodness me! Why didn't you keep up with us?"

Mrs. Parker showed her the double parlors. "In this closet," she said, "one could keep a skeleton or anæsthetic or coal—"

"But I am neither a doctor nor a dentist," said Miss Leeson, with a shiver.

Mrs. Parker gave her the incredulous, pitying, sneering, icy stare that she kept for those who failed to qualify as doctors or dentists, and led the way to the second-floor-back.

"Eight dollars?" said Miss Leeson. "Dear me! I'm not Hetty if I do look green. I'm just a poor little working girl. Show me something higher and lower."

Mr. Skidder jumped and strewed the floor with cigarette stubs at the rap on his door.

"Excuse me, Mr. Skidder," said Mrs. Parker, with her demon's smile at his pale looks. "I didn't know you were in. I asked the lady to have a look at your lambrequins."

"They're too lovely for anything," said Miss Leeson, smiling in exactly the way the angels do.

After they had gone Mr. Skidder got very busy erasing the tall, black-haired heroine from his latest (unproduced) play and inserted a small, roguish one with heavy, bright hair and vivacious features.

"Anna Held'll jump at it," said Mr. Skidder to himself, putting his feet up against the lambrequins and disappearing in a cloud of smoke like an aerial cuttlefish.

Presently the tocsin call of "Clara!" sounded to the world the state of Miss Leeson's purse. A dark goblin seized her, mounted a Stygian stairway, thrust her into a vault with a glimmer of light in its top and muttered the menacing and cabalistic words "two dollars!"

"I'll take it!" sighed Miss Leeson, sinking down upon the squeaky iron bed.

Every day Miss Leeson went out to work. At night she brought home papers with handwriting on them and made copies with her typewriter. Sometimes she had no work at night, and then she would sit on the steps of the high stoop with the other roomers. Miss Leeson was not intended for a skylight room when the plans were drawn for her creation. She was gay-hearted and full of tender, whimsical fancies. Once she let Mr. Skidder read to her three acts of his great (unpublished) comedy, "It's No Kid; or, The Heir of the Subway."

There was rejoicing among the gentlemen roomers whenever Miss Leeson had time to sit on the steps for an hour or two. But Miss Longnecker, the tall blonde who taught in a public school and said, "Well, really!" to everything you said, sat on the top step and sniffed. And Miss Dorn, who shot at the moving ducks at Coney every Sunday and worked in a department store, sat on the bottom step and sniffed. Miss Leeson sat on the middle step and the men would quickly group around her.

Especially Mr. Skidder, who had cast her in his mind for the star part in a private, romantic (unspoken) drama in real life. And especially Mr. Hoover, who was forty-five, fat, flush and foolish. And especially very young Mr. Evans, who set up a hollow cough to induce her to ask him to leave off cigarettes. The men voted her "the funniest and jolliest ever," but the sniffs on the top step and the lower step were implacable.

I pray you let the drama halt while chorus stalks to the footlights and drops an epicidian tear upon the fatness of Mr. Hoover. Tune the pipes to the tragedy of tallow, the bane of bulk, the calamity of corpulence. Tried out, Falstaff might have rendered more romance to the ton than would have Romeo's rickety ribs to the ounce. A lover may sigh, but he must not puff. To the train of Momus are the fat men remanded. In vain beats the faithfullest heart above a 52-inch belt. Avaunt, Hoover! Hoover, forty-five, flush and foolish, might carry off Helen herself; Hoover, forty-five, flush, foolish and fat is meat for perdition. There was never a chance for you, Hoover.

As Mrs. Parker's roomers sat thus one summer's evening, Miss Leeson looked up into the firmament and cried with her little gay laugh:

"Why, there's Billy Jackson! I can see him from down here, too."

All looked up—some at the windows of skyscrapers, some casting about for an airship, Jackson-guided.

"It's that star," explained Miss Leeson, pointing with a tiny finger. "Not the big one that twinkles—the steady blue one near it. I can see it every night through my skylight. I named it Billy Jackson."

"Well, really!" said Miss Longnecker. "I didn't know you were an astronomer, Miss Leeson."

"Oh, yes," said the small star gazer, "I know as much as any of them about the style of sleeves they're going to wear next fall in Mars."

"Well, really!" said Miss Longnecker. "That star you refer to is Gamma, of the constellation Cassiopeia. It is nearly of the second magnitude, and its meridian passage is——"

"Oh," said the very young Mr. Evans, "I think Billy Jackson is a much better name for it."

"Same here," said Mr. Hoover, loudly breathing defiance to Miss Longnecker. "I think Miss Leeson has just as much right to name stars as any of those old astrologers had."

"Well, really!" said Miss Longnecker.

"I wonder whether it's a shooting star," remarked Miss Dorn. "I hit nine ducks and a rabbit out of ten in the gallery at Coney Sunday."

"He doesn't show up very well from down here," said Miss Leeson. "You ought to see him from my room. You know you can see stars even in the daytime from the bottom of a well. At night my room is like the shaft of a coal mine, and it makes Billy Jackson look like the big diamond pin that Night fastens her kimono with."

There came a time after that when Miss Leeson brought no formidable papers home to copy. And when she went out in the morning, instead of working, she went from office to office and let her heart melt away in the drip of cold refusals transmitted through insolent office boys. This went on.

There came an evening when she wearily climbed Mrs. Parker's stoop at the hour when she always returned from her dinner at the restaurant. But she had had no dinner.

As she stepped into the hall Mr. Hoover met her and seized his chance. He asked her to marry him, and his fatness hovered above her like an avalanche. She dodged, and caught the balustrade. He tried for her hand, and she raised it and smote him weakly in the face. Step by step she went up, dragging herself by the railing. She passed Mr. Skidder's door as he was red-inking a stage direction for Myrtle Delorme (Miss Leeson) in his (unaccepted) comedy, to "pirouette across stage from L to the side of the Count." Up the carpeted ladder she crawled at last and opened the door of the skylight room.

She was too weak to light the lamp or to undress. She fell upon the iron cot, her fragile body scarcely hollowing the worn springs. And in that Erebus of a room she slowly raised her heavy eyelids, and smiled.

For Billy Jackson was shining down on her, calm and bright and constant through the skylight. There was no world about her. She was sunk in a pit of blackness, with but that small square of pallid light framing the star that she had so whimsically and oh, so ineffectually, named. Miss Longnecker must be right: It was Gamma, of the constellation Cassiopeia, and not Billy Jackson. And yet she could not let it be Gamma.

As she lay on her back, she tried twice to raise her arm. The third time she got two thin fingers to her lips and blew a kiss out of the black pit to Billy Jackson. Her arm fell back limply.

"Good-bye, Billy," she murmured, faintly. "You're millions of miles away and you won't even twinkle once. But you kept where I could see you most of the time up there when there wasn't anything else but darkness to look at, didn't you? . . . Millions of miles. . . . Good-bye, Billy Jackson."

Clara, the colored maid, found the door locked at 10 the next day, and they forced it open. Vinegar, and the slapping of wrists and burnt feathers proving of no avail, some one ran to 'phone for an ambulance.

In due time it backed up to the door with much gong-clanging, and the capable young medico, in his white linen coat, ready, active, confident, with his smooth face half debonair, half grim, danced up the steps.

"Ambulance call to 49," he said, briefly. "What's the trouble?"

"Oh, yes, doctor," sniffed Mrs. Parker, as though her trouble that there should be trouble in the house was the greater. "I can't think what can be the matter with her. Nothing we could do would bring her to. It's a young woman, a Miss Elsie—yes, a Miss Elsie Leeson. Never before in my house——"

"What room?" cried the doctor in a terrible voice, to which Mrs. Parker was a stranger.

"The skylight room. It——"

Evidently the ambulance doctor was familiar with the location of skylight rooms. He was gone up the stairs, four at a time. Mrs. Parker followed slowly, as her dignity demanded.

On the first landing she met him coming back bearing the astronomer in his arms. He stopped and let loose the practised scalpel of his tongue, not loudly. Gradually Mrs. Parker crumpled as a stiff garment that slips down from a nail. Ever afterwards there remained crumples in her mind and body. Sometimes her curious roomers would ask her what the doctor said to her.

"Let that be," she would answer. "If I can get forgiveness for having heard it I will be satisfied."

The ambulance physician strode with his burden through the pack of hounds that follow the curiosity chase, and even they fell back along the sidewalk abashed, for his face was that of one who bears his own dead.

They noticed that he did not lay down upon the bed prepared for it in the ambulance the form that he carried, and all that he said was: "Drive like h—l, Wilson," to the driver.

That is all. Is it a story? In the next morning's paper I saw a little news item, and the last sentence of it may help you (as it helped me) to weld the incidents together.

It recounted the reception into Bellevue Hospital of a young woman who had been removed from No. 49 East—— Street, suffering from debility induced by starvation. It concluded with these words:

"Dr. William Jackson, the ambulance physician who attended the case, says the patient will recover."

The Cop and the Anthem

ON his bench in Madison Square Soapy moved uneasily. When wild geese honk high of nights, and when women without sealskin coats grow kind to their husbands, and when Soapy moves uneasily on his bench in the park, you may know that winter is near at hand.

A dead leaf fell in Soapy's lap. That was Jack Frost's card. Jack is kind to the regular denizens of Madison Square, and gives fair warning of his annual call. At the corners of four streets he hands his pasteboard to the North Wind, footman of the mansion of All Outdoors, so that the inhabitants thereof may make ready.

Soapy's mind became cognizant of the fact that the time had come for him to resolve himself into a singular Committee of Ways and Means to provide against the coming rigor. And therefore he moved uneasily on his bench.

The hibernatorial ambitions of Soapy were not of the highest. In them were no considerations of Mediterranean cruises, of soporific Southern skies or drifting in the Vesuvian Bay. Three months on the Island was what his soul craved. Three months of assured board and bed and congenial company, safe from Boreas and bluecoats, seemed to Soapy the essence of things desirable.

For years the hospitable Blackwell's had been his winter quarters. Just as his more fortunate fellow New Yorkers had bought their tickets to Palm Beach and the Riviera each winter, so Soapy had made his humble arrangements for his annual hegira to the Island. And now the time was come. On the previous night three Sabbath newspapers, distrib-

14

uted beneath his coat, about his ankles and over his lap, had failed to repulse the cold as he slept on his bench near the spurting fountain in the ancient square. So the Island loomed big and timely in Soapy's mind. He scorned the provisions made in the name of charity for the city's dependents. In Soapy's opinion the Law was more benign than Philanthropy. There was an endless round of institutions, municipal and eleemosynary, on which he might set out and receive lodging and food accordant with the simple life. But to one of Soapy's proud spirit the gifts of charity are encumbered. If not in coin you must pay in humiliation of spirit for every benefit received at the hands of philanthropy. As Cæsar had his Brutus, every bed of charity must have its toll of a bath, every loaf of bread its compensation of a private and personal inquisition. Wherefore it is better to be a guest of the law, which, though conducted by rules, does not meddle unduly with a gentleman's private affairs.

Soapy, having decided to go to the Island, at once set about accomplishing his desire. There were many easy ways of doing this. The pleasantest was to dine luxuriously at some expensive restaurant; and then, after declaring insolvency, be handed over quietly and without uproar to a policeman. An accommodating magistrate would do the rest.

Soapy left his bench and strolled out of the square and across the level sea of asphalt, where Broadway and Fifth Avenue flow together. Up Broadway he turned, and halted at a glittering café, where are gathered together nightly the choicest products of the grape, the silkworm, and the protoplasm.

Soapy had confidence in himself from the lowest button of his vest upward. He was shaven, and his coat was decent and his neat black, ready-tied four-in-hand had been presented to him by a lady missionary on Thanksgiving Day. If he could reach a table in the restaurant unsuspected success would be his. The portion of him that would show above the table would raise no doubt in the waiter's mind. A roasted mallard duck, thought Soapy, would be about the thing—with a bottle of Chablis, and then Camembert, a demi-tasse and a cigar. One dollar for the cigar would be enough. The total would not be so high as to call forth any supreme manifestation of revenge from the café management; and yet the meat would leave him filled and happy for the journey to his winter refuge.

But as Soapy set foot inside the restaurant door the head waiter's eye fell upon his frayed trousers and decadent shoes. Strong and ready hands turned him about and conveyed him in silence and haste to the sidewalk and averted the ignoble fate of the menaced mallard.

Soapy turned off Broadway. It seemed that his route to the coveted Island was not to be an epicurean one. Some other way of entering limbo must be thought of.

At a corner of Sixth Avenue electric lights and cunningly displayed wares behind plate-glass made a shop window conspicuous. Soapy took a cobblestone and dashed it through the glass. People came running around the corner, a policeman in the lead. Soapy stood still, with his hands in his pockets, and smiled at the sight of brass buttons.

"Where's the man that done that?" inquired the officer, excitedly.

"Don't you figure out that I might have had something to do with it?" said Soapy, not without sarcasm, but friendly, as one greets good fortune.

The policeman's mind refused to accept Soapy even as a clue. Men who smash windows do not remain to parley with the law's minions. They take to their heels. The policeman saw a man halfway down the block running to catch a car. With drawn club he joined in the pursuit. Soapy, with disgust in his heart, loafed along, twice unsuccessful.

On the opposite side of the street was a restaurant of no great pretensions. It catered to large appetites and modest purses. Its crockery and atmosphere were thick; its soup and napery thin. Into this place Soapy took his accusive shoes and telltale trousers without challenge. At a table he sat and consumed beefsteak, flapjacks, doughnuts and pie. And then to the waiter he betrayed the fact that the minutest coin and himself were strangers.

"Now, get busy and call a cop," said Soapy. "And don't keep a gentleman waiting."

"No cop for youse," said the waiter, with a voice like butter cakes and an eye like the cherry in a Manhattan cocktail. "Hey, Con!"

Neatly upon his left ear on the callous pavement two waiters pitched Soapy. He arose joint by joint, as a carpenter's rule opens, and beat the dust from his clothes. Arrest seemed but a rosy dream. The Island seemed very far away. A policeman who stood before a drug store two doors away laughed and walked down the street.

Five blocks Soapy travelled before his courage permitted him to woo capture again. This time the opportunity presented what he fatuously termed to himself a "cinch." A young woman of a modest and pleasing guise was standing before a show window gazing with sprightly interest at its display of shaving mugs and ink-stands, and two yards from the window a large policeman of severe demeanor leaned against a water plug.

It was Soapy's design to assume the rôle of the despicable and execrated "masher." The refined and elegant appearance of his victim and the contiguity of the conscientious cop encouraged him to believe that he would soon feel the pleasant official clutch upon his arm that would insure his winter quarters on the right little, tight little isle.

Soapy straightened the lady missionary's ready-made tie, dragged his shrinking cuffs into the open, set his hat at a killing cant and sidled toward the young woman. He made eyes at her, was taken with sudden coughs and "hems," smiled, smirked and went brazenly through the impudent and contemptible litany of the "masher." With half an eye Soapy saw that the policeman was watching him fixedly. The young woman moved away a few steps, and again bestowed her absorbed attention upon the shaving mugs. Soapy followed, boldly stepping to her side, raised his hat and said:

"Ah there, Bedelia! Don't you want to come and play in my yard?"

The policeman was still looking. The persecuted young woman had but to beckon a finger and Soapy would be practically en route for his insular haven. Already he imagined he could feel the cozy warmth of the station-house. The young woman faced him and, stretching out a hand, caught Soapy's coat sleeve.

"Sure, Mike," she said, joyfully, "if you'll blow me to a pail of suds. I'd have spoke to you sooner, but the cop was watching."

With the young woman playing the clinging ivy to his oak Soapy walked past the policeman overcome with gloom. He seemed doomed to liberty.

At the next corner he shook off his companion and ran. He halted in the district where by night are found the lightest streets, hearts, vows and librettos. Women in furs and men in greatcoats moved gaily in the wintry air. A sudden fear seized Soapy that some dreadful enchantment had rendered him immune to arrest. The thought brought a little of panic upon it, and when he came upon another policeman lounging grandly in front of a transplendent theatre he caught at the immediate straw of "disorderly conduct."

On the sidewalk Soapy began to yell drunken gibberish at the top of his harsh voice. He danced, howled, raved, and otherwise disturbed the welkin.

The policeman twirled his club, turned his back to Soapy and remarked to a citizen.

" 'Tis one of them Yale lads celebratin' the goose egg they give to the Hartford College. Noisy; but no harm. We've instructions to lave them be."

Disconsolate, Soapy ceased his unavailing racket. Would never a policeman lay hands on him? In his fancy the Island seemed an unattainable Arcadia. He buttoned his thin coat against the chilling wind.

In a cigar store he saw a well-dressed man lighting a cigar at a swinging light. His silk umbrella he had set by the door on entering. Soapy stepped inside, secured the umbrella and sauntered off with it slowly. The man at the cigar light followed hastily.

"My umbrella," he said, sternly.

"Oh, is it?" sneered Soapy, adding insult to petit larceny. "Well, why don't you call a policeman? I took it. Your umbrella! Why don't you call a cop? There stands one on the corner."

The umbrella owner slowed his steps. Soapy did likewise, with a presentiment that luck would again run against him. The policeman looked at the two curiously.

"Of course," said the umbrella man—"that is—well, you know how these mistakes occur—I—if it's your umbrella I hope you'll excuse me—I picked it up this morning in a restaurant—If you recognize it as yours, why—I hope you'll——"

"Of course it's mine," said Soapy, viciously.

The ex-umbrella man retreated. The policeman hurried to assist a tall blonde in an opera cloak across the street in front of a street car that was approaching two blocks away.

Soapy walked eastward through a street damaged by improvements. He hurled the umbrella wrathfully into an excavation. He muttered against the men who wear helmets and carry clubs. Because he wanted to fall into their clutches, they seemed to regard him as a king who could do no wrong.

At length Soapy reached one of the avenues to the east where the glitter and turmoil was but faint. He set his face down this toward Madison Square, for the homing instinct survives even when the home is a park bench.

But on an unusually quiet corner Soapy came to a standstill. Here was an old church, quaint and rambling and gabled. Through one violet-stained window a soft light glowed, where, no doubt, the organist loitered over the keys, making sure of his mastery of the coming Sabbath anthem. For there drifted out to Soapy's ears sweet music that caught and held him transfixed against the convolutions of the iron fence.

The moon was above, lustrous and serene; vehicles and pedestrians were few; sparrows twittered sleepily in the eaves—for a little while the scene might have been a country churchyard. And the anthem that the organist played cemented Soapy to the iron fence, for he had known it well in the days when his life contained such things as mothers and roses and ambitions and friends and immaculate thoughts and collars.

The conjunction of Soapy's receptive state of mind and the influences about the old church wrought a sudden and wonderful change in his soul. He viewed with swift horror the pit into which he had tumbled, the degraded days, unworthy desires, dead hopes, wrecked faculties and base motives that made up his existence.

And also in a moment his heart responded thrillingly to this novel mood. An instantaneous and strong impulse moved him to battle with his desperate fate. He would pull himself out of the mire; he would make a man of himself again; he would conquer the evil that had taken possession of him. There was time; he was comparatively young yet; he would resurrect his old eager ambitions and pursue them without faltering. Those solemn but sweet organ notes had set up a revolution in him. To-morrow he would go into the roaring downtown district and find work. A fur importer had once offered him a place as driver. He would find him to-morrow and ask for the position. He would be somebody in the world. He would——

Soapy felt a hand laid on his arm. He looked quickly around into the broad face of a policeman.

"What are you doin' here?" asked the officer.

"Nothin'," said Soapy.

"Then come along," said the policeman.

"Three months on the Island," said the Magistrate in the Police Court the next morning.

Memoirs of a Yellow Dog

~~~~~~

I DON'T suppose it will knock any of you people off your perch to read a contribution from an animal. Mr. Kipling and a good many others have demonstrated the fact that animals can express themselves in remunerative English, and no magazine goes to press nowadays without an animal story in it, except the old-style monthlies that are still running pictures of Bryan and the Mont Pelée horror.

But you needn't look for any stuck-up literature in my piece, such as Bearoo, the bear, and Snakoo, the snake, and Tammanoo, the tiger, talk in the jungle books. A yellow dog that's spent most of his life in a cheap New York flat, sleeping in a corner on an old sateen underskirt (the one she spilled port wine on at the Lady Longshoremen's banquet), mustn't be expected to perform any tricks with the art of speech.

I was born a yellow pup; date, locality, pedigree and weight unknown. The first thing I can recollect, an old woman had me in a basket at Broadway and Twenty-third trying to sell me to a fat lady. Old Mother Hubbard was boosting me to beat the band as a genuine Pomeranian-Hambletonian-Red-Irish-Cochin-China-Stoke-Poges fox terrier. The fat lady chased a V around among the samples of grosgrain flannelette in her shopping bag till she cornered it, and gave up. From that moment I was a pet—a mamma's own wootsey squidlums. Say, gentle reader, did you ever have a 200-pound woman breathing a flavor of Camembert cheese and Peau d'Espagne pick you up and wallop her nose all over you, remarking all the time in an Emma Eames tone of voice: "Oh, oo's um oodlum, doodlum, woodlum, toodlum, bitsy-witsy skoodlums?"

From pedigreed yellow pup I grew up to be an anonymous yellow cur looking like a cross between an Angora cat and a box of lemons. But my mistress never tumbled. She thought that the two primeval pups that Noah chased into the ark were but a collateral branch of my ancestors. It took two policemen to keep her from entering me at the Madison Square Garden for the Siberian bloodhound prize.

I'll tell you about that flat. The house was the ordinary thing in New York, paved with Parian marble in the entrance hall and cobblestones above the first floor. Our flat was three—well, not flights—climbs up. My mistress rented it unfurnished, and put in the regular things—1903 antique upholstered parlor set, oil chromo of geishas in a Harlem tea house, rubber plant and husband.

By Sirius! there was a biped I felt sorry for. He was a little man with sandy hair and whiskers a good deal like mine. Henpecked?—well, toucans and flamingoes and pelicans all had their bills in him. He wiped the dishes and listened to my mistress tell about the cheap, ragged things the lady with the squirrel-skin coat on the second floor hung out on her line to dry. And every evening while she was getting supper she made him take me out on the end of a string for a walk.

If men knew how women pass the time when they are alone they'd never marry. Laura Lean Jibbey, peanut brittle, a little almond cream on the neck muscles, dishes unwashed, half an hour's talk with the iceman, reading a package of old letters, a couple of pickles and two bottles of malt extract, one hour peeking through a hole in the window shade into the flat across the airshaft—that's about all there is to it. Twenty minutes before time for him to come home from work she straightens up the house, fixes her rat so it won't show, and gets out a lot of sewing for a ten-minute bluff.

I led a dog's life in that flat. 'Most all day I lay there in my corner watching that fat woman kill time. I slept sometimes and had pipe dreams about being out chasing cats into basements and growling at old ladies with black mittens, as a dog was intended to do. Then she would pounce upon me with a lot of that drivelling poodle palaver and kiss me on the nose—but what could I do? A dog can't chew cloves.

I began to feel sorry for Hubby, dog my cats if I didn't. We looked so much alike that people noticed it when we went out; so we shook the streets that Morgan's cab drives down, and took to climbing the piles of last December's snow on the streets where cheap people live.

One evening when we were thus promenading, and I was trying to look like a prize St. Bernard, and the old man was trying to look like he wouldn't have murdered the first organ-grinder he heard play Mendelssohn's wedding-march, I looked up at him and said, in my way:

"What are you looking so sour about, you oakum trimmed lobster? She don't kiss you. You don't have to sit on her lap and listen to talk that would make the book of a musical comedy sound like the maxims of Epictetus. You ought to be thankful you're not a dog. Brace up, Benedick, and bid the blues begone."

The matrimonial mishap looked down at me with almost canine intelligence in his face.

"Why, doggie," says he, "good doggie. You almost look like you could speak. What is it, doggie—Cats."

Cats! Could speak!

But, of course, he couldn't understand. Humans were denied the speech of animals. The only common ground of communication upon which dogs and men can get together is in fiction.

In the flat across the hall from us lived a lady with a black-and-tan terrier. Her husband strung it and took it out every evening, but he always came home cheerful and whistling. One day I touched noses with the black-and-tan in the hall, and I struck him for an elucidation.

"See here, Wiggle-and-Skip," I says, "you know that it ain't the nature of a real man to play dry nurse to a dog in public. I never saw one leashed to a bow-wow yet that didn't look like he'd like to lick every other man that looked at him. But your boss comes in every day as perky and set up as an amateur prestidigitator doing the egg trick. How does he do it? Don't tell me he likes it."

"Him?" says the black-and-tan. "Why, he uses Nature's Own Remedy. He gets spifflicated. At first when we go out he's as shy as the man on the steamer who would rather play pedro when they make 'em all jackpots. By the time we've been in eight saloons he don't care whether the thing on the end of his line is a dog or a catfish. I've lost two inches of my tail trying to sidestep those swinging doors."

The pointer I got from that terrier—vaudeville please copy —set me to thinking.

One evening about 6 o'clock my mistress ordered him to get busy and do the ozone act for Lovey. I have concealed it until now, but that is what she called me. The black-and-tan was called "Tweetness." I consider that I have the bulge on him as far as you could chase a rabbit. Still "Lovey" is something of a nomenclatural tin can on the tail of one's self-respect.

At a quiet place on a safe street I tightened the line of my custodian in front of an attractive, refined saloon. I made a dead-ahead scramble for the doors, whining like a dog in the press despatches that lets the family know that little Alice is bogged while gathering lilies in the brook.

"Why, darn my eyes," says the old man, with a grin; "darn my eyes if the saffron-colored son of a seltzer lemonade ain't asking me in to take a drink. Lemme see—how long's it been since I saved shoe leather by keeping one foot on the foot-rest? I believe I'll——"

I knew I had him. Hot Scotches he took, sitting at a table. For an hour he kept the Campbells coming. I sat by his side rapping for the waiter with my tail, and eating free lunch such as mamma in her flat never equalled with her homemade truck bought at a delicatessen store eight minutes before papa comes home.

When the products of Scotland were all exhausted except the rye bread the old man unwound me from the table leg

and played me outside like a fisherman plays a salmon.
Out there he took off my collar and threw it into the street.

"Poor doggie," says he; "good doggie. She shan't kiss you
any more. 'S a darned shame. Good doggie, go away and get
run over by a street car and be happy."

I refused to leave. I leaped and frisked around the old
man's legs happy as a pug on a rug.

"You old flea-headed woodchuck-chaser," I said to him—
"you moon-baying, rabbit-pointing, egg-stealing old beagle,
can't you see that I don't want to leave you? Can't you see
that we're both Pups in the Wood and the missis is the cruel
uncle after you with the dish towel and me with the flea
liniment and pink bow to tie on my tail. Why not cut that
all out and be pards forever more?"

Maybe you'll say he didn't understand—maybe he didn't.
But he kind of got a grip on the Hot Scotches, and stood still
for a minute, thinking.

"Doggie," says he, finally, "we don't live more than a dozen
lives on this earth, and very few of us live to be more than
300. If I ever see that flat any more I'm a flat, and if you do
you're flatter; and that's no flattery. I'm offering 60 to 1 that
Westward Ho wins out by the length of a dachshund."

There was no string, but I frolicked along with my master
to the Twenty-third Street ferry. And the cats on the route
saw reason to give thanks that prehensile claws had been
given to them.

On the Jersey side my master said to a stranger who stood
eating a currant bun:

"Me and my doggie, we are bound for the Rocky Mountains."

But what pleased me most was when my old man pulled
both of my ears until I howled, and said:

"You common, monkey-headed, rat-tailed, sulphur-colored
son of a door mat, do you know what I'm going to call you?"

I thought of "Lovey," and I whined dolefully.

"I'm going to call you 'Pete,'" says my master; and if I'd
had five tails I couldn't have done enough wagging to do
justice to the occasion.

Springtime à la Carte

~~~~~~

IT was a day in March.

Never, never begin a story this way when you write one. No opening could possibly be worse. It is unimaginative, flat, dry, and likely to consist of mere wind. But in this instance it is allowable. For the following paragraph, which should have inaugurated the narrative, is too wildly extravagant and preposterous to be flaunted in the face of the reader without preparation.

Sarah was crying over her bill of fare.

Think of a New York girl shedding tears on the menu card!

To account for this you will be allowed to guess that the lobsters were all out, or that she had sworn ice-cream off during Lent, or that she had ordered onions, or that she had just come from a Hackett matinée. And then, all these theories being wrong, you will please let the story proceed.

The gentleman who announced that the world was an oyster which he with his sword would open made a larger hit than he deserved. It is not difficult to open an oyster with a sword. But did you ever notice any one try to open the terrestrial bivalve with a typewriter? Like to wait for a dozen raw opened that way?

Sarah had managed to pry apart the shells with her unhandy weapon far enough to nibble a wee bit at the cold and clammy world within. She knew no more shorthand than if she had been a graduate in stenography just let slip upon the world by a business college. So, not being able to stenog, she could not enter that bright galaxy of office talent. She was a free-lance typist and canvassed for odd jobs of copying.

The most brilliant and crowning feat of Sarah's battle with the world was the deal she made with Schulenberg's Home Restaurant. The restaurant was next door to the old red brick in which she hall-roomed. One evening after dining at Schulenberg's 40-cent, five-course *table d'hôte* (served as fast as you throw the five baseballs at the colored gentleman's head) Sarah took away with her the bill of fare. It was written in an almost unreadable script neither English nor German, and so arranged that if you were not careful you began with a toothpick and rice pudding and ended with soup and the day of the week.

The next day Sarah showed Schulenberg a neat card on which the menu was beautifully typewritten with the viands temptingly marshalled under their right and proper heads from "hors d'œuvre" to "not responsible for over-coats and umbrellas."

Schulenberg became a naturalized citizen on the spot. Before Sarah left him she had him willingly committed to an agreement. She was to furnish typewritten bills of fare for the twenty-one tables in the restaurant—a new bill for each day's dinner, and new ones for breakfast and lunch as often as changes occurred in the food or as neatness required.

In return for this Schulenberg was to send three meals per diem to Sarah's hall room by a waiter—an obsequious one if possible—and furnish her each afternoon with a pencil draft of what Fate had in store for Schulenberg's customers on the morrow.

Mutual satisfaction resulted from the agreement. Schulenberg's patrons now knew what the food they ate was called even if its nature sometimes puzzled them. And Sarah had food during a cold, dull winter, which was the main thing with her.

And then the almanac lied, and said that spring had come. Spring comes when it comes. The frozen snows of January still lay like adamant in the cross-town streets. The hand-organs still played "In the Good Old Summertime," with their December vivacity and expression. Men began to make thirty-day notes to buy Easter dresses. Janitors shut off steam. And when these things happen one may know that the city is still in the clutches of winter.

One afternoon Sarah shivered in her elegant hall bedroom; "house heated; scrupulously clean; conveniences; seen to be appreciated." She had no work to do except Schulenberg's menu cards. Sarah sat in her squeaky willow rocker, and looked out the window. The calendar on the wall kept crying to her: "Springtime is here, Sarah—springtime is here, I tell you. Look at me, Sarah, my figures show it. You've got a neat figure yourself, Sarah—a—nice springtime figure—why do you look out the window so sadly?"

Sarah's room was at the back of the house. Looking out the window she could see the windowless rear brick wall of the box factory on the next street. But the wall was clearest crystal; and Sarah was looking down a grassy lane shaded with cherry trees and elms and bordered with raspberry bushes and Cherokee roses.

Spring's real harbingers are too subtle for the eye and ear. Some must have the flowering crocus, the wood-starring dogwood, the voice of bluebird—even so gross a reminder as the farewell handshake of the retiring buckwheat and oyster before they can welcome the Lady in Green to their dull bosoms. But to old earth's choicest kind there come straight, sweet messages from his newest bride, telling them they shall be no stepchildren unless they choose to be.

On the previous summer Sarah had gone into the country and loved a farmer.

(In writing your story never hark back thus. It is bad art, and cripples interest. Let it march, march.)

Sarah stayed two weeks at Sunnybrook Farm. There she learned to love old Farmer Franklin's son Walter. Farmers have been loved and wedded and turned out to grass in less time. But young Walter Franklin was a modern agriculturist. He had a telephone in his cow house, and he could figure up exactly what effect next year's Canada wheat crop would have on potatoes planted in the dark of the moon.

It was in this shaded and raspberried lane that Walter had wooed and won her. And together they had sat and woven a crown of dandelions for her hair. He had immoderately praised the effect of the yellow blossoms against her brown tresses; and she had left the chaplet there, and walked back to the house swinging her straw sailor in her hands.

They were to marry in the spring—at the very first signs of spring, Walter said. And Sarah came back to the city to pound her typewriter.

A knock at the door dispelled Sarah's visions of that happy day. A waiter had brought the rough pencil draft of the Home Restaurant's next day fare in old Schulenberg's angular hand.

Sarah sat down to her typewriter and slipped a card between the rollers. She was a nimble worker. Generally in an hour and a half the twenty-one menu cards were written and ready.

To-day there were more changes on the bill of fare than usual. The soups were lighter; pork was eliminated from the entrées, figuring only with Russian turnips among the roasts. The gracious spirit of spring pervaded the entire menu. Lamb, that lately capered on the greening hillsides, was becoming exploited with the sauce that commemorated its gambols. The song of the oyster, though not silenced, was *diminuendo con amore*. The frying-pan seemed to be held, inactive, behind the beneficent bars of the broiler. The pie list swelled; the richer puddings had vanished; the sausage, with his drapery wrapped about him, barely lingered in a pleasant thanatopsis with the buckwheats and the sweet but doomed maple.

Sarah's fingers danced like midgets above a summer stream. Down through the courses she worked, giving each item its position according to its length with an accurate eye.

Just above the desserts came the list of vegetables. Carrots and peas, asparagus on toast, the perennial tomatoes and corn and succotash, lima beans, cabbage—and then——

Sarah was crying over her bill of fare. Tears from the depths of some divine despair rose in her heart and gathered

to her eyes. Down went her head on the little typewriter
stand; and the keyboard rattled a dry accompaniment to her
moist sobs.

For she had received no letter from Walter in two weeks,
and the next item on the bill of fare was dandelions—dandelions with some kind of egg—but bother the egg!—dandelions, with whose golden blooms Walter had crowned her
his queen of love and future bride—dandelions, the harbingers
of spring, her sorrow's crown of sorrow—reminder of her
happiest days.

Madam, I dare you to smile until you suffer this test:
Let the Marechal Niel roses that Percy brought you on
the night you gave him your heart be served as a salad with
French dressing before your eyes at a Schulenberg *table
d'hôte*. Had Juliet so seen her love tokens dishonored the
sooner would she have sought the lethean herbs of the good
apothecary.

But what witch is Spring! Into the great cold city of stone
and iron a message had to be sent. There was none to convey
it but the little hardy courier of the fields with his rough
green coat and modest air. He is a true soldier of fortune, this
dent-de-lion—this lion's tooth, as the French chefs call him.
Flowered, he will assist at love-making, wreathed in my
lady's nut-brown hair; young and callow and unblossomed,
he goes into the boiling pot and delivers the word of his
sovereign mistress.

By and by Sarah forced back her tears. The cards must
be written. But, still in a faint, golden glow from her dan-
delion dream, she fingered the typewriter keys absently for
a little while, with her mind and heart in the meadow lane
with her young farmer. But soon she came swiftly back
to the rock-bound lanes of Manhattan, and the typewriter
began to rattle and jump like a strike-breaker's motor car.

At 6 o'clock the waiter brought her dinner and carried
away the typewritten bill of fare. When Sarah ate she set
aside, with a sigh, the dish of dandelions with its crowning
ovarious accompaniment. As this dark mass had been trans-
formed from a bright and love-indorsed flower to be an ig-

nominious vegetable, so had her summer hopes wilted and perished. Love may, as Shakespeare said, feed on itself: but Sarah could not bring herself to eat the dandelions that had graced, as ornaments, the first spiritual banquet of her heart's true affection.

At 7:30 the couple in the next room began to quarrel; the man in the room above sought for A on his flute; the gas went a little lower; three coal wagons started to unload— the only sound of which the phonograph is jealous; cats on the back fences slowly retreated toward Mukden. By these signs Sarah knew that it was time for her to read. She got out "The Cloister and the Hearth," the best non-selling book of the month, settled her feet on her trunk, and began to wander with Gerard.

The front door bell rang. The landlady answered it. Sarah left Gerard and Denys treed by a bear and listened. Oh, yes; you would, just as she did!

And then a strong voice was heard in the hall below, and Sarah jumped for her door, leaving the book on the floor and the first round easily the bear's.

You have guessed it. She reached the top of the stairs just as her farmer came up, three at a jump, and reaped and garnered her, with nothing left for the gleaners.

"Why haven't you written—oh, why?" cried Sarah.

"New York is a pretty large town," said Walter Franklin. "I came in a week ago to your old address. I found that you went away on a Thursday. That consoled some; it eliminated the possible Friday bad luck. But it didn't prevent my hunting for you with police and otherwise ever since!"

"I wrote!" said Sarah, vehemently.

"Never got it!"

"Then how did you find me?"

The young farmer smiled a springtime smile.

"I dropped into that Home Restaurant next door this evening," said he. "I don't care who knows it; I like a dish of some kind of greens at this time of the year. I ran my eye down that nice typewritten bill of fare looking for something in that line. When I got below cabbage I turned my chair over and hollered for the proprietor. He told me where you lived."

"I remember," sighed Sarah, happily. "That was dande-lions below cabbage."

"I'd know that cranky capital W 'way above the line that your typewriter makes anywhere in the world," said Franklin.

"Why, there's no W in dandelions," said Sarah in surprise.

The young man drew the bill of fare from his pocket and pointed to a line.

Sarah recognised the first card she had typewritten that afternoon. There was still the rayed splotch in the upper right-hand corner where a tear had fallen. But over the spot where one should have read the name of the meadow plant, the clinging memory of their golden blossoms had allowed her fingers to strike strange keys.

Between the red cabbage and the stuffed green peppers was the item:

"DEAREST WALTER, WITH HARD-BOILED EGG."

The Green Door

SUPPOSE you should be walking down Broadway after dinner, with ten minutes allotted to the consummation of your cigar while you are choosing between a diverting trag-edy and something serious in the way of vaudeville. Suddenly a hand is laid upon your arm. You turn to look into the thrill-ing eyes of a beautiful woman, wonderful in diamonds and Russian sables. She thrusts hurriedly into your hand an ex-tremely hot buttered roll, flashes out a tiny pair of scissors, snips off the second button of your overcoat, meaningly ejaculates the one word, "parallelogram!" and swiftly flies down a cross street, looking back fearfully over her shoulder.

That would be pure adventure. Would you accept it? Not you. You would flush with embarrassment; you would sheepishly drop the roll and continue down Broadway, fumbling feebly for the missing button. This you would do unless you are one of the blessed few in whom the pure spirit of adventure is not dead.

True adventurers have never been plentiful. They who are set down in print as such have been mostly business men with newly invented methods. They have been out after the things they wanted—golden fleeces, holy grails, lady loves, treasure, crowns and fame. The true adventurer goes forth aimless and uncalculating to meet and greet unknown fate. A fine example was the Prodigal Son—when he started back home.

Half-adventurers—brave and splendid figures—have been numerous. From the Crusades to the Palisades they have enriched the arts of history and fiction and the trade of historical fiction. But each of them had a prize to win, a goal to kick, an axe to grind, a race to run, a new thrust in tierce to deliver, a name to carve, a crow to pick—so they were not followers of true adventure.

In the big city the twin spirits Romance and Adventure are always abroad seeking worthy wooers. As we roam the streets they slyly peep at us and challenge us in twenty different guises. Without knowing why, we look up suddenly to see in a window a face that seems to belong to our gallery of intimate portraits; in a sleeping thoroughfare we hear a cry of agony and fear coming from an empty and shuttered house; instead of at our familiar curb a cab-driver deposits us before a strange door, which one, with a smile, opens for us and bids us enter; a slip of paper, written upon, flutters down to our feet from the high lattices of Chance; we exchange glances of instantaneous hate, affection, and fear with hurrying strangers in the passing crowds; a sudden souse of rain—and our umbrella may be sheltering the daughter of the Full Moon and first cousin of the Sidereal System; at every corner handkerchiefs drop, fingers beckon, eyes besiege, and the lost, the lonely, the rapturous, the

mysterious, the perilous changing clues of adventure are
slipped into our fingers. But few of us are willing to hold
and follow them. We are grown stiff with the ramrod of
convention down our backs. We pass on; and some day we
come, at the end of a very dull life, to reflect that our romance has been a pallid thing of a marriage or two, a satin
rosette kept in a safe-deposit drawer, and a lifelong feud with
a steam radiator.

Rudolf Steiner was a true adventurer. Few were the evenings on which he did not go forth from his hall bedchamber
in search of the unexpected and the egregious. The most
interesting thing in life seemed to him to be what might lie
just around the next corner. Sometimes his willingness to
tempt fate led him into strange paths. Twice he had spent
the night in a station-house; again and again he had found
himself the dupe of ingenious and mercenary tricksters; his
watch and money had been the price of one flattering allure-
ment. But with undiminished ardor he picked up every glove
cast before him into the merry lists of adventure.

One evening Rudolf was strolling along a cross-town street
in the older central part of the city. Two streams of people
filled the sidewalks—the home-hurrying, and that restless contingent that abandons home for the specious welcome of the
thousand-candle-power *table d'hôte*.

The young adventurer was of pleasing presence, and
moved serenely and watchfully. By daylight he was a salesman in a piano store. He wore his tie drawn through a topaz
ring instead of fastened with a stick pin; and once he had
written to the editor of a magazine that "Junie's Love Test,"
by Miss Libbey, had been the book that had most influenced
his life.

During his walk a violent chattering of teeth in a glass
case on the sidewalk seemed at first to draw his attention
(with a qualm) to a restaurant before which it was set;
but a second glance revealed the electric letters of a dentist's sign high above the next door. A giant Negro, fantastically dressed in a red embroidered coat, yellow trousers

and a military cap, discreetly distributed cards to those of the passing crowd who consented to take them.

This mode of dentistic advertising was a common sight to Rudolf. Usually he passed the dispenser of the dentist's cards without reducing his store; but to-night the African slipped one into his hand so deftly that he retained it there smiling a little at the successful feat.

When he had travelled a few yards further he glanced at the card indifferently. Surprised, he turned it over and looked again with interest. One side of the card was blank; on the other was written in ink three words, "The Green Door." And then Rudolf saw, three steps in front of him, a man throw down the card the Negro had given him as he passed. Rudolf picked it up. It was printed with the dentist's name and address and the usual schedule of "plate work" and "bridge work" and "crowns," and specious promises of "painless" operations.

The adventurous piano salesman halted at the corner and considered. Then he crossed the street, walked down a block, recrossed and joined the upward current of people again. Without seeming to notice the Negro as he passed the second time, he carelessly took the card that was handed him. Ten steps away he inspected it. In the same handwriting that appeared on the first card "The Green Door" was inscribed upon it. Three or four cards were tossed to the pavement by pedestrians both following and leading him. These fell blank side up. Rudolf turned them over. Every one bore the printed legend of the dental "parlors."

Rarely did the arch sprite Adventure need to beckon twice to Rudolf Steiner, his true follower. But twice it had been done, and the quest was on.

Rudolf walked slowly back to where the giant Negro stood by the case of rattling teeth. This time as he passed he received no card. In spite of his gaudy and ridiculous garb, the Ethiopian displayed a natural barbaric dignity as he stood, offering the cards suavely to some, allowing others to pass unmolested. Every half minute he chanted a harsh, unintelligible phrase akin to the jabber of car conductors and grand opera. And not only did he withhold a card this time but it seemed to Rudolf that he received from the shining and massive black countenance a look of cold, almost contemptuous disdain.

The look stung the adventurer. He read in it a silent accusation that he had been found wanting. Whatever the mysterious written words on the cards might mean, the black had selected him twice from the throng for their recipient; and now seemed to have condemned him as deficient in the wit and spirit to engage the enigma.

Standing aside from the rush, the young man made a rapid estimate of the building in which he conceived that his adventure must lie. Five stories high it rose. A small restaurant occupied the basement.

The first floor, now closed, seemed to house millinery or furs. The second floor, by the winking electric letters, was the dentist's. Above this a polyglot babel of signs struggled to indicate the abodes of palmists, dressmakers, musicians, and doctors. Still higher up draped curtains and milk bottles white on the window sills proclaimed the regions of domesticity.

After concluding his survey Rudolf walked briskly up the high flight of stone steps into the house. Up two flights of the carpeted stairway he continued; and at its top paused. The hallway there was dimly lighted by two pale jets of gas —one far to his right, the other nearer, to his left. He looked toward the nearer light and saw, within its wan halo, a green door. For one moment he hesitated; then he seemed to see the contumelious sneer of the African juggler of cards; and then he walked straight to the green door and knocked against it.

Moments like those that passed before his knock was answered measure the quick breath of true adventure. What might not be behind those green panels! Gamesters at play; cunning rogues baiting their traps with subtle skill; beauty in love with courage, and thus planning to be sought by it; danger, death, love, disappointment, ridicule—any of these might respond to that temerarious rap.

A faint rustle was heard inside, and the door slowly opened. A girl not yet twenty stood there white-faced and tottering. She loosed the knob and swayed weakly, groping with one hand. Rudolf caught her and laid her on a faded couch that stood against the wall. He closed the door and took a swift glance around the room by the light of a flickering gas jet. Neat, but extreme poverty was the story that he read.

The girl lay still, as if in a faint. Rudolf looked around the room excitedly for a barrel. People must be rolled upon a barrel who—no, no; that was for drowned persons. He began to fan her with his hat. That was successful, for he struck her nose with the brim of his derby and she opened her eyes. And then the young man saw that hers, indeed, was the one missing face from his heart's gallery of intimate portraits. The frank, gray eyes, the little nose, turning pertly outward; the chestnut hair, curling like the tendrils of a pea vine, seemed the right end and reward of all his wonderful adventures. But the face was woefully thin and pale.

The girl looked at him calmly, and then smiled.

"Fainted, didn't I?" she asked, weakly. "Well, who wouldn't? You try going without anything to eat for three days and see!"

"Himmel!" exclaimed Rudolf, jumping up. "Wait till I come back."

He dashed out the green door and down the stairs. In twenty minutes he was back again kicking at the door with his toe for her to open it. With both arms he hugged an array of wares from the grocery and the restaurant. On the table he laid them—bread and butter, cold meats, cakes, pies, pickles, oysters, a roasted chicken, a bottle of milk and one of red-hot tea.

"This is ridiculous," said Rudolf, blusteringly, "to go without eating. You must quit making election bets of this kind. Supper is ready." He helped her to a chair at the table and asked: "Is there a cup for the tea?" "On the shelf by the window," she answered. When he turned again with the cup he saw her, with eyes shining rapturously, beginning upon a huge dill pickle that she had rooted out from

the paper bags with a woman's unerring instinct. He took
it from her, laughingly, and poured the cup full of milk.
"Drink that first," he ordered, "and then you shall have some
tea, and then a chicken wing. If you are very good you shall
have a pickle to-morrow. And now, if you'll allow me to be
your guest we'll have supper."

He drew up the other chair. The tea brightened the girl's
eyes and brought back some of her color. She began to eat
with a sort of dainty ferocity like some starved wild animal.
She seemed to regard the young man's presence and the aid
he had rendered her as a natural thing—not as though she
undervalued the conventions; but as one whose great stress
gave her the right to put aside the artificial for the human.
But gradually, with the return of strength and comfort, came
also a sense of the little conventions that belong; and she
began to tell him her little story. It was one of a thousand
such as the city yawns at every day—the shop girl's story of
insufficient wages, further reduced by "fines" that go to swell
the store's profits; of time lost through illness; and then of
lost positions, lost hope, and—the knock of the adventurer
upon the green door.

But to Rudolf the history sounded as big as the Iliad or the
crisis in "Junie's Love Test."

"To think of you going through all that," he exclaimed.

"It was something fierce," said the girl, solemnly.

"And you have no relatives or friends in the city?"

"None whatever."

"I am all alone in the world, too," said Rudolf, after a
pause.

"I am glad of that," said the girl, promptly; and somehow
it pleased the young man to hear that she approved of his
bereft condition.

Very suddenly her eyelids dropped and she sighed deeply.

"I'm awfully sleepy," she said, "and I feel so good."

Rudolf rose and took his hat.

"Then I'll say good-night. A long night's sleep will be fine
for you."

He held out his hand, and she took it and said "good-night." But her eyes asked a question so eloquently, so frankly and pathetically that he answered it with words.

"Oh, I'm coming back to-morrow to see how you are getting along. You can't get rid of me so easily."

Then, at the door, as though the way of his coming had been so much less important than the fact that he had come, she asked: "How did you come to knock at my door?"

He looked at her for a moment, remembering the cards, and felt a sudden jealous pain. What if they had fallen into other hands as adventurous as his? Quickly he decided that she must never know the truth. He would never let her know that he was aware of the strange expedient to which she had been driven by her great distress.

"One of our piano tuners lives in this house," he said. "I knocked at your door by mistake."

The last thing he saw in the room before the green door closed was her smile.

At the head of the stairway he paused and looked curiously about him. And then he went along the hallway to its other end; and, coming back, ascended to the floor above and continued his puzzled explorations. Every door that he found in the house was painted green.

Wondering, he descended to the sidewalk. The fantastic African was still there. Rudolf confronted him with his two cards in his hand.

"Will you tell me why you gave me these cards and what they mean?" he asked.

In a broad, good-natured grin the Negro exhibited a splendid advertisement of his master's profession.

"Dar it is, boss," he said, pointing down the street. "But I 'spect you is a little late for de fust act."

Looking the way he pointed Rudolf saw above the entrance to a theatre the blazing electric sign of its new play, "The Green Door."

"I'm informed dat it's a fust-rate show, sah," said the Negro. "De agent what represents it pussented me with a dollar, sah, to distribute a few of his cards along with de doctah's. May I offer you one of de doctah's cards, sah?"

At the corner of the block in which he lived Rudolf stopped for a glass of beer and a cigar. When he had come out with his lighted weed he buttoned his coat, pushed back his hat and said, stoutly, to the lamp post on the corner:

"All the same, I believe it was the hand of Fate that doped out the way for me to find her."

Which conclusion, under the circumstances, certainly admits Rudolf Steiner to the ranks of the true followers of Romance and Adventure.

After Twenty Years

THE policeman on the beat moved up the avenue impressively. The impressiveness was habitual and not for show, for spectators were few. The time was barely 10 o'clock at night, but chilly gusts of wind with a taste of rain in them had well nigh depeopled the streets.

Trying doors as he went, twirling his club with many intricate and artful movements, turning now and then to cast his watchful eye adown the pacific thoroughfare, the officer, with his stalwart form and slight swagger, made a fine picture of a guardian of the peace. The vicinity was one that kept early hours. Now and then you might see the lights of a cigar store or of an all-night lunch counter; but the majority of the doors belonged to business places that had long since been closed.

When about midway of a certain block the policeman suddenly slowed his walk. In the doorway of a darkened hardware store a man leaned, with an unlighted cigar in his mouth. As the policeman walked up to him the man spoke up quickly.

"It's all right, officer," he said, reassuringly. "I'm just waiting for a friend. It's an appointment made twenty years ago.

Sounds a little funny to you, doesn't it? Well, I'll explain if you'd like to make certain it's all straight. About that long ago there used to be a restaurant where this store stands— 'Big Joe' Brady's restaurant."

"Until five years ago," said the policeman. "It was torn down then."

The man in the doorway struck a match and lit his cigar. The light showed a pale, square-jawed face with keen eyes, and a little white scar near his right eyebrow. His scarfpin was a large diamond, oddly set.

"Twenty years ago to-night," said the man, "I dined here at 'Big Joe' Brady's with Jimmy Wells, my best chum, and the finest chap in the world. He and I were raised here in New York, just like two brothers, together. I was eighteen and Jimmy was twenty. The next morning I was to start for the West to make my fortune. You couldn't have dragged Jimmy out of New York; he thought it was the only place on earth. Well, we agreed that night that we would meet here again exactly twenty years from that date and time, no matter what our conditions might be or from what distance we might have to come. We figured that in twenty years each of us ought to have our destiny worked out and our fortunes made, whatever they were going to be."

"It sounds pretty interesting," said the policeman. "Rather a long time between meets, though, it seems to me. Haven't you heard from your friend since you left?"

"Well, yes, for a time we corresponded," said the other. "But after a year or two we lost track of each other. You see, the West is a pretty big proposition, and I kept hustling around over it pretty lively. But I know Jimmy will meet me here if he's alive, for he always was the truest, stanchest old chap in the world. He'll never forget. I came a thousand miles to stand in this door to-night, and it's worth it if my old partner turns up."

The waiting man pulled out a handsome watch, the lids of it set with small diamonds.

"Three minutes to ten," he announced. "It was exactly ten o'clock when we parted here at the restaurant door."

"Did pretty well out West, didn't you?" asked the policeman.

"You bet! I hope Jimmy has done half as well. He was a kind of plodder, though, good fellow as he was. I've had to compete with some of the sharpest wits going to get my pile. A man gets in a groove in New York. It takes the West to put a razor-edge on him."

The policeman twirled his club and took a step or two.

"I'll be on my way. Hope your friend comes around all right. Going to call time on him sharp?"

"I should say not!" said the other. "I'll give him half an hour at least. If Jimmy is alive on earth he'll be here by that time. So long, officer."

"Good-night, sir," said the policeman, passing on along his beat, trying doors as he went.

There was now a fine, cold drizzle falling, and the wind had risen from its uncertain puffs into a steady blow. The few foot passengers astir in that quarter hurried dismally and silently along with coat collars turned high and pocketed hands. And in the door of the hardware store the man who had come a thousand miles to fill an appointment, uncertain almost to absurdity, with the friend of his youth, smoked his cigar and waited.

About twenty minutes he waited, and then a tall man in a long overcoat, with collar turned up to his ears, hurried across from the opposite side of the street. He went directly to the waiting man.

"Is that you, Bob?" he asked, doubtfully.

"Is that you, Jimmy Wells?" cried the man in the door.

"Bless my heart!" exclaimed the new arrival, grasping both the other's hands with his own. "It's Bob, sure as fate. I was certain I'd find you here if you were still in existence. Well, well, well!—twenty years is a long time. The old restaurant's gone, Bob; I wish it had lasted, so we could have had another dinner there. How has the West treated you, old man?"

"Bully; it has given me everything I asked it for. You've changed lots, Jimmy. I never thought you were so tall by two or three inches."

"Oh, I grew a bit after I was twenty."

"Doing well in New York, Jimmy?"

"Moderately. I have a position in one of the city departments. Come on, Bob; we'll go around to a place I know of, and have a good long talk about old times."

The two men started up the street, arm in arm. The man from the West, his egotism enlarged by success, was beginning to outline the history of his career. The other, submerged in his overcoat, listened with interest.

At the corner stood a drug store, brilliant with electric lights. When they came into this glare each of them turned simultaneously to gaze upon the other's face.

The man from the West stopped suddenly and released his arm.

"You're not Jimmy Wells," he snapped. "Twenty years is a long time, but not long enough to change a man's nose from a Roman to a pug."

"It sometimes changes a good man into a bad one," said the tall man. "You've been under arrest for ten minutes, 'Silky' Bob. Chicago thinks you may have dropped over our way and wires us she wants to have a chat with you. Going quietly, are you? That's sensible. Now, before we go to the station here's a note I was asked to hand to you. You may read it here at the window. It's from Patrolman Wells."

The man from the West unfolded the little piece of paper handed him. His hand was steady when he began to read, but it trembled a little by the time he had finished. The note was rather short.

Bob: I was at the appointed place on time. When you struck the match to light your cigar I saw it was the face of the man wanted in Chicago. Somehow I couldn't do it myself, so I went around and got a plain clothes man to do the job.

JIMMY.

The Furnished Room

~~~~~~

RESTLESS, shifting, fugacious as time is a certain vast bulk of the population of the red brick district of the lower West Side. Homeless, they have a hundred homes. They flit from furnished room to furnished room, transients forever—transients in abode, transients in heart and mind. They sing "Home, Sweet Home" in ragtime; they carry their *lares et penates* in a bandbox; their vine is entwined about a picture hat; a rubber plant is their fig tree.

Hence the houses of this district, having had a thousand dwellers, should have a thousand tales to tell, mostly dull ones, no doubt; but it would be strange if there could not be found a ghost or two in the wake of all these vagrant guests.

One evening after dark a young man prowled among these crumbling red mansions, ringing their bells. At the twelfth he rested his lean hand-baggage upon the step and wiped the dust from his hatband and forehead. The bell sounded faint and far away in some remote, hollow depths.

To the door of this, the twelfth house whose bell he had rung, came a housekeeper who made him think of an unwholesome, surfeited worm that had eaten its nut to a hollow shell and now sought to fill the vacancy with edible lodgers.

He asked if there was a room to let.

"Come in," said the housekeeper. Her voice came from her throat; her throat seemed lined with fur. "I have the third-floor back, vacant since a week back. Should you wish to look at it?"

The young man followed her up the stairs. A faint light from no particular source mitigated the shadows of the halls.

They trod noiselessly upon a stair carpet that its own loom would have forsworn. It seemed to have become vegetable; to have degenerated in that rank, sunless air to lush lichen or spreading moss that grew in patches to the stair-case and was viscid under the foot like organic matter. At each turn of the stairs were vacant niches in the wall. Perhaps plants had once been set within them. If so they had died in that foul and tainted air. It may be that statues of the saints had stood there, but it was not difficult to conceive that imps and devils had dragged them forth in the darkness and down to the unholy depths of some furnished pit below.

"This is the room," said the housekeeper, from her furry throat. "It's a nice room. It ain't often vacant. I had some most elegant people in it last summer—no trouble at all, and paid in advance to the minute. The water's at the end of the hall. Sprowls and Mooney kept it three months. They done a vaudeville sketch. Miss B'retta Sprowls—you may have heard of her—Oh, that was just the stage names—right there over the dresser is where the marriage certificate hung, framed. The gas is here, and you see there is plenty of closet room. It's a room everybody likes. It never stays idle long."

"Do you have many theatrical people rooming here?" asked the young man.

"They comes and goes. A good proportion of my lodgers is connected with the theatres. Yes, sir, this is the theatrical district. Actor people never stays long anywhere. I get my share. Yes, they comes and they goes."

He engaged the room, paying for a week in advance. He was tired, he said, and would take possession at once. He counted out the money. The room had been made ready, she said, even to towels and water. As the housekeeper moved away he put, for the thousandth time, the question that he carried at the end of his tongue.

"A young girl—Miss Vashner—Miss Eloise Vashner—do you remember such a one among your lodgers? She would be singing on the stage, most likely. A fair girl, of medium height and slender, with reddish, gold hair and a dark mole near her left eyebrow."

"No, I don't remember the name. Them stage people has names they change as often as their rooms. They comes and they goes. No, I don't call that one to mind."

No. Always no. Five months of ceaseless interrogation and the inevitable negative. So much time spent by day in questioning managers, agents, schools and choruses; by night among the audiences of theatres from all-star casts down to music halls so low that he dreaded to find what he most hoped for. He who had loved her best had tried to find her. He was sure that since her disappearance from home this great, water-girt city held her somewhere, but it was like a monstrous quicksand, shifting its particles constantly, with no foundation, its upper granules of to-day buried to-morrow in ooze and slime.

The furnished room received its latest guest with a first glow of pseudo-hospitality, a hectic, haggard, perfunctory welcome like the specious smile of a demirep. The sophistical comfort came in reflected gleams from the decayed furniture, the ragged brocade upholstery of a couch and two chairs, a foot-wide cheap pier glass between the two windows, from one or two gilt picture frames and a brass bedstead in a corner.

The guest reclined, inert, upon a chair, while the room, confused in speech as though it were an apartment in Babel, tried to discourse to him of its divers tenantry.

A polychromatic rug like some brilliant-flowered, rectangular, tropical islet lay surrounded by a billowy sea of soiled matting. Upon the gay-papered wall were those pictures that pursue the homeless one from house to house— The Huguenot Lovers, The First Quarrel, The Wedding Breakfast, Psyche at the Fountain. The mantel's chastely severe outline was ingloriously veiled behind some pert drapery drawn rakishly askew like the sashes of the Amazonian ballet. Upon it was some desolate flotsam cast aside by the room's marooned when a lucky sail had borne them to a fresh port—a trifling vase or two, pictures of actresses, a medicine bottle, some stray cards out of a deck.

One by one, as the characters of a cryptograph become

explicit, the little signs left by the furnished room's procession of guests developed a significance. The threadbare space in the rug in front of the dresser told that lovely women had marched in the throng. The tiny fingerprints on the wall spoke of little prisoners trying to feel their way to sun and air. A splattered stain, raying like the shadow of a bursting bomb, witnessed where a hurled glass or bottle had splintered with its contents against the wall. Across the pier glass had been scrawled with a diamond in staggering letters the name "Marie." It seemed that the succession of dwellers in the furnished room had turned in fury—perhaps tempted beyond forbearance by its garish coldness—and wreaked upon it their passions. The furniture was chipped and bruised; the couch, distorted by bursting springs, seemed a horrible monster that had been slain during the stress of some grotesque convulsion. Some more potent upheaval had cloven a great slice from the marble mantel. Each plank in the floor owned its particular cant and shriek as from a separate and individual agony. It seemed incredible that all this malice and injury had been wrought upon the room by those who had called it for a time their home; and yet it may have been the cheated home instinct surviving blindly, the resentful rage at false household gods that had kindled their wrath. A hut that is our own we can sweep and adorn and cherish.

The young tenant in the chair allowed these thoughts to file, soft-shod, through his mind, while there drifted into the room furnished sounds and furnished scents. He heard in one room a tittering and incontinent, slack laughter; in others the monologue of a scold, the rattling of dice, a lullaby, and one crying dully; above him a banjo tinkled with spirit. Doors banged somewhere; the elevated trains roared intermittently; a cat yowled miserably upon a back fence. And he breathed the breath of the house—a dank savor rather than a smell— a cold, musty effluvium as from underground vaults mingled with the reeking exhalations of linoleum and mildewed and rotten woodwork.

Then suddenly, as he rested there, the room was filled with the strong, sweet odor of mignonette. It came as upon a single

buffet of wind with such sureness and fragrance and emphasis
that it almost seemed a living visitant. And the man cried
aloud: "What, dear?" as if he had been called, and sprang
up and faced about. The rich odor clung to him and wrapped
him around. He reached out his arms for it, all his senses for
the time confused and commingled. How could one be per-
emptorily called by an odor? Surely it must have been a
sound. But, was it not the sound that had touched, that had
caressed him?

"She has been in this room," he cried, and he sprang to
wrest from it a token, for he knew he would recognize the
smallest thing that had belonged to her or that she had
touched. This enveloping scent of mignonette, the odor that
she had loved and made her own—whence came it?

The room had been but carelessly set in order. Scattered
upon the flimsy dresser scarf were half a dozen hairpins—
those discreet, indistinguishable friends of womankind, feminine of gender, infinite mood and uncommunicative of tense.
These he ignored, conscious of their triumphant lack of identity. Ransacking the drawers of the dresser he came upon a
discarded, tiny, ragged handkerchief. He pressed it to his
face. It was racy and insolent with heliotrope; he hurled it
to the floor. In another drawer he found odd buttons, a
theatre programme, a pawnbroker's card, two lost marsh-
mallows, a book on the divination of dreams. In the last was
a woman's black satin hair bow, which halted him, poised
between ice and fire. But the black satin hair bow also is
femininity's demure, impersonal common ornament and tells
no tales.

And then he traversed the room like a hound on the scent,
skimming the walls, considering the corners of the bulging
matting on his hands and knees, rummaging mantel and
tables, the curtains and hangings, the drunken cabinet in
the corner, for a visible sign, unable to perceive that she was
there beside, around, against, within, above him, clinging to
him, wooing him, calling him so poignantly through the finer
senses that even his grosser ones became cognizant of the
call. Once again he answered loudly: "Yes, dear!" and turned,

wild-eyed, to gaze on vacancy, for he could not yet discern form and color and love and outstretched arms in the odor of mignonette. Oh, God! whence that odor, and since when have odors had a voice to call? Thus he groped.

He burrowed in crevices and corners, and found corks and cigarettes. These he passed in passive contempt. But once he found in a fold of the matting a half-smoked cigar, and this he ground beneath his heel with a green and trenchant oath. He sifted the room from end to end. He found dreary and ignoble small records of many a peripatetic tenant; but of her whom he sought, and who may have lodged there, and whose spirit seemed to hover there, he found no trace.

And then he thought of the housekeeper.

He ran from the haunted room downstairs and to a door that showed a crack of light. She came out to his knock. He smothered his excitement as best she could.

"Will you tell me, madam," he besought her, "who occupied the room I have before I came?"

"Yes, sir. I can tell you again. 'Twas Sprowls and Mooney, as I said. Miss B'retta Sprowls it was in the theatres, but Missis Mooney she was. My house is well known for respectability. The marriage certificate hung, framed, on a nail over—"

"What kind of a lady was Miss Sprowls—in looks, I mean?"

"Why, black-haired, sir, short, and stout, with a comical face. They left a week ago Tuesday."

"And before they occupied it?"

"Why, there was a single gentleman connected with the draying business. He left owing me a week. Before him was Missis Crowder and her two children, that stayed four months; and back of them was old Mr. Doyle, whose sons paid for him. He kept the room six months. That goes back a year, sir, and further I do not remember."

He thanked her and crept back to his room. The room was dead. The essence that had vivified it was gone. The perfume of mignonette had departed. In its place was the old, stale odor of mouldy house furniture, of atmosphere in storage.

The ebbing of his hope drained his faith. He sat staring at the yellow, swinging gaslight. Soon he walked to the bed and began to tear the sheets into strips. With the blade of his knife he drove them tightly into every crevice around windows and door. When all was snug and taut he turned out the light, turned the gas full on again and laid himself gratefully upon the bed.

It was Mrs. McCool's night to go with the can for beer. So she fetched it and sat with Mrs. Purdy in one of those subterranean retreats where housekeepers foregather and the worm dieth seldom.

"I rented out my third-floor-back this evening," said Mrs. Purdy, across a fine circle of foam. "A young man took it. He went up to bed two hours ago."

"Now, did ye, Mrs. Purdy, ma'am?" said Mrs. McCool, with intense admiration. "You do be a wonder for rentin' rooms of that kind. And did ye tell him, then?" she concluded in a husky whisper laden with mystery.

"Rooms," said Mrs. Purdy, in her furriest tones, "are furnished for to rent. I did not tell him, Mrs. McCool."

"'Tis right ye are, ma'am; 'tis by renting rooms we kape alive. Ye have the rale sense for business, ma'am. There be many people will rayjict the rentin' of a room if they be tould a suicide has been after dyin' in the bed of it."

"As you say, we has our living to be making," remarked Mrs. Purdy.

"Yis, ma'am; 'tis true. 'Tis just one wake ago this day I helped ye lay out the third-floor-back. A pretty slip of a colleen she was to be killin' herself wid the gas—a swate little face she had, Mrs. Purdy, ma'am."

"She'd a-been called handsome, as you say," said Mrs. Purdy, assenting but critical, "but for that mole she had a'growin' by her left eyebrow. Do fill up your glass again, Mrs. McCool."

The Pimienta Pancakes

WHILE we were rounding up a bunch of the Triangle-O cattle in the Frio bottoms a projecting branch of a dead mesquite caught my wooden stirrup and gave my ankle a wrench that laid me up in camp for a week.

On the third day of my compulsory idleness I crawled out near the grub wagon, and reclined helpless under the conversational fire of Judson Odom, the camp cook. Jud was a monologist by nature, whom Destiny, with customary blundering, had set in a profession wherein he was bereaved, for the greater portion of his time, of an audience.

Therefore, I was manna in the desert of Jud's obmutescence.

Betimes I was stirred by invalid longings for something to eat that did not come under the caption of "grub." I had visions of the maternal pantry "deep as first love, and wild with all regret," and then I asked:

"Jud, can you make pancakes?"

Jud laid down his sixshooter, with which he was preparing to pound an antelope steak, and stood over me in what I felt to be a menacing attitude. He further indorsed my impression that his pose was resentful by fixing upon me with his light blue eyes a look of cold suspicion.

"Say, you," he said, with candid, though not excessive, choler, "did you mean that straight, or was you trying to throw the gaff into me? Some of the boys been telling you about me and that pancake racket?"

"No, Jud," I said, sincerely, "I meant it. It seems to me I'd swap my pony and saddle for a stack of buttered brown pancakes with some first crop, open kettle, New Orleans sweetening. Was there a story about pancakes?"

Jud was mollified at once when he saw that I had not been dealing in allusions. He brought some mysterious bags and tin boxes from the grub wagon and set them in the shade of the hackberry where I lay reclined. I watched him as he began to arrange them leisurely and untie their many strings.

"No, not a story," said Jud, as he worked, "but just the logical disclosures in the case of me and that pink-eyed snoozer from Mired Mule Cañada and Miss Willella Learight. I don't mind telling you.

"I was punching then for old Bill Toomey, on the San Miguel. One day I gets all ensnared up in aspirations for to eat some canned grub that hasn't ever mooed or baaed or grunted or been in peck measures. So, I gets on my bronc and pushes the wind for Uncle Emsley Telfair's store at the Pimienta Crossing on the Nueces.

"About three in the afternoon I threw my bridle over a mesquite limb and walked the last twenty yards into Uncle Emsley's store. I got up on the counter and told Uncle Emsley that the signs pointed to the devastation of the fruit crop of the world. In a minute I had a bag of crackers and a long-handled spoon, with an open can each of apricots and pineapples and cherries and green-gages beside of me with Uncle Emsley busy chopping away with the hatchet at the yellow clings. I was feeling like Adam before the apple stampede, and was digging my spurs into the side of the counter and working with my twenty-four-inch spoon when I happened to look out of the window into the yard of Uncle Emsley's house, which was next to the store.

"There was a girl standing there—an imported girl with fixings on—philandering with a croquet maul and amusing herself by watching my style of encouraging the fruit canning industry.

"I slid off the counter and delivered up my shovel to Uncle Emsley.

"'That's my niece,' says he; 'Miss Willella Learight, down from Palestine on a visit. Do you want that I should make you acquainted?'

"'The Holy Land,' I says to myself, my thoughts milling

some as I tried to run 'em into the corral. 'Why not? There was sure angels in Pales— Why yes, Uncle Emsley,' I says out loud, 'I'd be awful edified to meet Miss Learight.'

"So Uncle Emsley took me out in the yard and gave us each other's entitlements.

"I never was shy about women. I never could understand why some men who can break a mustang before breakfast and shave in the dark, get all lefthanded and full of perspiration and excuses when they see a bolt of calico draped around what belongs in it. Inside of eight minutes me and Miss Willella was aggravating the croquet balls around as amiable as second cousins. She gave me a dig about the quantity of canned fruit I had eaten, and I got back at her, flatfooted, about how a certain lady named Eve started the fruit trouble in the first free-grass pasture—'Over in Palestine, wasn't it?' says I, as easy and pat as roping a one-year-old.

"That was how I acquired cordiality for the proximities of Miss Willella Learight; and the disposition grew larger as time passed. She was stopping at Pimienta Crossing for her health, which was very good, and for the climate, which was forty per cent. hotter than Palestine. I rode over to see her once every week for a while; and then I figured it out that if I doubled the number of trips I would see her twice as often.

"One week I slipped in a third trip; and that's where the pancakes and the pink-eyed snoozer busted into the game.

"That evening, while I set on the counter with a peach and two damsons in my mouth, I asked Uncle Emsley how Miss Willella was.

"'Why,' says Uncle Emsley, 'she's gone riding with Jackson Bird, the sheep man from over at Mired Mule Cañada.'

"I swallowed the peach seed and the two damson seeds. I guess somebody held the counter by the bridle while I got off; and then I walked out straight ahead till I butted against the mesquite where my roan was tied.

"'She's gone riding,' I whispered in my bronc's ear, 'with Birdstone Jack, the hired mule from Sheep Man's Cañada. Did you get that, old Leather-and-Gallops?'

"That bronc of mine wept, in his way. He'd been raised a cow pony and he didn't care for snoozers.

"I went back and said to Uncle Emsley: 'Did you say a sheep man?'

"'I said a sheep man,' says Uncle again. 'You must have heard tell of Jackson Bird. He's got eight sections of grazing and four thousand head of the finest Merinos south of the Arctic Circle.'

"I went out and sat on the ground in the shade of the store and leaned against a prickly pear. I sifted sand into my boots with unthinking hands while I soliloquized a quantity about this bird with the Jackson plumage to his name.

"I never had believed in harming sheep men. I see one, one day, reading a Latin grammar on hossback, and I never touched him! They never irritated me like they do most cowmen. You wouldn't go to work now, and impair and disfigure snoozers, would you, that eat on tables and wear little shoes and speak to you on subjects? I had always let 'em pass, just as you would a jack-rabbit; with a polite word and a guess about the weather, but no stopping to swap canteens. I never thought it was worth while to be hostile with a snoozer. And because I'd been lenient, and let 'em live, here was one going around riding with Miss Willella Learight!

"An hour by sun they come loping back, and stopped at Uncle Emsley's gate. The sheep person helped her off; and they stood throwing each other sentences all sprightful and sagacious for a while. And then this feathered Jackson flies up in his saddle and raises his little stewpot of a hat, and trots off in the direction of his mutton ranch. By this time I had turned the sand out of my boots and unpinned myself from the prickly pear; and by the time he gets half a mile out of Pimienta, I singlefoots up beside him on my bronc.

"I said that snoozer was pink-eyed, but he wasn't. His seeing arrangement was gray enough, but his eyelashes was pink and his hair was sandy, and that gave you the idea. Sheep man—he wasn't more than a lamb man, anyhow—a little thing with his neck involved in a yellow silk handkerchief, and shoes tied up in bowknots.

" 'Afternoon!' says I to him. 'You now ride with a equestrian who is commonly called Dead-Moral-Certainty Judson, on account of the way I shoot. When I want a stranger to know me I always introduce myself before the draw, for I never did like to shake hands with ghosts.'

" 'Ah,' says he, just like that—'Ah, I'm glad to know you, Mr. Judson. I'm Jackson Bird, from over at Mired Mule Ranch.'

"Just then one of my eyes saw a roadrunner skipping down the hill with a young tarantula in his bill, and the other eye noticed a rabbit-hawk sitting on a dead limb in a water-elm. I popped over one after the other with my forty-five, just to show him. 'Two out of three,' says I. 'Birds just naturally seem to draw my fire wherever I go.'

" 'Nice shooting,' says the sheep man, without a flutter. 'But don't you sometimes ever miss the third shot? Elegant fine rain that was last week for the young grass, Mr. Judson,' says he.

" 'Willie,' says I, riding over close to his palfrey, 'your infatuated parents may have denounced you by the name of Jackson, but you sure moulted into a twittering Willie—let us slough off this here analysis of rain and the elements, and get down to talk that is outside the vocabulary of parrots. That is a bad habit you have got of riding with young ladies over at Pimienta. I've known birds,' says I, 'to be served on toast for less than that. Miss Willella,' says I, 'don't ever want any nest made out of sheep's wool by a tomtit of the Jacksonian branch of ornithology. Now, are you going to quit, or do you wish for to gallop up against this Dead-Moral-Certainty attachment to my name, which is good for two hyphens and at least one set of funeral obsequies?'

"Jackson Bird flushed up some, and then he laughed.

" 'Why, Mr. Judson,' says he, 'you've got the wrong idea. I've called on Miss Learight a few times; but not for the purpose you imagine. My object is purely a gastronomical one.'

"I reached for my gun.

" 'Any coyote,' says I, 'that would boast of dishonorable—'

" 'Wait a minute,' says this Bird, 'till I explain. What would I do with a wife? If you ever saw that ranch of mine! I do my own cooking and mending. Eating—that's all the pleasure I get out of sheep raising. Mr. Judson, did you ever taste the pancakes that Miss Learight makes?'

" 'Me? No,' I told him. 'I never was advised that she was up to any culinary maneuvers.'

" 'They're golden sunshine,' says he, 'honey-browned by the ambrosial fires of Epicurus. I'd give two years of my life to get the recipe for making them pancakes. That's what I went to see Miss Learight for,' says Jackson Bird, 'but I haven't been able to get it from her. It's an old recipe that's been in the family for seventy-five years. They hand it down from one generation to another, but they don't give it away to outsiders. If I could get that recipe, so I could make them pancakes for myself on my ranch, I'd be a happy man,' says Bird.

" 'Are you sure,' I says to him, 'that it ain't the hand that mixes the pancakes that you're after?'

" 'Sure,' says Jackson. 'Miss Learight is a mighty nice girl, but I can assure you my intentions go no further than the gastro—' but he seen my hand going down to my holster and he changed his similitude—'than the desire to produce a copy of the pancake recipe,' he finishes.

" 'You ain't such a bad little man,' says I, trying to be fair. 'I was thinking some of making orphans of your sheep, but I'll let you fly away this time. But you stick to pancakes,' says I, 'as close as the middle one of a stack; and don't go and mistake sentiments for syrup, or there'll be singing at your ranch, and you won't hear it.'

" 'To convince you that I am sincere,' says the sheep man, 'I'll ask you to help me. Miss Learight and you being closer friends, maybe she would do for you what she wouldn't for me. If you will get me a copy of that pancake recipe, I give you my word that I'll never call upon her again.'

" 'That's fair,' I says, and I shook hands with Jackson Bird. 'I'll get it for you if I can, and glad to oblige.' And he turned off down the big pear flat on the Piedra, in the direction of Mired Mule; and I steered northwest for old Bill Toomey's ranch.

"It was five days afterward when I got another chance to ride over to Pimienta. Miss Willella and me passed a gratifying evening at Uncle Emsley's. She sang some, and exasperated the piano quite a lot with quotations from the operas. I gave imitations of a rattlesnake, and told her about Snaky McFee's new way of skinning cows, and described the trip I made to Saint Louis once. We was getting along in one another's estimations fine. Thinks I, if Jackson can now be persuaded to migrate, I win. I recollect his promise about the pancake receipt, and I thinks I will persuade it from Miss Willella and give it to him; and then if I catches Birdie off of Mired Mule again, I'll make him hop the twig.

"So, along about ten o'clock, I put on a wheedling smile and says to Miss Willella: 'Now, if there's anything I do like better than the sight of a red steer on green grass it's the taste of a nice hot pancake smothered in sugarhouse molasses.'

"Miss Willella gives a little jump on the piano stool, and looked at me curious.

"'Yes,' says she, 'they're real nice. What did you say was the name of that street in Saint Louis, Mr. Odom, where you lost your hat?'

"'Pancake Avenue,' says I, with a wink, to show her that I was on about the family receipt, and couldn't be side-corralled off of the subject. 'Come, now Miss Willella,' I says; 'let's hear how you make 'em. Pancakes is just whirling in my head like wagon wheels. Start her off, now—pound of flour, eight dozen eggs, and so on. How does the catalogue of constituents run?'

"'Excuse me for a moment, please,' says Miss Willella, and she gives me a quick kind of sideways look, and slides off the stool. She ambled out into the other room, and directly Uncle Emsley comes in in his shirt sleeves, with a pitcher of water. He turns around to get a glass on the table, and I see a forty-five in his hip pocket. 'Great post-holes!' thinks I, 'but here's a family thinks a heap of cooking receipts, protecting it with firearms. I've known outfits that wouldn't do that much by a family feud.'

" 'Drink this here down,' says Uncle Emsley, handing me the glass of water. 'You've rid too far to-day, Jud, and got yourself over-excited. Try to think about something else now.'

" 'Do you know how to make them pancakes, Uncle Emsley?' I asked.

" 'Well, I'm not as apprised in the anatomy of them as some,' says Uncle Emsley, 'but I reckon you take a sifter of plaster of paris and a little dough and saleratus and corn meal, and mix 'em with eggs and buttermilk as usual. Is old Bill going to ship beeves to Kansas City again this spring, Jud?'

"That was all the pancake specifications I could get that night. I didn't wonder that Jackson Bird found it uphill work. So I dropped the subject and talked with Uncle Emsley a while about hollow-horn and cyclones. And then Miss Willella came and said 'Goodnight,' and I hit the breeze for the ranch.

"About a week afterward I met Jackson Bird riding out of Pimienta as I rode in, and we stopped in the road for a few frivolous remarks.

" 'Got the bill of particulars for them flapjacks yet?' I asked him.

" 'Well, no,' says Jackson. 'I don't seem to have any success in getting hold of it. Did you try?'

" 'I did,' says I, 'and 'twas like trying to dig a prairie dog out of his hole with a peanut hull. That pancake receipt must be a jooka-lorum, the way they hold on to it.'

" 'I'm 'most ready to give it up,' says Jackson, so discouraged in his pronunciations that I felt sorry for him; 'but I did want to know how to make them pancakes to eat on my lonely ranch,' says he. 'I lie awake at nights thinking how good they are.'

" 'You keep on trying for it,' I tells him, 'and I'll do the same. One of us is bound to get a rope over its horns before long. Well, so-long, Jacksy.'

"You see, by this time we was on the peacefullest of

terms. When I saw that he wasn't after Miss Willella I had more endurable contemplations of that sandy-haired snoozer. In order to help out the ambitions of his appetite I kept on trying to get that receipt from Miss Willella. But every time I would say 'pancakes' she would get sort of remote and fidgety about the eye, and try to change the subject. If I held her to it she would slide out and round up Uncle Emsley with his pitcher of water and hip-pocket howitzer.

"One day I galloped over to the store with a fine bunch of blue verbenas that I cut out of a herd of wild flowers over on Poisoned Dog Prairie. Uncle Emsley looked at 'em with one eye shut and says:

" 'Haven't ye heard the news?'

" 'Cattle up?' I asks.

" 'Willella and Jackson Bird was married in Palestine yesterday,' says he. 'Just got a letter this morning.'

"I dropped them flowers in a cracker-barrel, and let the news trickle in my ears and down toward my upper left-hand shirt pocket until it got to my feet.

" 'Would you mind saying that over again once more, Uncle Emsley?' says I. 'Maybe my hearing has got wrong, and you only said that prime heifers was 4.80 on the hoof, or something like that.'

" 'Married yesterday,' says Uncle Emsley, 'and gone to Waco and Niagara Falls on a wedding tour. Why, didn't you see none of the signs all along? Jackson Bird has been courting Willella ever since that day he took her out riding.'

" 'Then,' says I, in a kind of a yell, 'what was all this zizzaparoola he gives me about pancakes? Tell me *that*.'

"When I said 'pancakes' Uncle Emsley sort of dodged and stepped back.

" 'Somebody's been dealing me pancakes from the bottom of the deck,' I says, 'and I'll find out. I believe you know. Talk up,' says I, 'or we'll mix a panful of batter right here.'

"I slid over the counter after Uncle Emsley. He grabbed at his gun, but it was in a drawer, and he missed it two inches. I got him by the front of his shirt and shoved him in a corner.

" 'Talk pancakes,' says I, 'or be made into one. Does Miss Willella make 'em?'

" 'She never made one in her life and I never saw one,' says Uncle Emsley, soothing. 'Calm down now, Jud—calm down. You've got excited, and that wound in your head is contaminating your sense of intelligence. Try not to think about pancakes.'

" 'Uncle Emsley,' says I, 'I'm not wounded in the head except so far as my natural cogitative instincts run to runts. Jackson Bird told me he was calling on Miss Willella for the purpose of finding out her system of producing pancakes, and he asked me to help him get the bill of lading of the ingredients. I done so, with the results as you see. Have I been sodded down with Johnson grass by a pink-eyed snoozer, or what?'

" 'Slack up your grip on my dress shirt,' says Uncle Emsley, 'and I'll tell you. Yes, it looks like Jackson Bird has gone and humbugged you some. The day after he went riding with Willella he came back and told me and her to watch out for you whenever you got to talking about pancakes. He said you was in camp once where they was cooking flapjacks, and one of the fellows cut you over the head with a frying pan. Jackson said that whenever you got over-hot or excited that wound hurt you and made you kind of crazy, and you went raving about pancakes. He told us to just get you worked off of the subject and soothed down, and you wouldn't be dangerous. So, me and Willella done the best by you we knew how. Well, well,' says Uncle Emsley, 'that Jackson Bird is sure a seldom kind of a snoozer.' "

During the progress of Jud's story he had been slowly but deftly combining certain portions of the contents of his sacks and cans. Toward the close of it he set before me the finished product—a pair of red-hot, rich-hued pancakes on a tin plate. From some secret hoarding place he also brought a lump of excellent butter and a bottle of golden syrup.

"How long ago did these things happen?" I asked him.

"Three years," said Jud. "They're living on the Mired Mule Ranch now. But I haven't seen either of 'em since. They say

Jackson Bird was fixing his ranch up fine with rocking chairs and window curtains all the time he was putting me up the pancake tree. Oh, I got over it after a while. But the boys kept the racket up."

"Did you make these cakes by the famous recipe?" I asked.

"Didn't I tell you there wasn't no receipt?" said Jud. "The boys hollered pancakes till they got pancake hungry, and I cut this receipt out of a newspaper. How does the truck taste?"

"They're delicious," I answered. "Why don't you have some, too, Jud?" I was sure I heard a sigh.

"Me?" said Jud. "I don't never eat 'em."

The Reformation of Calliope

CALLIOPE CATESBY was in his humors again. Ennui was upon him. This goodly promontory, the earth—particularly that portion of it known as Quicksand—was to him no more than a pestilent congregation of vapors. Overtaken by the megrims, the philosopher may seek relief in soliloquy; my lady find solace in tears; the flaccid Easterner scold at the millinery bills of his women folk. Such recourse was insufficient to the denizens of Quicksand. Calliope, especially, was wont to express his ennui according to his lights.

Over night Calliope had hung out signals of approaching low spirits. He had kicked his own dog on the porch of the Occidental Hotel, and refused to apologize. He had become capricious and fault-finding in conversation. While strolling about he reached often for twigs of mesquite and chewed the leaves fiercely. That was always an ominous act. Another symptom alarming to those who were familiar with the different stages of his doldrums was his increasing politeness and a tendency to use formal phrases. A husky softness succeeded the usual penetrating drawl in his tones. A dangerous courtesy marked his manners. Later, his smile became crooked, the left side of his mouth slanting upward, and Quicksand got ready to stand from under.

At this stage Calliope generally began to drink. Finally, about midnight, he was seen going homeward, saluting those whom he met with exaggerated but inoffensive courtesy. Not yet was Calliope's melancholy at the danger point. He would seat himself at the window of the room he occupied over Silvester's tonsorial parlors and there chant lugubrious and tuneless ballads until morning, accompanying the noises by appropriate maltreatment of a jingling guitar. More magnanimous than Nero, he would thus give musical warning of the forthcoming municipal upheaval that Quicksand was scheduled to endure.

A quiet, amiable man was Calliope Catesby at other times —quiet to indolence, and amiable to worthlessness. At best he was a loafer and a nuisance; at worst he was the Terror of Quicksand. His ostensible occupation was something subordinate in the real estate line; he drove the beguiled Easterner in buckboards out to look over lots and ranch property. Originally he came from one of the Gulf States, his lank six feet, slurring rhythm of speech, and sectional idioms giving evidence of his birthplace.

And yet, after taking on Western adjustments, this languid pine-box whittler, cracker barrel hugger, shady corner lounger of the cotton fields and sumac hills of the South became famed as a bad man among men who had made a life-long study of the art of truculence.

At nine the next morning Calliope was fit. Inspired by his own barbarous melodies and the contents of his jug, he was ready primed to gather fresh laurels from the diffident brow of Quicksand. Encircled and crisscrossed with cartridge belts, abundantly garnished with revolvers, and copiously drunk, he poured forth into Quicksand's main street. Too chivalrous to surprise and capture a town by silent sortie, he paused at the nearest corner and emitted his slogan—that fearful, brassy yell, so reminiscent of the steam piano, that had gained for him the classic appellation that had superseded his own baptismal name. Following close upon his vociferation came three shots from his forty-five by way of limbering up the guns and testing his aim. A yellow dog, the personal property of Colonel Swazey, the proprietor of the Occidental, fell feet upward in the dust with one farewell yelp. A Mexican who was crossing the street from the Blue Front grocery, carrying in his hand a bottle of kerosene, was stimulated to a sudden and admirable burst of speed, still grasping the neck of the shattered bottle. The new gilt weathercock on Judge Riley's lemon and ultra-marine two-story residence shivered, flapped, and hung by a splinter, the sport of the wanton breezes.

The artillery was in trim. Calliope's hand was steady. The high, calm ecstasy of habitual battle was upon him, though slightly embittered by the sadness of Alexander in that his conquests were limited to the small world of Quicksand.

Down the street went Calliope, shooting right and left. Glass fell like hail; dogs vamosed; chickens flew, squawking; feminine voices shrieked concernedly to youngsters at large. The din was perforated at intervals by the *staccato* of the Terror's guns, and was drowned periodically by the brazen screech that Quicksand knew so well. The occasions of Calliope's low spirits were legal holidays in Quicksand. All along the main street in advance of his coming clerks were putting up shutters and closing doors. Business would languish for a space. The right of way was Calliope's, and as he advanced, observing the dearth of opposition and the few opportunities for distraction, his ennui perceptibly increased.

But some four squares farther down lively preparations were being made to minister to Mr. Catesby's love for interchange of compliments and repartee. On the previous night numerous messengers had hastened to advise Buck Patterson, the City Marshal, of Calliope's impending eruption. The patience of that official, often strained in extending leniency toward the disturber's misdeeds, had been overtaxed. In Quicksand some indulgence was accorded the natural ebullition of human nature. Providing that the lives of the more useful citizens were not recklessly squandered, or too much property needlessly laid waste, the community sentiment was against a too strict enforcement of the law. But Calliope had raised the limit. His outbursts had been too frequent and too violent to come within the classification of a normal and sanitary relaxation of spirit.

Buck Patterson had been expecting and awaiting in his little ten-by-twelve frame office that preliminary yell announcing that Calliope was feeling blue. When the signal came the City Marshal rose to his feet and buckled on his guns. Two deputy sheriffs and three citizens who had proven the edible qualities of fire also stood up, ready to bandy with Calliope's leaden jocularities.

"Gather that fellow in," said Buck Patterson, setting forth the lines of the campaign. "Don't have no talk, but shoot as soon as you can get a show. Keep behind cover and bring him down. He's a nogood 'un. It's up to Calliope to turn up his toes this time, I reckon. Go to him all spraddled out, boys. And don't git too reckless, for what Calliope shoots at he hits."

Buck Patterson, tall, muscular, and solemn-faced, with his bright "City Marshal" badge shining on the breast of his blue flannel shirt, gave his posse directions for the onslaught upon Calliope. The plan was to accomplish the downfall of the Quicksand Terror without loss to the attacking party, if possible.

The splenetic Calliope, unconscious of retributive plots, was steaming down the channel, cannonading on either side, when he suddenly became aware of breakers ahead. The City Marshal and one of the deputies rose up behind some drygoods boxes half a square to the front and opened fire. At the same time the rest of the posse, divided, shelled him from two side streets up which they were cautiously manœuvring from a well-executed detour.

The first volley broke the lock of one of Calliope's guns, cut a neat underbit in his right ear, and exploded a cartridge in his crossbelt, scorching his ribs as it burst. Feeling braced up by this unexpected tonic to his spiritual depression, Calliope executed a fortissimo note from his upper registers, and returned the fire like an echo. The upholders of the law dodged at his flash, but a trifle too late to save one of the deputies a bullet just above the elbow, and the marshal a bleeding cheek from a splinter that a ball tore from a box he had ducked behind.

And now Calliope met the enemy's tactics in kind. Choosing with a rapid eye the street from which the weakest and least accurate fire had come, he invaded it at double-quick, abandoning the unprotected middle of the street. With rare cunning the opposing force in that direction—one of the deputies and two of the valorous volunteers—waited, concealed by beer barrels, until Calliope had passed their retreat, and then peppered him from the rear. In another moment they were reinforced by the marshal and his other men, and then Calliope felt that in order to successfully prolong the delights of the controversy he must find some means of reducing the great odds against him. His eye fell upon a structure that seemed to hold out this promise, providing he could reach it.

Not far away was the little railroad station, its building a strong box house, ten by twenty feet, resting upon a platform four feet above ground. Windows were in each of its walls. Something like a fort it might become to a man thus sorely pressed by superior numbers.

Calliope made a bold and rapid spurt for it, the marshal's crowd "smoking" him as he ran. He reached the haven in safety, the station agent leaving the building by a window, like a flying squirrel, as the garrison entered the door.

Patterson and his supporters halted under protection of a pile of lumber and held consultations. In the station was an unterrified desperado who was an excellent shot and carried an abundance of ammunition. For thirty yards on each side of the besieged was a stretch of bare, open ground. It was a sure thing that the man who attempted to enter that unprotected area would be stopped by one of Calliope's bullets.

The City Marshal was resolved. He had decided that Calliope Catesby should no more wake the echoes of Quicksand

with his strident whoop. He had so announced. Officially and
personally he felt imperatively bound to put the soft pedal
on that instrument of discord. It played bad tunes.

Standing near was a hand truck used in the manipulation
of small freight. It stood by a shed full of sacked wool, con-
signment from one of the sheep ranches. On this truck the
marshal and his men piled three heavy sacks of wool. Stoop-
ing low, Buck Patterson started for Calliope's fort, slowly
pushing this loaded truck before him for protection. The
posse, scattering broadly, stood ready to nip the besieged in
case he should show himself in an effort to repel the jug-
gernaut of justice that was creeping upon him. Only once
did Calliope make demonstration. He fired from a window
and some tufts of wool spurted from the marshal's trust-
worthy bulwark. The return shots from the posse pattered
against the window frame of the fort. No loss resulted on
either side.

The marshal was too deeply engrossed in steering his pro-
tected battleship to be aware of the approach of the morning
train until he was within a few feet of the platform. The
train was coming up on the other side of it. It stopped only
one minute at Quicksand. What an opportunity it would offer
to Calliope! He had only to step out the other door, mount
the train, and away.

Abandoning his breastworks, Buck, with his gun ready,
dashed up the steps and into the room, driving open the
closed door with one heave of his weighty shoulder. The
members of the posse heard one shot fired inside, and then
there was silence.

At length the wounded man opened his eyes. After a blank
space he again could see and hear and feel and think. Turning his eyes about, he found himself lying on a wooden bench.
A tall man with a perplexed countenance, wearing a big
badge with "City Marshal" engraved upon it, stood over him.
A little old woman in black, with a wrinkled face and sparkling black eyes was holding a wet handkerchief against one
of his temples. He was trying to get these facts fixed in his

mind and connected with past events, when the old woman began to talk.

"There now, great, big, strong man! That bullet never tetched ye! Jest skeeted along the side of your head and sort of paralyzed ye for a spell. I've heerd of sech things afor! Con-cussion is what they names it. Abel Wadkins used to kill squirrels that way—barkin' em, Abe called it. You jest been barked, sir, and you'll be all right in a little bit. Feel lots better already, don't ye! You just lay still a while longer and let me bathe your head. You don't know me, I reckon, and 'tain't surprisin' that you shouldn't. I come in on that train from Alabama to see my son. Big son, ain't he? Lands! you wouldn't hardly think he'd ever been a baby, would ye? This is my son, sir."

Half turning, the old woman looked up at the standing man, her worn face lighting with a proud and wonderful smile. She reached out one veined and calloused hand and took one of her son's. Then smiling cheerily down at the prostrate man, she continued to dip the handkerchief in the waiting-room tin washbasin and gently apply it to his temple. She had the benevolent garrulity of old age.

"I ain't seen my son before," she continued, "in eight years. One of my nephews, Elkanah Price, he's a conductor on one of them railroads, and he got me a pass to come out here. I can stay a whole week on it, and then it'll take me back again. Jest think, now, that little boy of mine has got to be a officer—a city marshal of a whole town! That's something like a constable, ain't it? I never knowed he was a officer; he didn't say nothin' about it in his letters. I reckon he thought his old mother'd be skeered about the danger he was in. But, laws! I never was much of a hand to get skeered. 'Tain't no use. I heard them guns a-shootin' while I was gittin' off them cars, and I see smoke a-comin' out of the depot, but I jest walked right along. Then I see son's face lookin' out through the window. I knowed him at oncet. He met me at the door, and squeezed me 'most to death. And there you was, sir, a-lyin' there jest like you was dead, and I 'lowed we'd see what might be done to help sot you up."

"I think I'll sit up now," said the concussion patient. "I'm feeling pretty fair by this time."

He sat, somewhat weakly yet, leaning against the wall. He was a rugged man, big-boned and straight. His eyes, steady and keen, seemed to linger upon the face of the man standing so still above him. His look wandered often from the face he studied to the marshal's badge upon the other's breast.

"Yes, yes, you'll be all right," said the old woman, patting his arm, "if you don't get to cuttin' up ag'in, and havin' folks shootin' at you. Son told me about you, sir, while you was layin' senseless on the floor. Don't you take it as meddlesome fer an old woman with a son as big as you to talk about it. And you mustn't hold no grudge ag'in my son for havin' to shoot at ye. A officer has got to take up for the law—it's his duty—and them that acts bad and lives wrong has to suffer. Don't blame my son any, sir—'tain't his fault. He's always been a good boy—good when he was growin' up, and kind and 'bedient and well-behaved. Won't you let me advise you, sir, not to do so no more? Be a good man, and leave liquor alone and live peaceably and godly. Keep away from bad company and work honest and sleep sweet."

The black-mittened hand of the old pleader gently touched the breast of the man she addressed. Very earnest and candid her old, worn face looked. In her rusty black dress and antique bonnet she sat, near the close of a long life, and epitomized the experience of the world. Still the man to whom she spoke gazed above her head, contemplating the silent son of the old mother.

"What does the marshal say?" he asked. "Does he believe the advice is good? Suppose the marshal speaks up and says if the talk's all right?"

The tall man moved uneasily. He fingered the badge on his breast for a moment, and then he put an arm around the old woman and drew her close to him. She smiled the unchanging mother smile of three-score years, and patted his big brown hand with her crooked, mittened fingers while her son spake.

"I say this," he said, looking squarely into the eyes of the other man, "that if I was in your place I'd follow it. If I was a drunken, desp'rate character, without shame or hope, I'd follow it. If I was in your place and you was in mine I'd say: 'Marshal, I'm willin' to swear if you'll give me the chance I'll quit the racket. I'll drop the tanglefoot and the gun play, and won't play hoss no more. I'll be a good citizen and go to work and quit my foolishness. So help me God!' That's what I'd say to you if you was marshal and I was in your place."

"Hear my son talkin'," said the old woman, softly. "Hear him, sir. You promise to be good and he won't do you no harm. Forty-one year ago his heart first beat ag'in mine, and it's beat true ever since."

The other man rose to his feet, trying his limbs and stretching his muscles.

"Then," said he, "if you was in my place and said that, and I was marshal, I'd say: 'Go free, and do your best to keep your promise.'"

"Lawsy!" exclaimed the old woman, in a sudden flutter, "ef I didn't clear forget that trunk of mine! I see a man settin' it on the platform jest as I seen son's face in the window, and it went plum out of my head. There's eight jars of home-made quince jam in that trunk that I made myself. I wouldn't have nothin' happen to them jars for a red apple."

Away to the door she trotted, spry and anxious, and then Calliope Catesby spoke out to Buck Patterson:

"I just couldn't help it, Buck. I seen her through the window a-comin' in. She had never heard a word 'bout my tough ways. I didn't have the nerve to let her know I was a worth-less cuss bein' hunted down by the community. There you was lyin' where my shot laid you, like you was dead. The idea struck me sudden, and I just took your badge off and fastened it onto myself, and I fastened my reputation onto you. I told her I was the marshal and you was a holy terror. You can take your badge back now, Buck."

With shaking fingers Calliope began to unfasten the disc of metal from his shirt.

"Easy there!" said Buck Patterson. "You keep that badge right where it is, Calliope Catesby. Don't you dare to take it off till the day your mother leaves this town. You'll be City Marshal of Quicksand as long as she's here to know it. After I stir around town a bit and put 'em on I'll guarantee that nobody won't give the thing away to her. And say, you leather-headed, rip-roarin', low-down son of a locoed cyclone, you follow that advice she gave me! I'm goin' to take some of it myself, too."

"Buck," said Calliope, feelingly, "ef I don't I hope I may——"

"Shut up," said Buck. "She's a-comin' back."

The Passing of Black Eagle

FOR some months of a certain year a grim bandit infested the Texas border along the Rio Grande. Peculiarly striking to the optic nerve was this notorious marauder. His personality secured him the title of "Black Eagle, the Terror of the Border." Many fearsome tales are on record concerning the doings of him and his followers. Suddenly, in the space of a single minute, Black Eagle vanished from earth. He was never heard of again. His own band never even guessed the mystery of his disappearance. The border ranches and settlements feared he would come again to ride and ravage the mesquite flats. He never will. It is to disclose the fate of Black Eagle that this narrative is written.

The initial movement of the story is furnished by the foot of a bartender in St. Louis. His discerning eye fell upon the form of Chicken Ruggles as he pecked with avidity at the free lunch. Chicken was a "hobo." He had a long nose like the bill of a fowl, an inordinate appetite for poultry, and a habit of gratifying it without expense, which accounts for the name given him by his fellow vagrants.

Physicians agree that the partaking of liquors at meal times is not a healthy practice. The hygiene of the saloon promulgates the opposite. Chicken had neglected to purchase a drink to accompany his meal. The bartender rounded the counter, caught the injudicious diner by the ear with a lemon squeezer, led him to the door and kicked him into the street.

Thus the mind of Chicken was brought to realize the signs of coming winter. The night was cold; the stars shone with unkindly brilliancy; people were hurrying along the streets in two egotistic, jostling streams. Men had donned their overcoats, and Chicken knew to an exact percentage the increased difficulty of coaxing dimes from those buttoned-in vest pockets. The time had come for his annual exodus to the south.

A little boy, five or six years old, stood looking with covetous eyes in a confectioner's window. In one small hand he held an empty two-ounce vial; in the other he grasped tightly something flat and round, with a shining milled edge. The scene presented a field of operations commensurate to Chicken's talents and daring. After sweeping the horizon to make sure that no official tug was cruising near, he insidiously accosted his prey. The boy, having been early taught by his household to regard altruistic advances with extreme suspicion, received the overtures coldly.

Then Chicken knew that he must make one of those desperate, nerve-shattering plunges into speculation that fortune sometimes requires of those who would win her favor. Five cents was his capital, and this he must risk against the chance of winning what lay within the close grasp of the youngster's chubby hand. It was a fearful lottery, Chicken knew. But he must accomplish his end by strategy, since he had a wholesome terror of plundering infants by force. Once, in a park, driven by hunger, he had committed an onslaught upon a bottle of peptonized infant's food in the possession of an occupant of a baby carriage. The outraged infant had so promptly opened its mouth and pressed the button that communicated with the welkin that help arrived, and Chicken did his thirty days in a snug coop. Wherefore he was, as he said, "leary of kids."

Beginning artfully to question the boy concerning his choice of sweets, he gradually drew out the information he wanted. Mamma said he was to ask the drug-store man for ten cents' worth of paregoric in the bottle; he was to keep his hand shut tight over the dollar; he must not stop to talk to any one in the street; he must ask the drug-store man to wrap up the change and put it in the pocket of his trousers. Indeed, they had pockets—two of them! And he liked chocolate creams best.

Chicken went into the store and turned plunger. He invested his entire capital in C. A. N. D. Y. stocks, simply to pave the way to the greater risk following.

He gave the sweets to the youngster, and had the satisfaction of perceiving that confidence was established. After that it was easy to obtain leadership of the expedition, to take the investment by the hand and lead it to a nice drug store he knew of in the same block. There Chicken, with a parental air, passed over the dollar and called for the medicine, while the boy crunched his candy, glad to be relieved of the responsibility of the purchase. And then the successful investor, searching his pockets, found an overcoat button —the extent of his winter trousseau—and, wrapping it carefully, placed the ostensible change in the pocket of confiding juvenility. Setting the youngster's face homeward, and patting him benevolently on the back—for Chicken's heart was as soft as those of his feathered namesakes—the speculator quit the market with a profit of 1,700 per cent. on his invested capital.

Two hours later an Iron Mountain freight engine pulled out of the railroad yards, Texas bound, with a string of empties. In one of the cattle cars, half buried in excelsior, Chicken lay at ease. Beside him in his nest was a quart bottle of very poor whisky and a paper bag of bread and cheese. Mr. Ruggles, in his private car, was on his trip south for the winter season.

For a week that car was trundled southward, shifted, laid over, and manipulated after the manner of rolling stock, but Chicken stuck to it, leaving it only at necessary times to satisfy his hunger and thirst. He knew it must go down to the cattle country, and San Antonio, in the heart of it, was his goal. There the air was salubrious and mild; the people indulgent and long-suffering. The bartenders there would not kick him. If he should eat too long or too often at one place they would swear at him as if by rote and without heat. They swore so drawlingly, and they rarely paused short of their full vocabulary, which was copious, so that Chicken had often gulped a good meal during the process of the vituperative prohibition. The season there was always spring-like; the plazas were pleasant at night, with music and gayety: except during the slight and infrequent cold snaps one could sleep comfortably out of doors in case the interiors should develop inhospitality.

At Texarkana his car was switched to the I. and G. N. Then still southward it trailed until, at length, it crawled across the Colorado bridge at Austin, and lined out, straight as an arrow, for the run to San Antonio.

When the freight halted at that town Chicken was fast asleep. In ten minutes the train was off again for Laredo, the end of the road. Those empty cattle cars were for distribution along the line at points from which the ranches shipped their stock.

When Chicken awoke his car was stationary. Looking out between the slats he saw it was a bright, moonlit night. Scrambling out, he saw his car with three others abandoned on a little siding in a wild and lonesome country. A cattle pen and chute stood on one side of the track. The railroad bisected a vast, dim ocean of prairie, in the midst of which Chicken, with his futile rolling stock, was as completely stranded as was Robinson with his land-locked boat.

A white post stood near the rails. Going up to it, Chicken read the letters at the top, S. A. 90. Laredo was nearly as far to the south. He was almost a hundred miles from any town. Coyotes began to yelp in the mysterious sea around him. Chicken felt lonesome. He had lived in Boston without an education, in Chicago without nerve, in Philadelphia without a sleeping place, in New York without a pull, and in Pittsburgh sober, and yet he had never felt so lonely as now.

Suddenly through the intense silence, he heard the whicker of a horse. The sound came from the side of the track toward the east, and Chicken began to explore timorously in that direction. He stepped high along the mat of curly mesquite grass, for he was afraid of everything there might be in this wilderness—snakes, rats, brigands, centipedes, mirages, cowboys, fandangoes, tarantulas, tamales—he had read of them in the story papers. Rounding a clump of prickly pear that reared high its fantastic and menacing array of rounded heads, he was struck to shivering terror by a snort and a thunderous plunge, as the horse, himself startled, bounded away some fifty yards, and then resumed his grazing. But here was the one thing in the desert that Chicken did not fear. He had been reared on a farm; he had handled horses, understood them, and could ride.

Approaching slowly and speaking soothingly, he followed the animal, which, after its first flight, seemed gentle enough, and secured the end of the twenty-foot lariat that dragged after him in the grass. It required him but a few moments to contrive the rope into an ingenious nose-bridle, after the style of the Mexican *borsal*. In another he was upon the horse's back and off at a splendid lope, giving the animal free choice of direction. "He will take me somewhere," said Chicken to himself.

It would have been a thing of joy, that untrammelled gallop over the moonlit prairie, even to Chicken, who loathed exertion, but that his mood was not for it. His head ached; a growing thirst was upon him; the "somewhere" whither his lucky mount might convey him was full of dismal peradventure.

And now he noted that the horse moved to a definite goal. Where the prairie lay smooth he kept his course straight as an arrow's toward the east. Deflected by hill or arroyo or impracticable spinous brakes, he quickly flowed again into the current, charted by his unerring instinct. At last, upon the side of a gentle rise, he suddenly subsided to a complacent walk. A stone's cast away stood a little mott of coma trees; beneath it a *jacal* such as the Mexicans erect—a one-room house of upright poles daubed with clay and roofed with grass or tule reeds. An experienced eye would have estimated the spot as the headquarters of a small sheep ranch. In the moonlight the ground in the nearby corral showed pulverized to a level smoothness by the hoofs of the sheep. Everywhere was carelessly distributed the paraphernalia of the place—ropes, bridles, saddles, sheep pelts, wool sacks, feed troughs, and camp litter. The barrel of drinking water stood in the end of the two-horse wagon near the door. The harness was piled, promiscuous, upon the wagon tongue, soaking up the dew.

Chicken slipped to earth, and tied the horse to a tree. He halloed again and again, but the house remained quiet. The door stood open, and he entered cautiously. The light was sufficient for him to see that no one was at home. He struck a match and lighted a lamp that stood on a table. The room was that of a bachelor ranchman who was content with the necessaries of life. Chicken rummaged intelligently until he found what he had hardly dared hope for—a small brown jug that still contained something near a quart of his desire.

Half an hour later, Chicken—now a gamecock of hostile aspect—emerged from the house with unsteady steps. He had drawn upon the absent ranchman's equipment to replace his own ragged attire. He wore a suit of coarse brown ducking, the coat being a sort of rakish bolero, jaunty to a degree. Boots he had donned, and spurs that whirred with every lurching step. Buckled around him was a belt full of cartridges with a six-shooter in each of its two holsters.

Prowling about, he found blankets, a saddle and bridle with which he caparisoned his steed. Again mounting, he rode swiftly away, singing a loud and tuneless song.

Bud King's band of desperadoes, outlaws and horse and cattle thieves were in camp at a secluded spot on the bank of the Frio. Their depredations in the Rio Grande country, while no bolder than usual, had been advertised more extensively, and Captain Kinney's company of rangers had been ordered down to look after them. Consequently, Bud King, who was a wise general, instead of cutting out a hot trail for the upholders of the law, as his men wished to do, retired for the time to the prickly fastnesses of the Frio valley.

Though the move was a prudent one, and not incompatible with Bud's well-known courage, it raised dissension among the members of the band. In fact, while they thus lay ingloriously *perdu* in the brush, the question of Bud King's fitness for the leadership was argued, with closed doors, as it were, by his followers. Never before had Bud's skill or efficiency been brought to criticism; but his glory was waning (and such is glory's fate) in the light of a newer star. The sentiment of the band was crystallizing into the opinion that Black Eagle could lead them with more luster, profit, and distinction.

This Black Eagle—sub-titled the "Terror of the Border"— had been a member of the gang about three months.

One night while they were in camp on the San Miguel water-hole a solitary horseman on the regulation fiery steed dashed in among them. The newcomer was of a portentous and devastating aspect. A beak-like nose with a predatory curve projected above a mass of bristling, blue-black whiskers. His eye was cavernous and fierce. He was spurred, sombreroed, booted, garnished with revolvers, abundantly drunk, and very much unafraid. Few people in the country drained by the Rio Bravo would have cared thus to invade alone the camp of Bud King. But this fell bird swooped fearlessly upon them and demanded to be fed.

Hospitality in the prairie country is not limited. Even if your enemy pass your way you must feed him before you shoot him. You must empty your larder into him before you empty your lead. So the stranger of undeclared intentions was set down to a mighty feast.

A talkative bird he was, full of most marvellous loud tales and exploits, and speaking a language at times obscure but never colorless. He was a new sensation to Bud King's men, who rarely encountered new types. They hung, delighted, upon his vainglorious boasting, the spicy strangeness of his lingo, his contemptuous familiarity with life, the world, and remote places, and the extravagant frankness with which he conveyed his sentiments.

To their guest the band of outlaws seemed to be nothing more than a congregation of country bumpkins whom he was "stringing for grub" just as he would have told his stories at the back door of a farmhouse to wheedle a meal. And, indeed, his ignorance was not without excuse, for the "bad man" of the Southwest does not run to extremes. Those brigands might justly have been taken for a little party of peaceable rustics assembled for a fish-fry or pecan gathering. Gentle of manner, slouching of gait, soft-voiced, unpicturesquely clothed; not one of them presented to the eye any witness of the desperate records they had earned.

For two days the glittering stranger within the camp was feasted. Then, by common consent, he was invited to become a member of the band. He consented, presenting for enrollment the prodigious name of "Captain Montressor." This was immediately overruled by the band, and "Piggy" substituted as a compliment to the awful and insatiate appetite of its owner.

Thus did the Texas border receive the most spectacular brigand that ever rode its chaparral.

For the next three months Bud King conducted business as usual, escaping encounters with law officers and being content with reasonable profits. The band ran off some very good companies of horses from the ranges, and a few bunches of fine cattle which they got safely across the Rio Grande and disposed of to fair advantage. Often the band would ride into the little villages and Mexican settlements, terrorizing the inhabitants and plundering for the provisions and ammunition they needed. It was during these bloodless raids that Piggy's ferocious aspect and frightful voice gained him a renown more widespread and glorious than those other gentle-voiced and sad-faced desperadoes could have acquired in a lifetime.

The Mexicans, most apt in nomenclature, first called him The Black Eagle, and used to frighten the babes by threatening them with tales of the dreadful robber who carried off little children in his great beak. Soon the name extended, and Black Eagle, the Terror of the Border, became a recognized factor in exaggerated newspaper reports and ranch gossip.

The country from the Nueces to the Rio Grande was a wild but fertile stretch, given over to the sheep and cattle ranches. Range was free; the inhabitants were few; the law was mainly a letter, and the pirates met with little opposition until the flaunting and garish Piggy gave the band undue advertisement. Then Kinney's ranger company headed for those precincts, and Bud King knew that it meant grim and sudden war or else temporary retirement. Regarding the risk to be unnecessary, he drew off his band to an almost inaccessible spot on the bank of the Frio. Wherefore, as has been said, dissatisfaction arose among the members, and impeachment proceedings against Bud were premeditated, with Black Eagle in high favor for the succession. Bud King was not unaware of the sentiment, and he called aside Cactus Taylor, his trusted lieutenant, to discuss it.

"If the boys," said Bud, "ain't satisfied with me, I'm willin' to step out. They're buckin' against my way of handlin' 'em. And 'specially because I concludes to hit the brush while Sam Kinney is ridin' the line. I saves 'em from bein' shot or sent up on a state contract, and they up and says I'm no good."

"It ain't so much that," explained Cactus, "as it is they're plum locoed about Piggy. They want them whiskers and that nose of his to split the wind at the head of the column."

"There's somethin' mighty seldom about Piggy," declared Bud, musingly. "I never yet see anything on the hoof that he exactly grades up with. He can shore holler a plenty, and he straddles a hoss from where you laid the chunk. But he ain't never been smoked yet. You know, Cactus, we ain't had a row since he's been with us. Piggy's all right for skearin' the greaser kids and layin' waste a cross-roads store. I reckon he's the finest canned oyster buccaneer and cheese pirate that ever was, but how's his appetite for fightin'? I've knowed some citizens you'd think was starvin' for trouble get a bad case of dyspepsy the first dose of lead they had to take."

"He talks all spraddled out," said Cactus, " 'bout the rookuses he's been in. He claims to have saw the elephant and hearn the owl."

"I know," replied Bud, using the cow-puncher's expressive phrase of skepticism, "but it sounds to me!"

This conversation was held one night in camp while the other members of the band—eight in number—were sprawling around the fire, lingering over their supper. When Bud and Cactus ceased talking they heard Piggy's formidable voice holding forth to the others as usual while he was engaged in checking, though never satisfying, his ravening appetite.

"Wat's de use," he was saying, "of chasin' little red cowses and hosses 'round for t'ousands of miles? Dere ain't nuttin' in it. Gallopin' t'rough dese bushes and briers, and gettin' a t'irst dat a brewery couldn't put out, and missin' meals! Say! You know what I'd do if I was main finger of dis bunch? I'd stick up a train. I'd blow de express car and make hard dollars where you guys get wind. Youse makes me tired. Dis sook-cow kind of cheap sport gives me a pain."

Later on, a deputation waited on Bud. They stood on one leg, chewed mesquite twigs and circumlocuted, for they hated to hurt his feelings. Bud foresaw their business, and made it easy for them. Bigger risks and larger profits was what they wanted.

The suggestion of Piggy's about holding up a train had fired their imagination and increased their admiration for the dash and boldness of the instigator. They were such simple, artless, and custom-bound bush-rangers that they had never before thought of extending their habits beyond the running off of livestock and the shooting of such of their acquaintances as ventured to interfere.

Bud acted "on the level," agreeing to take a subordinate place in the gang until Black Eagle should have been given a trial as leader.

After a great deal of consultation, studying of timetables and discussion of the country's topography, the time and place for carrying out their new enterprise was decided upon. At that time there was a feedstuff famine in Mexico and a cattle famine in certain parts of the United States, and there was a brisk international trade. Much money was being shipped along the railroads that connected the two republics. It was agreed that the most promising place for the contemplated robbery was at Espina, a little station on the I. and G. N., about forty miles north of Laredo. The train stopped there one minute; the country around was wild and unsettled; the station consisted of but one house in which the agent lived.

Black Eagle's band set out, riding by night. Arriving in the vicinity of Espina they rested their horses all day in a thicket a few miles distant.

The train was due at Espina at 10:30 P.M. They could rob the train and be well over the Mexican border with their booty by daylight the next morning.

To do Black Eagle justice, he exhibited no signs of flinching from the responsible honors that had been conferred upon him.

He assigned his men to their respective posts with discretion, and coached them carefully as to their duties. On each side of the track four of the band were to lie concealed in the chaparral. Gotch-Ear Rodgers was to stick up the station agent. Bronco Charlie was to remain with the horses, holding them in readiness. At a spot where it was calculated the engine would be when the train stopped, Bud King was to lie hidden on one side, and Black Eagle himself on the other. The two would get the drop on the engineer and fireman, force them to descend and proceed to the rear. Then the express car would be looted, and the escape made. No one was to move until Black Eagle gave the signal by firing his revolver. The plan was perfect.

At ten minutes to train time every man was at his post, effectually concealed by the thick chaparral that grew almost to the rails. The night was dark and lowering, with a fine drizzle falling from the flying gulf clouds. Black Eagle crouched behind a bush within five yards of the track. Two six-shooters were belted around him. Occasionally he drew a large black bottle from his pocket and raised it to his mouth.

A star appeared far down the track which soon waxed into the headlight of the approaching train. It came on with an increasing roar; the engine bore down upon the ambushing desperadoes with a glare and a shriek like some avenging monster come to deliver them to justice. Black Eagle flattened himself upon the ground. The engine, contrary to their calculations, instead of stopping between him and Bud King's place of concealment, passed fully forty yards farther before it came to a stand.

The bandit leader rose to his feet and peered around the bush. His men all lay quiet, awaiting the signal. Immediately opposite Black Eagle was a thing that drew his attention. Instead of being a regular passenger train it was a mixed one. Before him stood a box car, the door of which, by some means, had been left slightly open. Black Eagle went up to it and pushed the door farther open. An odor came forth—a damp, rancid, familiar, musty, intoxicating, beloved odor stirring strongly at old memories of happy days and travels. Black Eagle sniffed at the witching smell as the returned wanderer smells of the rose that twines his boyhood's cottage home. Nostalgia seized him. He put his hand inside. Excelsior —dry, springy, curly, soft, enticing, covered the floor. Outside the drizzle had turned to a chilling rain.

The train bell clanged. The bandit chief unbuckled his belt and cast it, with its revolvers, upon the ground. His spurs followed quickly, and his broad sombrero. Black Eagle was moulting. The train started with a rattling jerk. The ex-Terror of the Border scrambled into the box car and closed the door. Stretched luxuriously upon the excelsior, with the black bottle clasped closely to his breast, his eyes closed, and a foolish, happy smile upon his terrible features Chicken Ruggles started upon his return trip.

Undisturbed, with the band of desperate bandits lying motionless, awaiting the signal to attack, the train pulled out from Espina. As its speed increased, and the black masses of chaparral went whizzing past on either side, the express messenger, lighting his pipe, looked through his window and remarked, feelingly:

"What a jim-dandy place for a hold-up!"

A Retrieved Reformation

A GUARD came to the prison shoe-shop, where Jimmy Valentine was assiduously stitching uppers, and escorted him to the front office. There the warden handed Jimmy his pardon, which had been signed that morning by the governor. Jimmy took it in a tired kind of way. He had served nearly ten months of a four-year sentence. He had expected to stay only about three months, at the longest. When a man with as many friends on the outside as Jimmy Valentine had is received in the "stir" it is hardly worth while to cut his hair.

"Now, Valentine," said the warden, "you'll go out in the morning. Brace up, and make a man of yourself. You're not a bad fellow at heart. Stop cracking safes, and live straight."

"Me?" said Jimmy, in surprise. "Why, I never cracked a safe in my life."

"Oh, no," laughed the warden. "Of course not. Let's see, now. How was it you happened to get sent up on that Springfield job? Was it because you wouldn't prove an alibi for fear of compromising somebody in extremely high-toned society? Or was it simply a case of a mean old jury that had it in for you? It's always one or the other with you innocent victims."

"Me?" said Jimmy, still blankly virtuous. "Why, warden, I never was in Springfield in my life!"

"Take him back, Cronin," smiled the warden, "and fix him up with outgoing clothes. Unlock him at seven in the morning, and let him come to the bull-pen. Better think over my advice, Valentine."

At a quarter past seven on the next morning Jimmy stood in the warden's outer office. He had on a suit of the villainously fitting, ready-made clothes and a pair of the stiff, squeaky shoes that the state furnishes to its discharged compulsory guests.

The clerk handed him a railroad ticket and the five-dollar bill with which the law expected him to rehabilitate himself into good citizenship and prosperity. The warden gave him a cigar, and shook hands. Valentine, 9762, was chronicled on the books "Pardoned by Governor," and Mr. James Valentine walked out into the sunshine.

Disregarding the song of the birds, the waving green trees, and the smell of the flowers, Jimmy headed straight for a restaurant. There he tasted the first sweet joys of liberty in the shape of a broiled chicken and a bottle of white wine—followed by a cigar a grade better than the one the warden had given him. From there he proceeded leisurely to the depot. He tossed a quarter into the hat of a blind man sitting by the door, and boarded his train. Three hours set him down in a little town near the state line. He went to the café of one Mike Dolan and shook hands with Mike, who was alone behind the bar.

"Sorry we couldn't make it sooner, Jimmy, me boy," said Mike. "But we had that protest from Springfield to buck against, and the governor nearly balked. Feeling all right?"

"Fine," said Jimmy. "Got my key?"

He got his key and went upstairs, unlocking the door of a room at the rear. Everything was just as he had left it. There on the floor was still Ben Price's collar-button that had been torn from that eminent detective's shirt-band when they had overpowered Jimmy to arrest him.

Pulling out from the wall a folding-bed, Jimmy slid back

a panel in the wall and dragged out a dust-covered suit-case. He opened this and gazed fondly at the finest set of burglar's tools in the East. It was a complete set, made of specially tempered steel, the latest designs in drills, punches, braces and bits, jimmies, clamps, and augers, with two or three novelties invented by Jimmy himself, in which he took pride. Over nine hundred dollars they had cost him to have made at ——, a place where they make such things for the profession.

In half an hour Jimmy went downstairs and through the café. He was now dressed in tasteful and well-fitting clothes, and carried his dusted and cleaned suit-case in his hand.

"Got anything on?" asked Mike Dolan, genially.

"Me?" said Jimmy, in a puzzled tone. "I don't understand. I'm representing the New York Amalgamated Short Snap Biscuit Cracker and Frazzled Wheat Company."

This statement delighted Mike to such an extent that Jimmy had to take a seltzer-and-milk on the spot. He never touched "hard" drinks.

A week after the release of Valentine, 9762, there was a neat job of safe-burglary done in Richmond, Indiana, with no clue to the author. A scant eight hundred dollars was all that was secured. Two weeks after that a patented, improved, burglar-proof safe in Logansport was opened like a cheese to the tune of fifteen hundred dollars, currency; securities and silver untouched. That began to interest the rogue-catchers. Then an old-fashioned bank-safe in Jefferson City became active and threw out of its crater an eruption of bank-notes amounting to five thousand dollars. The losses were now high enough to bring the matter up into Ben Price's class of work. By comparing notes, a remarkable similarity in the methods of the burglaries was noticed. Ben Price investigated the scenes of the robberies, and was heard to remark:

"That's Dandy Jim Valentine's autograph. He's resumed business. Look at that combination knob—jerked out as easy as pulling up a radish in wet weather. He's got the only clamps that can do it. And look how clean those tumblers were punched out! Jimmy never has to drill but one hole.

Yes, I guess I want Mr. Valentine. He'll do his bit next time without any short-time or clemency foolishness."

Ben Price knew Jimmy's habits. He had learned them while working up the Springfield case. Long jumps, quick get-aways, no confederates, and a taste for good society—these ways had helped Mr. Valentine to become noted as a successful dodger of retribution. It was given out that Ben Price had taken up the trail of the elusive cracksman, and other people with burglar-proof safes felt more at ease.

One afternoon Jimmy Valentine and his suit-case climbed out of the mail-hack in Elmore, a little town five miles off the railroad down in the black-jack country of Arkansas. Jimmy, looking like an athletic young senior just home from college, went down the board sidewalk toward the hotel.

A young lady crossed the street, passed him at the corner and entered a door over which was the sign "The Elmore Bank." Jimmy Valentine looked into her eyes, forgot what he was, and became another man. She lowered her eyes and colored slightly. Young men of Jimmy's style and looks were scarce in Elmore.

Jimmy collared a boy that was loafing on the steps of the bank as if he were one of the stock-holders, and began to ask him questions about the town, feeding him dimes at intervals. By and by the young lady came out, looking royally unconscious of the young man with the suit-case, and went her way.

"Isn't that young lady Miss Polly Simpson?" asked Jimmy, with specious guile.

"Naw," said the boy. "She's Annabel Adams. Her pa owns this bank. What'd you come to Elmore for? Is that a gold watch-chain? I'm going to get a bulldog. Got any more dimes?"

Jimmy went to the Planters' Hotel, registered as Ralph D. Spencer, and engaged a room. He leaned on the desk and declared his platform to the clerk. He said he had come to Elmore to look for a location to go into business. How was the shoe business, now, in the town? He had thought of the shoe business. Was there an opening?

The clerk was impressed by the clothes and manner of Jimmy. He, himself, was something of a pattern of fashion to the thinly gilded youth of Elmore, but he now perceived his shortcomings. While trying to figure out Jimmy's manner of tying his four-in-hand he cordially gave information.

Yes, there ought to be a good opening in the shoe line. There wasn't an exclusive shoe-store in the place. The dry-goods and general stores handled them. Business in all lines was fairly good. Hoped Mr. Spencer would decide to locate in Elmore. He would find it a pleasant town to live in, and the people very sociable.

Mr. Spencer thought he would stop over in the town a few days and look over the situation. No, the clerk needn't call the boy. He would carry up his suit-case himself; it was rather heavy.

Mr. Ralph Spencer, the phœnix that arose from Jimmy Valentine's ashes—ashes left by the flame of a sudden and alternative attack of love—remained in Elmore, and prospered. He opened a shoe-store and secured a good run of trade.

Socially he was also a success, and made many friends. And he accomplished the wish of his heart. He met Miss Annabel Adams, and became more and more captivated by her charms.

At the end of a year the situation of Mr. Ralph Spencer was this: he had won the respect of the community, his shoe-store was flourishing, and he and Annabel were engaged to be married in two weeks. Mr. Adams, the typical, plodding, country banker, approved of Spencer. Annabel's pride in him almost equalled her affection. He was as much at home in the family of Mr. Adams and that of Annabel's married sister as if he were already a member.

One day Jimmy sat down in his room and wrote this let-ter, which he mailed to the safe address of one of his old friends in St. Louis:

DEAR OLD PAL:

I want you to be at Sullivan's place, in Little Rock, next

Wednesday night at nine o'clock. I want you to wind up some little matters for me. And, also, I want to make you a present of my kit of tools. I know you'll be glad to get them— you couldn't duplicate the lot for a thousand dollars. Say, Billy, I've quit the old business—a year ago. I've got a nice store. I'm making an honest living, and I'm going to marry the finest girl on earth two weeks from now. It's the only life, Billy—the straight one. I wouldn't touch a dollar of another man's money now for a million. After I get married I'm going to sell out and go West, where there won't be so much danger of having old scores brought up against me. I tell you, Billy, she's an angel. She believes in me; and I wouldn't do another crooked thing for the whole world. Be sure to be at Sully's, for I must see you. I'll bring along the tools with me.

Your old friend,

JIMMY.

On the Monday night after Jimmy wrote this letter, Ben Price jogged unobtrusively into Elmore in a livery buggy. He lounged about town in his quiet way until he found out what he wanted to know. From the drug-store across the street from Spencer's shoe-store he got a good look at Ralph D. Spencer.

"Going to marry the banker's daughter are you, Jimmy?" said Ben to himself, softly. "Well, I don't know!"

The next morning Jimmy took breakfast at the Adamses. He was going to Little Rock that day to order his wedding-suit and buy something nice for Annabel. That would be the first time he had left town since he came to Elmore. It had been more than a year now since those last professional "jobs," and he thought he could safely venture out.

After breakfast quite a family party went down town together—Mr. Adams, Annabel, Jimmy, and Annabel's married sister with her two little girls, aged five and nine. They came by the hotel where Jimmy still boarded, and he ran up to his room and brought along his suit-case. Then they went on to the bank. There stood Jimmy's horse and buggy and Dolph Gibson, who was going to drive him over to the railroad station.

All went inside the high, carved oak railings into the banking-room—Jimmy included, for Mr. Adams's future son-in-law was welcome anywhere. The clerks were pleased to be greeted by the good-looking, agreeable young man who was going to marry Miss Annabel. Jimmy set his suit-case down. Annabel, whose heart was bubbling with happiness and lively youth, put on Jimmy's hat and picked up the suit-case. "Wouldn't I make a nice drummer?" said Annabel. "My! Ralph, how heavy it is. Feels like it was full of gold bricks."

"Lot of nickel-plated shoe-horns in there," said Jimmy, coolly, "that I'm going to return. Thought I'd save express charges by taking them up. I'm getting awfully economical."

The Elmore Bank had just put in a new safe and vault. Mr. Adams was very proud of it, and insisted on an inspection by every one. The vault was a small one, but it had a new patented door. It fastened with three solid steel bolts thrown simultaneously with a single handle, and had a time-lock. Mr. Adams beamingly explained its workings to Mr. Spencer, who showed a courteous but not too intelligent interest. The two children, May and Agatha, were delighted by the shining metal and funny clock and knobs.

While they were thus engaged Ben Price sauntered in and leaned on his elbow, looking casually inside between the railings. He told the teller that he didn't want anything; he was just waiting for a man he knew.

Suddenly there was a scream or two from the women, and a commotion. Unperceived by the elders, May, the nine-year-old girl, in a spirit of play, had shut Agatha in the vault. She had then shot the bolts and turned the knob of the combination as she had seen Mr. Adams do.

The old banker sprang to the handle and tugged at it for a moment. "The door can't be opened," he groaned. "The clock hasn't been wound nor the combination set."

Agatha's mother screamed again, hysterically.

"Hush!" said Mr. Adams, raising his trembling hand. "All be quiet for a moment. Agatha!" he called as loudly as he could. "Listen to me." During the following silence they could just hear the faint sound of the child wildly shrieking in the dark vault in a panic of terror.

"My precious darling!" wailed the mother. "She will die of fright! Open the door! Oh, break it open! Can't you men do something?"

"There isn't a man nearer than Little Rock who can open that door," said Mr. Adams, in a shaky voice. "My God! Spencer, what shall we do? That child—she can't stand it long in there. There isn't enough air, and, besides, she'll go into convulsions from fright."

Agatha's mother, frantic now, beat the door of the vault with her hands. Somebody wildly suggested dynamite. Annabel turned to Jimmy, her large eyes full of anguish, but not yet despairing. To a woman nothing seems quite impossible to the powers of the man she worships.

"Can't you do something, Ralph—*try*, won't you?"

He looked at her with a queer, soft smile on his lips and in his keen eyes.

"Annabel," he said, "give me that rose you are wearing, will you?"

Hardly believing that she heard him aright, she unpinned the bud from the bosom of her dress, and placed it in his hand. Jimmy stuffed it into his vestpocket, threw off his coat and pulled up his shirtsleeves. With that act Ralph D. Spencer passed away and Jimmy Valentine took his place.

"Get away from the door, all of you," he commanded, shortly.

He set his suit-case on the table, and opened it out flat. From that time on he seemed to be unconscious of the presence of any one else. He laid out the shining, queer instruments swiftly and orderly, whistling softly to himself as he always did when at work. In a deep silence and immovable, the others watched him as if under a spell.

In a minute Jimmy's pet drill was biting smoothly into the steel door. In ten minutes—breaking his own burglarious record—he threw back the bolts and opened the door.

Agatha, almost collapsed, but safe, was gathered into her mother's arms.

Jimmy Valentine put on his coat, and walked outside the railings toward the front door. As he went he thought he heard a far-away voice that he once knew call "Ralph!" But he never hesitated.

At the door a big man stood somewhat in his way.

"Hello, Ben!" said Jimmy, still with his strange smile. "Got around at last, have you? Well, let's go. I don't know that it makes much difference, now."

And then Ben Price acted rather strangely.

"Guess you're mistaken, Mr. Spencer," he said. "Don't believe I recognize you. Your buggy's waiting for you, ain't it?"

And Ben Price turned and strolled down the street.

Whistling Dick's Christmas Stocking

IT was with much caution that Whistling Dick slid back the door of the box-car, for Article 5716, City Ordinances, authorized (perhaps unconstitutionally) arrest on suspicion, and he was familiar of old with this ordinance. So, before climbing out, he surveyed the field with all the care of a good general.

He saw no change since his last visit to this big, almsgiving, long-suffering city of the South, the cold weather paradise of the tramps. The levee where his freight-car stood was pimpled with dark bulks of merchandise. The breeze reeked with the well-remembered, sickening smell of the old tarpaulins that covered bales and barrels. The dun river slipped along among the shipping with an oily gurgle. Far down toward Chalmette he could see the great bend in the stream, outlined by the row of electric lights. Across the river Algiers lay, a long, irregular blot, made darker by the dawn which lightened the sky beyond. An industrious tug or two, coming for some early sailing ship, gave a few appalling toots, that seemed to be the signal for breaking day. The Italian luggers were creeping nearer their landing, laden with early vegetables and shellfish. A vague roar, subterranean in quality, from dray wheels and street cars, began to make itself heard and felt; and the ferryboats, the Mary Anns of water craft, stirred sullenly to their menial morning tasks.

Whistling Dick's red head popped suddenly back into the car. A sight too imposing and magnificent for his gaze had been added to the scene. A vast, incomparable policeman rounded a pile of rice sacks and stood within twenty yards of the car. The daily miracle of the dawn, now being performed above Algiers, received the flattering attention of this specimen of municipal official splendor. He gazed with unbiased dignity at the faintly glowing colors until, at last, he turned to them his broad back, as if convinced that legal interference was not needed, and the sunrise might proceed unchecked. So he turned his face to the rice bags, and, drawing a flat flask from an inside pocket, he placed it to his lips and regarded the firmament.

Whistling Dick, professional tramp, possessed a half-friendly acquaintance with this officer. They had met several times before on the levee at night, for the officer, himself a lover of music, had been attracted by the exquisite whistling of the shiftless vagabond. Still, he did not care, under the present circumstances, to renew the acquaintance. There is a difference between meeting a policeman upon a lonely wharf and whistling a few operatic airs with him, and being caught by him crawling out of a freight-car. So Dick waited, as even a New Orleans policeman must move on some time—perhaps it is a retributive law of nature—and before long "Big Fritz" majestically disappeared between the trains of cars.

Whistling Dick waited as long as his judgment advised, and then slid swiftly to the ground. Assuming as far as possible the air of an honest laborer who seeks his daily toil, he moved across the network of railway lines, with the in-

tention of making his way by quiet Girod Street to a certain
bench in Lafayette Square, where, according to appointment,
he hoped to rejoin a pal known as "Slick," this adventurous
pilgrim having preceded him by one day in a cattle-car into
which a loose slat had enticed him.

As Whistling Dick picked his way where night still lingered among the big, reeking, musty warehouses, he gave
way to the habit that had won for him his title. Subdued, yet
clear, with each note as true and liquid as a bobolink's, his
whistle tinkled about the dim, cold mountains of brick like
drops of rain falling into a hidden pool. He followed an air,
but it swam mistily into a swirling current of improvisation.
You could cull out the trill of mountain brooks, the staccato
of green rushes shivering above chilly lagoons, the pipe of
sleepy birds.

Rounding a corner, the whistler collided with a mountain
of blue and brass.

"So," observed the mountain calmly, "you are already pack.
Und dere vill not pe frost before two veeks yet! Und you haf
forgotten how to vistle. Dere was a valse note in dot last bar."

"Whatcher know about it?" said Whistling Dick, with
tentative familiarity; "you wit yer little Gherman-band nix-
cumrous chunes. Whatcher know about music? Pick yer ears,
and listen agin. Here's de way I whistled it—see?"

He puckered his lips, but the big policeman held up his
hand.

"Shtop," he said, "und learn der right way. Und learn
also dot a rolling shtone can't vistle for a cent."

Big Fritz's heavy moustache rounded into a circle, and
from its depths came a sound deep and mellow as that from
a flute. He repeated a few bars of the air the tramp had been
whistling. The rendition was cold, but correct, and he empha-
sized the note he had taken exception to.

"Dot p is p natural, and not p vlat. Py der vay, you petter
pe glad I meet you. Von hour later, und I vould haf to put
you in a gage to vistle mit der chail pirds. Der orders are
to bull all der pums after sunrise."

"To which?"

"To bull der pums—eferybody mitout fisible means. Dirty days is der price, or fifteen tollars."

"Is dat straight, or a game you givin' me?"

"It's der pest tip you efer had. I gif it to you pecause I pelief you are not so bad as der rest. Und pecause you can vistle 'Der Freischütz' bezzer dan I myself gan. Don't run against any more bolicemans aroundt der corners, but go away from town a few tays. Goot-pye."

So Madame Orleans had at last grown weary of the strange and ruffled brood that came yearly to nestle beneath her charitable pinions.

After the big policeman had departed, Whistling Dick stood for an irresolute minute, feeling all the outraged indignation of a delinquent tenant who is ordered to vacate his premises. He had pictured to himself a day of dreamful ease when he should have joined his pal; a day of lounging on the wharf, munching the bananas and cocoanuts scattered in unloading the fruit steamers; and then a feast along the free-lunch counters from which the easy-going owners were too good-natured or too generous to drive him away, and afterward a pipe in one of the little flowery parks and a snooze in some shady corner of the wharf. But here was a stern order to exile, and one that he knew must be obeyed. So, with a wary eye open for the gleam of brass buttons, he began his retreat toward a rural refuge. A few days in the country need not necessarily prove disastrous. Beyond the possibility of a slight nip of frost, there was no formidable evil to be looked for.

However, it was with a depressed spirit that Whistling Dick passed the old French market on his chosen route down the river. For safety's sake he still presented to the world his portrayal of the part of the worthy artisan on his way to labor. A stall-keeper in the market, undeceived, hailed him by the generic name of his ilk, and "Jack" halted, taken by surprise. The vendor, melted by this proof of his own acuteness, bestowed a foot of Frankfurter and half a loaf, and thus the problem of breakfast was solved.

When the streets, from topographical reasons, began to

shun the river bank the exile mounted to the top of the levee, and on its well-trodden path pursued his way. The suburban eye regarded him with cold suspicion, individuals reflected the stern spirit of the city's heartless edict. He missed the seclusion of the crowded town and the safety he could always find in the multitude.

At Chalmette, six miles upon his desultory way, there suddenly menaced him a vast and bewildering industry. A new port was being established; the dock was being built, compresses were going up; picks and shovels and barrows struck at him like serpents from every side. An arrogant foreman bore down upon him, estimating his muscles with the eye of a recruiting-sergeant. Brown men and black men all about him were toiling away. He fled in terror.

By noon he had reached the country of the plantations, the great, sad, silent levels bordering the mighty river. He overlooked fields of sugar-cane so vast that their farthest limits melted into the sky. The sugar-making season was well advanced, and the cutters were at work, the wagons creaked drearily after them; the Negro teamsters inspired the mules to greater speed with mellow and sonorous imprecations. Dark-green groves, blurred by the blue of distance, showed where the plantation-houses stood. The tall chimneys of the sugar-mills caught the eye miles distant, like lighthouses at sea.

At a certain point Whistling Dick's unerring nose caught the scent of frying fish. Like a pointer to a quail, he made his way down the levee side straight to the camp of a credulous and ancient fisherman, whom he charmed with song and story, so that he dined like an admiral, and then like a philosopher annihilated the worst three hours of the day by a nap under the trees.

When he awoke and again continued his hegira, a frosty sparkle in the air succeeded the drowsy warmth of the day, and as this portent of a chilly night translated itself to the brain of Sir Peregrine, he lengthened his stride and bethought him of shelter. He traveled a road that faithfully followed the convolutions of the levee, running along its base, but whither he knew not. Bushes and rank grass crowded it to the wheel ruts, and out of his ambuscade the pests of the lowlands swarmed after him, humming a keen vicious soprano. And as the night grew nearer, although colder, the whine of the mosquitoes became a greedy, petulant snarl that shut out all other sounds. To his right, against the heavens, he saw a green light moving, and, accompanying it, the masts and funnels of a big incoming steamer, moving as upon a screen at a magic-lantern show. And there were mysterious marshes at his left, out of which came queer gurgling cries and a choked croaking. The whistling vagrant struck up a merry warble to offset these melancholy influences, and it is likely that. never before, since Pan himself jigged it on his reeds, had such sounds been heard in those depressing solitudes.

A distant clatter in the rear quickly developed into the swift beat of horses' hoofs, and Whistling Dick stepped aside into the dew-wet grass to clear the track. Turning his head, he saw approaching a fine team of stylish grays drawing a double surrey. A stout man with a white moustache occupied the front seat, giving all his attention to the rigid lines in his hands. Behind him sat a placid, middle-aged lady and a brilliant-looking girl hardly arrived at young ladyhood. The laprobe had slipped partly from the knees of the gentleman driving, and Whistling Dick saw two stout canvas bags between his feet—bags such as, while loafing in cities, he had seen warily transferred between express wagons and bank doors. The remaining space in the vehicle was filled with parcels of various sizes and shapes.

As the surrey swept even with the sidetracked tramp, the bright-eyed girl, seized by some merry, madcap impulse, leaned out toward him with a sweet, dazzling smile, and cried, "Mer-ry Christ-mas!" in a shrill, plaintive treble.

Such a thing had not often happened to Whistling Dick, and he felt handicapped in devising the correct response. But lacking time for reflection, he let his instinct decide, and snatching off his battered derby, he rapidly extended it at arm's length, and drew it back with a continuous motion, and shouted a loud, but ceremonious, "Ah, there!" after the flying surrey.

The sudden movement of the girl had caused one of the parcels to become unwrapped, and something limp and black fell from it into the road. The tramp picked it up and found it to be a new black silk stocking, long and fine and slender. It crunched crisply, and yet with a luxurious softness, between his fingers.

"Ther bloomin' little skeezicks!" said Whistling Dick, with a broad grin bisecting his freckled face. "W'ot d'yer think of dat, now! Mer-ry Chris-mus! Sounded like a cuckoo clock, dat's what she did. Dem guys is swells, too, bet yer life, an' der old 'un stacks dem sacks of dough down under his trotters like dey was common as dried apples. Been shoppin' fer Chris-mus, and de kid's lost one of her new socks w'ot she was goin' to hold up Santy wid. De bloomin' little skeezicks! Wit' her 'Mer-ry Chris-mus!' W'ot 'd yer t'ink! Same as to say, 'Hello, Jack, how goes it?' and as swell as Fift' Av'noo, and as easy as a blowout in Cincinnat'."

Whistling Dick folded the stocking carefully and stuffed it into his pocket.

It was nearly two hours later when he came upon signs of habitation. The buildings of an extensive plantation were brought into view by a turn in the road. He easily selected the planter's residence in a large square building with two wings, with numerous good-sized, well-lighted windows, and broad verandas running around its full extent. It was set upon a smooth lawn, which was faintly lit by the far-reaching rays of the lamps within. A noble grove surrounded it, and old-fashioned shrubbery grew thickly about the walls and fences. The quarters of the hands and the mill buildings were situated at a distance in the rear.

The road was now enclosed on each side by a fence, and presently, as Whistling Dick drew nearer the houses, he suddenly stopped and sniffed the air.

"If dere ain't a hobo stew cookin' somewhere in dis immediate precinct," he said to himself, "me nose has quit tellin' de trut'."

Without hesitation he climbed the fence to windward. He found himself in an apparently disused lot, where piles of old bricks were stacked, and rejected, decaying lumber. In a corner he saw the faint glow of a fire that had become little more than a bed of living coals, and he thought he could see some dim human forms sitting or lying about it. He drew nearer, and by the light of a little blaze that suddenly flared up he saw plainly the fat figure of a ragged man in an old brown sweater and cap.

"Dat man," said Whistling Dick to himself softly, "is a dead ringer for Boston Harry. I'll try him wit' de high sign."

He whistled one or two bars of a rag-time melody, and the air was immediately taken up, and then quickly ended with a peculiar run. The first whistler walked confidently up to the fire. The fat man looked up and spake in a loud, asthmatic wheeze:

"Gents, the unexpected but welcome addition to our circle is Mr. Whistling Dick, an old friend of mine for whom I fully vouches. The waiter will lay another cover at once. Mr. W. D. will join us at supper, during which function he will enlighten us in regard to the circumstances that give us the pleasure of his company."

"Chewin' de stuffin' out'n de dictionary, as usual, Boston," said Whistling Dick; "but t'anks all de same for de invitashun. I guess I finds meeself here about de same way as yous guys. A cop gimme de tip dis mornin'. Yous workin' on dis farm?"

"A guest," said Boston sternly, "shouldn't never insult his entertainers until he's filled up wid grub. 'Tain't good business sense. Workin'!—but I will restrain myself. We five— me, Deaf Pete, Blinky, Goggles, and Indiana Tom—got put on to this scheme of Noo Orleans to work visiting gentlemen upon her dirty streets, and we hit the road last evening just as the tender hues of twilight had flopped down upon the daisies and things. Blinky, pass the empty oyster-can at your left to the empty gentleman at your right."

For the next ten minutes the gang of roadsters paid their undivided attention to the supper. In an old five-gallon kerosene can they had cooked a stew of potatoes, meat, and

onions which they partook of from smaller cans they had
found scattered about the vacant lot.

Whistling Dick had known Boston Harry of old, and knew
him to be one of the shrewdest and most successful of his
brotherhood. He looked like a prosperous stock-drover or a
solid merchant from some country village. He was stout and
hale, with a ruddy, always smoothly shaven face. His clothes
were strong and neat, and he gave special attention to his
decent-appearing shoes. During the past ten years he had acquired a reputation for working a larger number of successfully managed confidence games than any of his acquaintances, and he had not a day's work to be counted against
him. It was rumored among his associates that he had saved
a considerable amount of money. The four other men were
fair specimens of the slinking, ill-clad, noisome genus who
carried their labels of "suspicious" in plain view.

After the bottom of the large can had been scraped, and
pipes lit at the coals, two of the men called Boston aside
and spake with him lowly and mysteriously. He nodded de-
cisively, and then said aloud to Whistling Dick:

"Listen, sonny, to some plain talky-talk. We five are on
a lay. I've guaranteed you to be square, and you're to come
in on the profits equal with the boys, and you've got to help.
Two hundred hands on this plantation are expecting to be
paid a week's wages to-morrow morning. To-morrow's Christmas, and they want to lay off. Says the boss: 'Work from five
to nine in the morning to get a train load of sugar off, and
I'll pay every man cash down for the week and a day extra.'
They say: 'Hooray for the boss! It goes.' He drives to Noo
Orleans to-day, and fetches back the cold dollars. Two thousand and seventy-four fifty is the amount. I got the figures
from a man who talks too much, who got 'em from the book-
keeper. The boss of this plantation thinks he's going to pay
this wealth to the hands. He's got it down wrong; he's going
to pay it to us. It's going to stay in the leisure class, where
it belongs. Now, half of this haul goes to me, and the other
half the rest of you may divide. Why the difference? I represent the brains. It's my scheme. Here's the way we're going

to get it. There's some company at supper in the house, but they'll leave about nine. They've just happened in for an hour or so. If they don't go pretty soon, we'll work the scheme anyhow. We want all night to get away good with the dollars. They're heavy. About nine o'clock Deaf Pete and Blinky'll go down the road about a quarter beyond the house, and set fire to a big cane-field there that the cutters haven't touched yet. The wind's just right to have it roaring in two minutes. The alarm'll be given, and every man Jack about the place will be down there in ten minutes, fighting fire. That'll leave the money sacks and the women alone in the house for us to handle. You've heard cane burn? Well, there's mighty few women can screech loud enough to be heard above its crackling. The thing's dead safe. The only danger is in being caught before we can get far enough away with the money. Now, if you——"

"Boston," interrupted Whistling Dick, rising to his feet, "t'anks for de grub yous fellers has given me, but I'll be movin' on now."

"What do you mean?" asked Boston, also rising.

"W'y, you can count me outer dis deal. You oughter know that. I'm on de bum all right enough, but dat other t'ing don't go wit' me. Burglary is no good. I'll say good night and many t'anks fer——"

Whistling Dick had moved away a few steps as he spoke, but he stopped very suddenly. Boston had covered him with a short revolver of roomy calibre.

"Take your seat," said the tramp leader. "I'd feel mighty proud of myself if I let you go and spoil the game. You'll stick right in this camp until we finish the job. The end of that brick pile is your limit. You go two inches beyond that, and I'll have to shoot. Better take it easy, now."

"It's my way of doin'," said Whistling Dick. "Easy goes. You can depress de muzzle of dat twelve-incher, and run 'em back on de trucks. I remains, as de newspapers says, 'in yer midst.'"

"All right," said Boston, lowering his piece, as the other returned and took his seat again on a projecting plank in a pile of timber. "Don't try to leave; that's all. I wouldn't miss this chance even if I had to shoot an old acquaintance to make it go. I don't want to hurt anybody specially, but this thousand dollars I'm going to get will fix me for fair. I'm going to drop the road, and start a saloon in a little town I know about. I'm tired of being kicked around."

Boston Harry took from his pocket a cheap silver watch and held it near the fire.

"It's a quarter to nine," he said. "Pete, you and Blinky start. Go down the road past the house and fire the cane in a dozen places. Then strike for the levee, and come back on it, instead of the road, so you won't meet anybody. By the time you get back the men will all be striking out for the fire, and we'll break for the house and collar the dollars. Everybody cough up what matches he's got."

The two surly tramps made a collection of all the matches in the party, Whistling Dick contributing his quota with propitiatory alacrity, and then they departed in the dim starlight in the direction of the road.

Of the three remaining vagrants, two, Goggles and Indiana Tom, reclined lazily upon convenient lumber and regarded Whistling Dick with undisguised disfavor. Boston, observing that the dissenting recruit was disposed to remain peaceably, relaxed a little of his vigilance. Whistling Dick arose presently and strolled leisurely up and down keeping carefully within the territory assigned him.

"Dis planter chap," he said, pausing before Boston Harry, "w'ot makes yer t'ink he's got de tin in de house wit' 'im?"

"I'm advised of the facts in the case," said Boston. "He drove to Noo Orleans and got it, I say, to-day. Want to change your mind now and come in?"

"Naw, I was just askin'. Wot kind o' team did de boss drive?"

"Pair of grays."

"Double surrey?"

"Yep."

"Women folks along?"

"Wife and kid. Say, what morning paper are you trying to pump news for?"

"I was just conversin' to pass de time away. I guess dat team passed me in de road dis evenin'. Dat's all."

As Whistling Dick put his hands into his pockets and continued his curtailed beat up and down by the fire, he felt the silk stocking he had picked up in the road.

"Ther bloomin' little skeezicks," he muttered, with a grin.

As he walked up and down he could see, through a sort of natural opening or lane among the trees, the planter's residence some seventy-five yards distant. The side of the house toward him exhibited spacious, well-lighted windows through which a soft radiance streamed, illuminating the broad veranda and some extent of the lawn beneath.

"What's that you said?" asked Boston, sharply.

"Oh, nuttin' 't all," said Whistling Dick, lounging carelessly, and kicking meditatively at a little stone on the ground.

"Just as easy," continued the warbling vagrant softly to himself, "an' sociable an' swell, an' sassy, wit' her 'Mer-ry Chris-mus.' Wot d'yer t'ink, now!"

Dinner, two hours late, was being served in the Bellemeade plantation dining-room.

The dining-room and all its appurtenances spoke of an old régime that was here continued rather than suggested to the memory. The plate was rich to the extent that its age and quaintness alone saved it from being showy; there were interesting names signed in the corners of the pictures on the walls; the viands were of the kind that bring a shine into the eyes of gourmets. The service was swift, silent, lavish, as in the days when the waiters were assets like the plate. The names by which the planter's family and their visitors addressed one another were historic in the annals of two nations. Their manners and conversation had that most difficult kind of ease—the kind that still preserves punctilio. The planter himself seemed to be the dynamo that generated the larger portion of the gaiety and wit. The younger ones at the board found it more than difficult to turn back on him his guns of raillery and banter. It is true, the young men attempted to storm his works repeatedly, incited by the hope of gaining the approbation of their fair companions; but even when they sped a well-aimed shaft, the planter forced them to feel defeat by the tremendous discomfiting thunder of the laughter with which he accompanied his retorts. At the head of the table, serene, matronly, benevolent, reigned the mistress of the house, placing here and there the right smile, the right word, the encouraging glance.

The talk of the party was too desultory, too evanescent to follow, but at last they came to the subject of the tramp nuisance, one that had of late vexed the plantations for many miles around. The planter seized the occasion to direct his good-natured fire of raillery at the mistress, accusing her of encouraging the plague. "They swarm up and down the river every winter," he said. "They overrun New Orleans, and we catch the surplus, which is generally the worst part. And, a day or two ago, Madame New Orleans, suddenly discovering that she can't go shopping without brushing her skirts against great rows of the vagabonds sunning themselves on the banquettes, says to the police: 'Catch 'em all,' and the police catch a dozen or two, and the remaining three or four thousand overflow up and down the levees, and madame there"—pointing tragically with the carving-knife at her—"feeds them. They won't work, they defy my overseers, and they make friends with my dogs; and you, madame, feed them before my eyes, and intimidate me when I would interfere. Tell us, please, how many to-day did you thus incite to future laziness and depredation?"

"Six, I think," said madame, with a reflective smile; "but you know two of them offered to work, for you heard them yourself."

The planter's disconcerting laugh rang out again.

"Yes, at their own trades. And one was an artificial-flower maker, and the other a glass-blower. Oh, they were looking for work! Not a hand would they consent to lift to labor of any other kind."

"And another one," continued the soft-hearted mistress,

"used quite good language. It was really extraordinary for one of his class. And he carried a watch. And had lived in Boston. I don't believe they are all bad. They have always seemed to me to rather lack development. I always look upon them as children with whom wisdom has remained at a standstill while whiskers have continued to grow. We passed one this evening as we were driving home who had a face as good as it was incompetent. He was whistling the intermezzo from 'Cavalleria' and blowing the spirit of Mascagni himself into it."

A bright-eyed young girl who sat at the left of the mistress leaned over and said in a confidential undertone:

"I wonder, Mamma, if that tramp we passed on the road found my stocking, and do you think he will hang it up to-night? Now I can hang up but one. Do you know why I wanted a new pair of silk stockings when I have plenty? Well, old Aunt Judy says, if you hang up two that have never been worn, Santa Claus will fill one with good things, and Monsieur Pambe will place in the other payment for all the words you have spoken—good or bad—on the day before Christmas. That's why I've been unusually nice and polite to everyone to-day. Monsieur Pambe, you know, is a witch gentleman; he——"

The words of the young girl were interrupted by a startling thing.

Like the wraith of some burned-out shooting star, a black streak came crashing through the window-pane and upon the table, where it shivered into fragments a dozen pieces of crystal and china ware, and then glanced between the heads of the guests to the wall, imprinting therein a deep, round indentation, at which, to-day, the visitor to Bellemeade marvels as he gazes upon it and listens to this tale as it is told.

The women screamed in many keys, and the men sprang to their feet, and would have laid their hands upon their swords had not the verities of chronology forbidden.

The planter was the first to act; he sprang to the intruding missile and held it up to view.

"By Jupiter!" he cried. "A meteoric shower of hosiery!

Has communication at last been established with Mars?"

"I should say—ahem!—Venus," ventured a young gentle-man visitor, looking hopefully for approbation toward the unresponsive young-lady visitors.

The planter held at arm's length the unceremonious visitor —a long dangling black stocking. "It's loaded," he announced.

As he spoke he reversed the stocking, holding it by the toe, and down from it dropped a roundish stone, wrapped about by a piece of yellowish paper. "Now for the first inter-stellar message of the century!" he cried; and nodding to the company, who had crowded about him, he adjusted his glasses with provoking deliberation, and examined it closely. When he finished he had changed from the jolly host to the practical, decisive man of business. He immediately struck a bell, and said to the silent-footed mulatto man who responded: "Go and tell Mr. Wesley to get Reeves and Maurice and about ten stout hands they can rely upon, and come to the hall door at once. Tell him to have the men arm themselves, and bring plenty of ropes and plough lines. Tell him to hurry." And then he read aloud from the paper these words:

TO THE GENT OF DE HOUS:

Dere is five tuff hoboes xcept meself in the vaken lot near de road war de old brick piles is. Dey got me stuck up wid a gun see and I taken dis means of comunikaten. 2 of der lads is gone down to set fire to de cain field below de hous and when yous fellers goes to turn de hoes on it de hole gang is goin to rob de house of de money yoo gotto pay off wit say git a move on ye say de kid dropt dis sock in der rode tel her mery crismus de same as she told me. Ketch de bums down de rode first and den sen a relefe core to get me out of soke youres truly,

WHISTLEN DICK.

There was some quiet, but rapid, maneuvering at Belle-meade during the ensuing half hour, which ended in five disgusted and sullen tramps being captured and locked se-curely in an out-house pending the coming of the morning and retribution. For another result, the visiting young gentlemen had secured the unqualified worship of the visiting young ladies by their distinguished and heroic conduct. For still another, behold Whistling Dick, the hero, seated at the planter's table, feasting upon viands his experience had never before included, and waited upon by admiring femininity in shapes of such beauty and "swellness" that even his ever-full mouth could scarcely prevent him from whistling. He was made to disclose in detail his adventure with the evil gang of Boston Harry, and how he cunningly wrote the note and wrapped it around the stone and placed it in the toe of the stocking, and, watching his chance, sent it silently, with a wonderful centrifugal momentum, like a comet, at one of the big lighted windows of the dining-room.

The planter vowed that the wanderer should wander no more; that his was a goodness and an honesty that should be rewarded, and that a debt of gratitude had been made that must be paid; for had he not saved them from a doubtless imminent loss, and maybe a greater calamity? He assured Whistling Dick that he might consider himself a charge upon the honor of Bellemeade; that a position suited to his powers would be found for him at once, and hinted that the way would be heartily smoothed for him to rise to as high places of emolument and trust as the plantation afforded.

But now, they said, he must be weary, and the immediate thing to consider was rest and sleep. So the mistress spoke to a servant, and Whistling Dick was conducted to a room in the wing of the house occupied by the servants. To this room, in a few minutes, was brought a portable tin bathtub filled with water, which was placed on a piece of oiled cloth upon the floor. There the vagrant was left to pass the night.

By the light of the candle he examined the room. A bed, with the covers neatly turned back, revealed snowy pillows and sheets. A worn, but clean, red carpet covered the floor. There was a dresser with a beveled mirror, a washstand with a flowered bowl and pitcher; the two or three chairs were softly upholstered. A little table held books, papers, and a day-old cluster of roses in a jar. There were towels on a rack and soap in a white dish.

Whistling Dick set his candle on a chair and placed his hat carefully under the table. After satisfying what we must suppose to have been his curiosity by a sober scrutiny, he removed his coat, folded it, and laid it upon the floor, near the wall, as far as possible from the unused bathtub. Taking his coat for a pillow, he stretched himself luxuriously upon the carpet.

When, on Christmas morning, the first streaks of dawn broke above the marshes, Whistling Dick awoke and reached instinctively for his hat. Then he remembered that the skirts of Fortune had swept him into their folds on the night previous, and he went to the window and raised it, to let the fresh breath of the morning cool his brow and fix the yet dream-like memory of his good luck within his brain.

As he stood there, certain dread and ominous sounds pierced the fearful hollow of his ear.

The force of plantation workers, eager to complete the shortened task allotted to them, were all astir. The mighty din of the ogre Labor shook the earth, and the poor tattered and forever disguised Prince in search of his fortune held tight to the window-sill even in the enchanted castle, and trembled.

Already from the bosom of the mill came the thunder of rolling barrels of sugar, and (prison-like sounds) there was a great rattling of chains as the mules were harried with stimulant imprecations to their places by the wagon-tongues. A little vicious "dummy" engine, with a train of flat cars in tow, stewed and fumed on the plantation tap of the narrow-gauge railroad, and a toiling, hurrying, hallooing stream of workers were dimly seen in the half darkness loading the train with the weekly output of sugar. Here was a poem, an epic—nay, a tragedy—with work, the curse of the world, for its theme.

The December air was frosty, but the sweat broke out upon Whistling Dick's face. He thrust his head out of the window and looked down. Fifteen feet below him, against the wall of the house, he could make out that a border of flowers grew, and by that token he over-hung a bed of soft earth.

Softly as a burglar goes, he clambered out upon the sill, lowered himself until he hung by his hands alone, and then dropped safely. No one seemed to be about upon this side of the house. He dodged low and skimmed swiftly across the yard to the low fence. It was an easy matter to vault this, for a terror urged him such as lifts the gazelle over the thorn bush when the lion pursues. A crash through the dew-drenched weeds on the roadside, a clutching, slippery rush up the grassy side of the levee to the footpath at the summit, and—he was free!

The east was blushing and brightening. The wind, himself a vagrant rover, saluted his brother upon the cheek. Some wild geese, high above, gave cry. A rabbit skipped along the path before him, free to turn to the right or to the left as his mood should send him. The river slid past, and certainly no one could tell the ultimate abiding place of its waters.

A small, ruffled, brown-breasted bird, sitting upon a dog-wood sapling, began a soft, throaty, tender little piping in praise of the dew which entices foolish worms from their holes; but suddenly he stopped, and sat with his head turned sidewise, listening.

From the path along the levee there burst forth a jubilant, stirring, buoyant, thrilling whistle, loud and keen and clear as the cleanest notes of the piccolo. The soaring sound rippled and thrilled and arpeggioed as the songs of wild birds do not; but it had a wild free grace that, in a way, reminded the small brown bird of something familiar, but exactly what he could not tell. There was in it the bird call, or reveille, that all birds know; but a great waste of lavish, unmeaning things that art had added and arranged, besides, and that were quite puzzling and strange; and the little brown bird sat with his head on one side until the sound died away in the distance.

The little bird did not know that the part of that strange warbling that he understood was just what kept the warbler without his breakfast; but he knew very well that the part he did not understand did not concern him, so he gave a little flutter of his wings and swooped down like a brown bullet upon a big fat worm that was wriggling along the levee path.

Caught

〜〜〜〜〜〜〜〜〜〜〜〜〜〜〜〜〜〜〜〜〜〜〜〜〜

THE plans for the detention of the flying president Miraflores and his companion at the coast line seemed hardly likely to fail. Dr. Zavalla himself had gone to the port of Alazan to establish a guard at that point. At Coralio the Liberal patriot Varras could be depended upon to keep close watch. Goodwin held himself responsible for the district about Coralio.

The news of the president's flight had been disclosed to no one in the coast towns save trusted members of the ambitious political party that was desirous of succeeding to power. The telegraph wire running from San Mateo to the coast had been cut far up on the mountain trail by an emissary of Zavalla's. Long before this could be repaired and word received along it from the capital the fugitives would have reached the coast and the question of escape or capture been solved.

Goodwin had stationed armed sentinels at frequent intervals along the shore for a mile in each direction from Coralio. They were instructed to keep a vigilant lookout during the night to prevent Miraflores from attempting to embark stealthily by means of some boat or sloop found by chance at the water's edge. A dozen patrols walked the streets of Coralio unsuspected, ready to intercept the truant official should he show himself there.

Goodwin was very well convinced that no precautions had been overlooked. He strolled about the streets that bore such high-sounding names and were but narrow, grass-covered lanes, lending his own aid to the vigil that had been intrusted to him by Bob Englehart.

The town had begun the tepid round of its nightly diversions. A few leisurely dandies, clad in white duck, with flowing neckties, and swinging slim bamboo canes, threaded the grassy by-ways toward the houses of their favored señoritas. Those who wooed the art of music dragged tirelessly at whining concertinas, or fingered lugubrious guitars at doors and windows. An occasional soldier from the *cuartel*, with flapping straw hat, without coat or shoes, hurried by, balancing his long gun like a lance in one hand. From every density of the foliage the giant tree frogs sounded their loud and irritating clatter. Further out, where the by-ways perished at the brink of the jungle, the guttural cries of marauding baboons and the coughing of the alligators in the black estuaries fractured the vain silence of the wood.

By ten o'clock the streets were deserted. The oil lamps that had burned, a sickly yellow, at random corners, had been extinguished by some economical civic agent. Coralio lay sleeping calmly between toppling mountains and encroaching sea like a stolen babe in the arms of its abductors. Somewhere over in that tropical darkness—perhaps already threading the profundities of the alluvial lowlands—the high adventurer and his mate were moving toward land's end. The game of Fox-in-the-Morning should be coming soon to its close.

Goodwin, at his deliberate gait, passed the long, low *cuartel* where Coralio's contingent of Anchuria's military force slumbered, with its bare toes pointed heavenward. There was a law that no civilian might come so near the headquarters of that citadel of war after nine o'clock, but Goodwin was always forgetting the minor statutes.

"*Quién vive?*" shrieked the sentinel, wrestling prodigiously with his lengthy musket.

"*Americano,*" growled Goodwin, without turning his head, and passed on, unhalted.

To the right he turned, and to the left up the street that ultimately reached the Plaza Nacional. When within the toss of a cigar stump from the intersecting Street of the Holy Sepulchre, he stopped suddenly in the pathway.

He saw the form of a tall man, clothed in black and carrying a large valise, hurry down the cross-street in the direction of the beach. And Goodwin's second glance made him aware of a woman at the man's elbow on the farther side, who seemed to urge forward, if not even to assist, her companion in their swift but silent progress. They were no Coralians, those two.

Goodwin followed at increased speed, but without any of the artful tactics that are so dear to the heart of the sleuth. The American was too broad to feel the instinct of the detective. He stood as an agent for the people of Anchuria, and but for political reasons he would have demanded then and there the money. It was the design of his party to secure the imperilled fund, to restore it to the treasury of the country, and to declare itself in power without bloodshed or resistance.

The couple halted at the door of the Hotel de los Extranjeros, and the man struck upon the wood with the impatience of one unused to his entry being stayed. Madama was long in response; but after a time her light showed, the door was opened, and the guests housed.

Goodwin stood in the quiet street, lighting another cigar. In two minutes a faint gleam began to show between the slats of the jalousies in the upper story of the hotel. "They have engaged rooms," said Goodwin to himself. "So, then, their arrangements for sailing have yet to be made."

At that moment there came along one Esteban Delgado, a barber, an enemy to existing government, a jovial plotter against stagnation in any form. This barber was one of Coralio's saddest dogs, often remaining out of doors as late as eleven, post meridian. He was a partisan Liberal; and he greeted Goodwin with flatulent importance as a brother in the cause. But he had something important to tell.

"What think you, Don Frank!" he cried, in the universal

tone of the conspirator. "I have to-night shaved *la barba*—
what you call the 'weeskers' of the *Presidente* himself, of this
countree! Consider! He sent for me to come. In the poor
casita of an old woman he awaited me—in a verree leetle
house in a dark place. *Caramba!*—el Señor Presidente to
make himself thus secret and obscured! I think he desired
not to be known—but, *carajo!* can you shave a man and not
see his face? This gold piece he gave me, and said it was
to be all quite still. I think, Don Frank, there is what you
call a chip over the bug."

"Have you ever seen President Miraflores before?" asked
Goodwin.

"But once," answered Estebán. "He is tall; and he had
weeskers verree black and sufficient."

"Was any one else present when you shaved him?"

"An old Indian woman, Señor, that belonged with the *casa*,
and one señorita—a ladee of so much beautee!—*ah, Dios!*"

"All right, Estebán," said Goodwin. "It's very lucky that
you happened along with your tonsorial information. The
new administration will be likely to remember you for this."

Then in a few words he made the barber acquainted with
the crisis into which the affairs of the nation had culminated,
and instructed him to remain outside, keeping watch upon
the two sides of the hotel that looked upon the street, and
observing whether any one should attempt to leave the house
by any door or window. Goodwin himself went to the door
through which the guests had entered, opened it and stepped
inside.

Madama had returned downstairs from her journey above
to see after the comfort of her lodgers. Her candle stood upon
the bar. She was about to take a thimbleful of rum as a
solace for having her rest disturbed. She looked up without
surprise or alarm as her third caller entered.

"Ah! it is the Señor Goodwin. Not often does he honor
my poor house by his presence."

"I must come oftener," said Goodwin, with the Goodwin
smile. "I hear that your cognac is the best between Belize

to the north and Rio to the south. Set out the bottle, Madama, and let us have the proof in *un vasito* for each of us."

"My *aguardiente*," said Madama, with pride, "is the best. It grows, in beautiful bottles, in the dark places among the banana-trees. *Si, Señor*. Only at midnight can they be picked by sailor-men who bring them, before daylight comes, to your back door. Good *aguardiente* is a verree difficult fruit to handle, Señor Goodwin."

Smuggling, in Coralio, was much nearer than competition to being the life of trade. One spoke of it slyly, yet with a certain conceit, when it had been well accomplished.

"You have guests in the house to-night," said Goodwin, laying a silver dollar upon the counter.

"Why not?" said Madama, counting the change. "Two, one señor, not quite old, and one señorita of sufficient handsomeness. To their rooms they have ascended, not desiring the to-eat nor the to-drink. Two rooms—*Número* 9 and *Número* 10."

"I was expecting that gentleman and that lady," said Goodwin. "I have important *negocios* that must be transacted. Will you allow me to see them?"

"Why not?" sighed Madama, placidly. "Why should not Señor Goodwin ascend and speak to his friends? *Está bueno*. Room *Número* 9 and room *Número* 10."

Goodwin loosened in his coat pocket the American revolver that he carried, and ascended the steep, dark stairway.

In the hallway above, the saffron light from a hanging lamp allowed him to select the gaudy numbers on the doors. He turned the knob of Number 9, entered and closed the door behind him.

If that was Isabel Guilbert seated by the table in that poorly furnished room, report had failed to do her charms justice. She rested her head upon one hand. Extreme fatigue was signified in every line of her figure; and upon her countenance a deep perplexity was written. Her eyes were gray-irised, and of that mould that seems to have belonged to the orbs of all the famous queens of hearts. Their whites were singularly clear and brilliant, concealed above the irises by heavy horizontal lids, and showing a snowy line below them. Such eyes denote great nobility, vigor, and, if you can conceive of it, a most generous selfishness. She looked up when the American entered with an expression of surprised inquiry, but without alarm.

Goodwin took off his hat and seated himself, with his characteristic deliberate ease, upon a corner of the table. He held a lighted cigar between his fingers. He took this familiar course because he was sure that preliminaries would be wasted upon Miss Guilbert. He knew her history, and the small part that the conventions had played in it.

"Good evening," he said. "Now, madame, let us come to business at once. You will observe that I mention no names, but I know who is in the next room, and what he carries in that valise. That is the point which brings me here. I have come to dictate terms of surrender."

The lady neither moved nor replied, but steadily regarded the cigar in Goodwin's hand.

"We," continued the dictator, thoughtfully regarding the neat buckskin shoe on his gently swinging foot—"I speak for a considerable majority of the people—demand the return of the stolen funds belonging to them. Our terms go very little further than that. They are very simple. As an accredited spokesman, I promise that our interference will cease if they are accepted. Give up the money, and you and your companion will be permitted to proceed wherever you will. In fact, assistance will be given you in the matter of securing a passage by any outgoing vessel you may choose. It is on my personal responsibility that I add congratulations to the gentleman in Number 10 upon his taste in feminine charms."

Returning his cigar to his mouth, Goodwin observed her, and saw that her eyes followed it and rested upon it with icy and significant concentration. Apparently she had not heard a word he had said. He understood, tossed the cigar out the window, and, with an amused laugh, slid from the table to his feet.

"That is better," said the lady. "It makes it possible for me to listen to you. For a second lesson in good manners, you might now tell me by whom I am being insulted."

"I am sorry," said Goodwin, leaning one hand on the table, "that my time is too brief for devoting much of it to a course of etiquette. Come, now; I appeal to your good sense. You have shown yourself, in more than one instance, to be well aware of what is to your advantage. This is an occasion that demands the exercise of your undoubted intelligence. There is no mystery here. I am Frank Goodwin; and I have come for the money. I entered this room at a venture. Had I entered the other I would have had it before now. Do you want it in words? The gentleman in Number 10 has betrayed a great trust. He has robbed his people of a large sum, and it is I who will prevent their losing it. I do not say who that gentleman is; but if I should be forced to see him and he should prove to be a certain high official of the republic, it will be my duty to arrest him. The house is guarded. I am offering you liberal terms. It is not absolutely necessary that I confer personally with the gentleman in the next room. Bring me the valise containing the money, and we will call the affair ended."

The lady arose from her chair, and stood for a moment, thinking deeply.

"Do you live here, Mr. Goodwin?" she asked, presently.

"Yes."

"What is your authority for this intrusion?"

"I am an instrument of the republic. I was advised by wire of the movements of the—gentleman in Number 10."

"May I ask you two or three questions? I believe you to be a man more apt to be truthful than—timid. What sort of a town is this—Coralio, I think they call it?"

"Not much of a town," said Goodwin, smiling. "A banana town, as they run. Grass huts, 'dobes, five or six two-story houses, accommodations limited, population half-breed Spanish and Indian, Caribs and blackamoors. No sidewalks to speak of, no amusements. Rather unmoral. That's an offhand sketch, of course."

"Are there any inducements, say in a social or in a business way, for people to reside here?"

"Oh, yes," answered Goodwin, smiling broadly. "There are no afternoon teas, no hand-organs, no department stores—and there is no extradition treaty."

"He told me," went on the lady, speaking as if to herself, and with a slight frown, "that there were towns on this coast of beauty and importance; that there was a pleasing social order—especially an American colony of cultured residents."

"There is an American colony," said Goodwin, gazing at her in some wonder. "Some of the members are all right. Some are fugitives from justice from the States. I recall two exiled bank presidents, one army paymaster under a cloud, a couple of manslayers, and a widow—arsenic, I believe, was the suspicion in her case. I myself complete the colony, but, as yet, I have not distinguished myself by any particular crime."

"Do not lose hope," said the lady, dryly; "I see nothing in your actions to-night to guarantee your further obscurity. Some mistake has been made; I do not know just where. But *him* you shall not disturb to-night. The journey has fatigued him so that he has fallen asleep, I think, in his clothes. You talk of stolen money! I do not understand you. Some mistake has been made. I will convince you. Remain where you are and I will bring you the valise that you seem to covet so, and show it to you."

She moved toward the closed door that connected the two rooms, but stopped, and half turned and bestowed upon Goodwin a grave, searching look that ended in a quizzical smile.

"You force my door," she said, "and you follow your ruffianly behavior with the basest accusations; and yet"—she hesitated, as if to reconsider what she was about to say—"and yet—it is a puzzling thing—I am sure there has been some mistake."

She took a step toward the door, but Goodwin stayed her by a light touch upon her arm. I have said before that women turned to look at him in the streets. He was the viking sort of man, big, good-looking, and with an air of kindly truculence. She was dark and proud, glowing or pale as her mood moved her. I do not know if Eve were light or dark, but if such a woman had stood in the garden I know that the apple would have been eaten. This woman was to be Goodwin's fate, and he did not know it; but he must have felt the first throes of destiny, for, as he faced her, the knowledge of what report named her turned bitter in his throat.

"If there has been any mistake," he said, hotly, "it was yours. I do not blame the man who has lost his country, his honor, and is about to lose the poor consolation of his stolen riches as much as I blame you, for, by Heaven! I can very well see how he was brought to it. I can understand, and pity him. It is such women as you that strew this degraded coast with wretched exiles, that make men forget their trusts, that drag——"

The lady interrupted him with a weary gesture.

"There is no need to continue your insults," she said, coldly, "I do not understand what you are saying, nor do I know what mad blunder you are making; but if the inspection of the contents of a gentleman's portmanteau will rid me of you, let us delay it no longer."

She passed quickly and noiselessly into the other room, and returned with the heavy leather valise, which she handed to the American with an air of patient contempt.

Goodwin set the valise quickly upon the table and began to unfasten the straps. The lady stood by, with an expression of infinite scorn and weariness upon her face.

The valise opened wide to a powerful, sidelong wrench. Goodwin dragged out two or three articles of clothing, exposing the bulk of its contents—package after package of tightly packed United States bank and treasury notes of large denomination. Reckoning from the high figures written upon the paper bands that bound them, the total must have come closely upon the hundred thousand mark.

Goodwin glanced swiftly at the woman, and saw, with surprise and a thrill of pleasure that he wondered at, that she had experienced an unmistakable shock. Her eyes grew wide, she gasped, and leaned heavily against the table. She had been ignorant, then, he inferred, that her companion had looted the government treasury. But why, he angrily asked himself, should he be so well pleased to think this wandering and unscrupulous singer not so black as report had painted her?

A noise in the other room startled them both. The door swung open, and a tall, elderly, dark complexioned man, recently shaven, hurried into the room.

All the pictures of President Miraflores represent him as the possessor of a luxuriant supply of dark and carefully tended whiskers; but the story of the barber, Estebán, had prepared Goodwin for the change.

The man stumbled in from the dark room, his eyes blinking at the lamplight, and heavy from sleep.

"What does this mean?" he demanded in excellent English, with a keen and perturbed look at the American—"robbery?"

"Very near it," answered Goodwin. "But I rather think I'm in time to prevent it. I represent the people to whom this money belongs, and I have come to convey it back to them." He thrust his hand into a pocket of his loose linen coat.

The other man's hand went quickly behind him.

"Don't draw," called Goodwin, sharply; "I've got you covered from my pocket."

The lady stepped forward, and laid one hand upon the shoulder of her hesitating companion. She pointed to the table. "Tell me the truth—the truth," she said, in a low voice. "Whose money is that?"

The man did not answer. He gave a deep, long-drawn sigh, leaned and kissed her on the forehead, stepped back into the other room and closed the door.

Goodwin foresaw his purpose, and jumped for the door, but the report of the pistol echoed as his hand touched the knob. A heavy fall followed, and some one swept him aside and struggled into the room of the fallen man.

A desolation, thought Goodwin, greater than that derived

from the loss of cavalier and gold must have been in the heart of the enchantress to have wrung from her, in that moment, the cry of one turning to the all-forgiving, all-comforting earthly consoler—to have made her call out from that bloody and dishonored room—"Oh, mother, mother, mother!"

But there was an alarm outside. The barber, Esteban, at the sound of the shot, had raised his voice; and the shot itself had aroused half the town. A pattering of feet came up the street, and official orders rang out on the still air. Goodwin had a duty to perform. Circumstances had made him the custodian of his adopted country's treasure. Swiftly cramming the money into the valise, he closed it, leaned far out of the window and dropped it into a thick orange-tree in the little inclosure below.

They will tell you in Coralio, as they delight in telling the stranger, of the conclusion of that tragic flight. They will tell you how the upholders of the law came apace when the alarm was sounded—the *Comandante* in red slippers and a jacket like a head waiter's and girded sword, the soldiers with their interminable guns, followed by outnumbering officers struggling into their gold lace and epaulettes; the barefooted policemen (the only capables in the lot), and ruffled citizens of every hue and description.

They say that the countenance of the dead man was marred sadly by the effects of the shot; but he was identified as the fallen president by both Goodwin and the barber Esteban. On the next morning messages began to come over the mended telegraph wire; and the story of the flight from the capital was given out to the public. In San Mateo the revolutionary party had seized the sceptre of government, without opposition, and the *vivas* of the mercurial populace quickly effaced the interest belonging to the unfortunate Miraflores.

They will relate to you how the new government sifted the towns and raked the roads to find the valise containing Anchuria's surplus capital, which the president was known to have carried with him, but all in vain. In Coralio Señor Goodwin himself led the searching party which combed that town as carefully as a woman combs her hair; but the money was not found.

So they buried the dead man, without honors, back of the town near the little bridge that spans the mangrove swamp; and for a *real* a boy will show you his grave. They say that the old woman in whose hut the barber shaved the president placed the wooden slab at his head, and burned the inscription upon it with a hot iron.

You will hear also that Señor Goodwin, like a tower of strength, shielded Doña Isabel Guilbert through those subsequent distressful days; and that his scruples as to her past career (if he had any) vanished; and her adventuresome waywardness (if she had any) left her, and they were wedded and were happy.

The American built a home on a little foot hill near the town. It is a conglomerate structure of native woods that, exported, would be worth a fortune, and of brick, palm, glass, bamboo and adobe. There is a paradise of nature about it; and something of the same sort within. The natives speak of its interior with hands uplifted in admiration. There are floors polished like mirrors and covered with hand-woven Indian rugs of silk fibre, tall ornaments and pictures, musical instruments and papered walls—"figure-it-to-yourself!" they exclaim.

But they cannot tell you in Coralio (as you shall learn) what became of the money that Frank Goodwin dropped into the orange-tree. But that shall come later; for the palms are fluttering in the breeze, bidding us to sport and gaiety.

The Sleuths

~~~~~~

IN the big city a man will disappear with the suddenness and completeness of the flame of a candle that is blown out. All the agencies of inquisition—the hounds of the trail, the sleuths of the city's labyrinths, the closet detectives of theory and induction—will be invoked to the search. Most often the man's face will be seen no more. Sometimes he will reappear in Sheboygan or in the wilds of Terre Haute, calling himself one of the synonyms of "Smith," and without memory of events up to a certain time, including his grocer's bill. Sometimes it will be found, after dragging the rivers, and polling the restaurants to see if he may be waiting for a well-done sirloin, that he has moved next door.

This snuffing out of a human being like the erasure of a chalk man from a blackboard is one of the most impressive themes in dramaturgy.

The case of Mary Snyder, in point, should not be without interest.

A man of middle age, of the name of Meeks, came from the West to New York to find his sister, Mrs. Mary Snyder, a widow, aged fifty-two, who had been living for a year in a tenement house in a crowded neighborhood.

At her address he was told that Mary Snyder had moved away longer than a month before. No one could tell him her new address.

On coming out Mr. Meeks addressed a policeman who was standing on the corner, and explained his dilemma.

"My sister is very poor," he said, "and I am anxious to find her. I have recently made quite a lot of money in a lead

mine, and I want her to share my prosperity. There is no use
in advertising her, because she cannot read."

The policeman pulled his mustache and looked so thought-
ful and mighty that Meeks could almost feel the joyful tears
of his sister Mary dropping upon his bright blue tie.

"You go down in the Canal Street neighborhood," said
the policeman, "and get a job drivin' the biggest dray you
can find. There's old women always gettin' knocked over by
drays down there. You might see 'er among 'em. If you don't
want to do that you better go 'round to headquarters and
get 'em to put a fly cop onto the dame."

At police headquarters, Meeks received ready assistance.
A general alarm was sent out and copies of a photograph of
Mary Snyder that her brother had were distributed among
the stations. In Mulberry Street the chief assigned Detective Mullins to the case.

The detective took Meeks aside and said:

"This is not a very difficult case to unravel. Shave off your
whiskers, fill your pockets with good cigars, and meet me in
the café of the Waldorf at three o'clock this afternoon."

Meeks obeyed. He found Mullins there. They had a bottle
of wine, while the detective asked questions concerning the
missing woman.

"Now," said Mullins, "New York is a big city, but we've
got the detective business systematized. There are two ways
we can go about finding your sister. We will try one of 'em
first. You say she's fifty-two?"

"A little past," said Meeks.

The detective conducted the Westerner to a branch advertising office of one of the largest dailies. There he wrote
the following "ad" and submitted it to Meeks.

"Wanted, at once—one hundred attractive chorus girls for
a new musical comedy. Apply all day at No.——Broadway."

Meeks was indignant.

"My sister," said he, "is a poor, hard-working elderly
woman. I do not see what aid an advertisement of this kind
would be toward finding her."

"All right," said the detective. "I guess you don't know

New York. But if you've got a grouch against this scheme we'll try the other one. It's a sure thing. But it'll cost you more."

"Never mind the expense," said Meeks; "we'll try it."

The sleuth led him back to the Waldorf. "Engage a couple of bedrooms and a parlor," he advised, "and let's go up."

This was done, and the two were shown to a superb suite on the fourth floor. Meeks looked puzzled. The detective sank into a velvet armchair, and pulled out his cigar case.

"I forgot to suggest, old man," he said, "that you should have taken the rooms by the month. They wouldn't have stuck you so much for 'em."

"By the month!" exclaimed Meeks. "What do you mean?"

"Oh, it'll take time to work the game this way. I told you it would cost you more. We'll have to wait till spring. There'll be a new city directory out then. Very likely your sister's name and address will be in it."

Meeks rid himself of the city detective at once. On the next day some one advised him to consult Shamrock Jolnes, New York's famous private detective, who demanded fabulous fees, but performed miracles in the way of solving mysteries and crimes.

After waiting for two hours in the anteroom of the great detective's apartment, Meeks was shown into his presence. Jolnes sat in a purple dressing-gown at an inlaid ivory chess table, with a magazine before him, trying to solve the mystery of "They." The famous sleuth's thin, intellectual face, piercing eyes, and rate per word are too well known to need description.

Meeks set forth his errand. "My fee, if successful, will be $500," said Shamrock Jolnes.

Meeks bowed his agreement to the price.

"I will undertake your case, Mr. Meeks," said Jolnes, finally. "The disappearance of people in this city has always been an interesting problem to me. I remember a case that I brought to a successful outcome a year ago. A family bearing the name of Clark disappeared suddenly from a small flat in which they were living. I watched the flat building for two months for a clue. One day it struck me that a certain milkman and a grocer's boy always walked backward when they carried their wares upstairs. Following out by induction the idea that this observation gave me, I at once located the missing family. They had moved into the flat across the hall and changed their name to Kralc."

Shamrock Jolnes and his client went to the tenement house where Mary Snyder had lived, and the detective demanded to be shown the room in which she had lived. It had been occupied by no tenant since her disappearance.

The room was small, dingy, and poorly furnished. Meeks seated himself dejectedly on a broken chair, while the great detective searched the walls and floors and the few sticks of old, rickety furniture for a clue.

At the end of half an hour Jolnes had collected a few seemingly unintelligible articles—a cheap black hatpin, a piece torn off a theatre programme, and the end of a small torn card on which was the word "Left" and the characters "C 12."

Shamrock Jolnes leaned against the mantel for ten minutes, with his head resting upon his hand, and an absorbed look upon his intellectual face. At the end of that time he exclaimed, with animation:

"Come, Mr. Meeks; the problem is solved. I can take you directly to the house where your sister is living. And you may have no fears concerning her welfare, for she is amply provided with funds—for the present at least."

Meeks felt joy and wonder in equal proportions.

"How did you manage it?" he asked, with admiration in his tones.

Perhaps Jolnes's only weakness was a professional pride in his wonderful achievements in induction. He was ever ready to astound and charm his listeners by describing his methods.

"By elimination," said Jolnes, spreading his clues upon a little table, "I got rid of certain parts of the city to which Mrs. Snyder might have removed. You see this hatpin? That eliminates Brooklyn. No woman attempts to board a car at the Brooklyn Bridge without being sure that she carries a hatpin with which to fight her way into a seat. And now I will demonstrate to you that she could not have gone to Harlem. Behind this door are two hooks in the wall. Upon one of these Mrs. Snyder has hung her bonnet, and upon the other her shawl. You will observe that the bottom of the hanging shawl has gradually made a soiled streak against the plastered wall. The mark is clean-cut, proving that there is no fringe on the shawl. Now, was there ever a case where a middle-aged woman, wearing a shawl, boarded a Harlem train without there being a fringe on the shawl to catch in the gate and delay the passengers behind her? So we eliminate Harlem.

"Therefore I conclude that Mrs. Snyder has not moved very far away. On this torn piece of card you see the word 'Left,' the letter 'C,' and the number '12.' Now, I happen to know that No. 12 Avenue C is a first-class boarding house, far beyond your sister's means—as we suppose. But then I find this piece of a theatre programme, crumpled into an odd shape. What meaning does it convey? None to you, very likely, Mr. Meeks; but it is eloquent to one whose habits and training take cognizance of the smallest things.

"You have told me that your sister was a scrub woman. She scrubbed the floors of offices and hallways. Let us assume that she procured such work to perform in a theatre. Where is valuable jewellery lost the oftenest, Mr. Meeks? In the theatres, of course. Look at that piece of programme, Mr. Meeks. Observe the round impression in it. It has been wrapped around a ring—perhaps a ring of great value. Mrs. Snyder found the ring while at work in the theatre. She hastily tore off a piece of a programme, wrapped the ring carefully, and thrust it into her bosom. The next day she disposed of it, and with her increased means, looked about her for a more comfortable place in which to live. When I reach thus far in the chain I see nothing impossible about No. 12 Avenue C. It is there we will find your sister, Mr. Meeks."

Shamrock Jolnes concluded his convincing speech with the smile of a successful artist. Meeks's admiration was too great for words. Together they went to No. 12 Avenue C. It was an old-fashioned brownstone house in a prosperous and respectable neighborhood.

They rang the bell, and on inquiry were told that no Mrs. Snyder was known there, and that not within six months had a new occupant come to the house.

When they reached the sidewalk again, Meeks examined the clues which he had brought away from his sister's old room.

"I am no detective," he remarked to Jolnes as he raised the piece of theatre programme to his nose, "but it seems to me that instead of a ring having been wrapped in this paper it was one of those round peppermint drops. And this piece with the address on it looks to me like the end of a seat coupon—No. 12, row C, left aisle."

Shamrock Jolnes had a far-away look in his eyes.

"I think you would do well to consult Juggins," said he.

"Who is Juggins?" asked Meeks.

"He is the leader," said Jolnes, "of a new modern school of detectives. Their methods are different from ours, but it is said that Juggins has solved some extremely puzzling cases. I will take you to him."

They found the greater Juggins in his office. He was a small man with light hair, deeply absorbed in reading one of the bourgeois works of Nathaniel Hawthorne.

The two great detectives of different schools shook hands with ceremony, and Meeks was introduced.

"State the facts," said Juggins, going on with his reading.

When Meeks ceased, the greater one closed his book and said:

"Do I understand that your sister is fifty-two years of age, with a large mole on the side of her nose, and that she is a very poor widow, making a scanty living by scrubbing, and with a very homely face and figure?"

"That describes her exactly," admitted Meeks. Juggins rose and put on his hat.

"In fifteen minutes," he said, "I will return, bringing you her present address."

Shamrock Jolnes turned pale, but forced a smile.

Within the specified time Juggins returned and consulted a little slip of paper held in his hand.

"Your sister, Mary Snyder," he announced calmly, "will be found at No. 162 Chilton Street. She is living in the back hall bedroom five flights up. The house is only four blocks from here," he continued, addressing Meeks. "Suppose you go and verify the statement and then return here. Mr. Jolnes will await you, I dare say."

Meeks hurried away. In twenty minutes he was back again, with a beaming face.

"She is there and well!" he cried. "Name your fee!"

"Two dollars," said Juggins.

When Meeks had settled his bill and departed, Shamrock Jolnes stood with his hat in his hand before Juggins.

"If it would not be asking too much," he stammered—"if you would favor me so far—would you object to——"

"Certainly not," said Juggins, pleasantly. "I will tell you how I did it. You remember the description of Mrs. Snyder? Did you ever know a woman like that who wasn't paying weekly instalments on an enlarged crayon portrait of herself? The biggest factory of that kind in the country is just around the corner. I went there and got her address off the books. That's all."

Makes the Whole World Kin

∼∼∼∼∼∼∼∼∼∼∼∼∼∼∼∼∼∼∼∼∼∼∼∼∼∼∼∼∼∼

THE burglar stepped inside the window quickly, and then he took his time. A burglar who respects his art always takes his time before taking anything else.

The house was a private residence. By its boarded front door and untrimmed Boston ivy the burglar knew that the mistress of it was sitting on some oceanside piazza telling a sympathetic man in a yachting cap that no one had ever understood her sensitive, lonely heart. He knew by the light in the third-story front windows, and by the lateness of the season, that the master of the house had come home, and would soon extinguish his light and retire. For it was September of the year and of the soul, in which season the house's good man comes to consider roof gardens and stenographers as vanities, and to desire the return of his mate and the more durable blessings of decorum and the moral excellencies.

The burglar lighted a cigarette. The guarded glow of the match illuminated his salient points for a moment. He belonged to the third type of burglars.

This third type has not yet been recognized and accepted. The police have made us familiar with the first and second. Their classification is simple. The collar is the distinguishing mark.

When a burglar is caught who does not wear a collar he is described as a degenerate of the lowest type, singularly vicious and depraved, and is suspected of being the desperate criminal who stole the handcuffs out of Patrolman Hennessy's pocket in 1878 and walked away to escape arrest.

The other well-known type is the burglar who wears a

collar. He is always referred to as a Raffles in real life. He is invariably a gentleman by daylight, breakfasting in a dress suit, and posing as a paperhanger, while after dark he plies his nefarious occupation of burglary. His mother is an extremely wealthy and respected resident of Ocean Grove, and when he is conducted to his cell he asks at once for a nail file and the *Police Gazette*. He always has a wife in every State in the Union and fiancées in all the Territories, and the newspapers print his matrimonial gallery out of their stock of cuts of the ladies who were cured by only one bottle after having been given up by five doctors, experiencing great relief after the first dose.

The burglar wore a blue sweater. He was neither a Raffles nor one of the chefs from Hell's Kitchen. The police would have been baffled had they attempted to classify him. They have not yet heard of the respectable, unassuming burglar who is neither above nor below his station.

This burglar of the third class began to prowl. He wore no masks, dark lanterns, or gum shoes. He carried a 38-calibre revolver in his pockets, and he chewed peppermint gum thoughtfully.

The furniture of the house was swathed in its summer dust protectors. The silver was far away in safe-deposit vaults. The burglar expected no remarkable "haul." His objective point was that dimly lighted room where the master of the house should be sleeping heavily after whatever solace he had sought to lighten the burden of his loneliness. A "touch" might be made there to the extent of legitimate, fair professional profits—loose money, a watch, a jeweled stickpin—nothing exorbitant or beyond reason. He had seen the window left open and had taken the chance.

The burglar softly opened the door of the lighted room. The gas was turned low. A man lay in the bed asleep. On the dresser lay many things in confusion—a crumpled roll of bills, a watch, keys, three poker chips, crushed cigars, a pink silk hair bow, and an unopened bottle of bromo-seltzer for a bulwark in the morning.

The burglar took three steps toward the dresser. The man

in the bed suddenly uttered a squeaky groan and opened his eyes. His right hand slid under his pillow, but remained there.

"Lay still," said the burglar in conversational tone. Burglars of the third type do not hiss. The citizen in the bed looked at the round end of the burglar's pistol and lay still.

"Now hold up both your hands," commanded the burglar.

The citizen had a little, pointed, brown-and-gray beard, like that of a painless dentist. He looked solid, esteemed, irritable, and disgusted. He sat up in bed and raised his right hand above his head.

"Up with the other one," ordered the burglar. "You might be amphibious and shoot with your left. You can count two, can't you? Hurry up, now."

"Can't raise the other one," said the citizen with a contortion of his lineaments.

"What's the matter with it?"

"Rheumatism in the shoulder."

"Inflammatory?"

"Was. The inflammation has gone down."

The burglar stood for a moment or two, holding his gun on the afflicted one. He glanced at the plunder on the dresser and then, with a half-embarrassed air back at the man in the bed. Then he, too, made a sudden grimace.

"Don't stand there making faces," snapped the citizen, bad-humoredly. "If you've come to burgle why don't you do it? There's some stuff lying around."

"'Scuse me," said the burglar, with a grin; "but it just socked me one, too. It's good for you that rheumatism and me happens to be old pals. I got it in my left arm, too. Most anybody but me would have popped you when you wouldn't hoist that left claw of yours."

"How long have you had it?" inquired the citizen.

"Four years. I guess that ain't all. Once you've got it, it's you for a rheumatic life—that's my judgment."

"Ever try rattlesnake oil?" asked the citizen interestedly.

"Gallons," said the burglar. "If all the snakes I've used the oil of was strung out in a row they'd reach eight times as far as Saturn, and the rattles could be heard at Valparaiso, Indiana, and back."

"Some use Chiselum's Pills," remarked the citizen.

"Fudge!" said the burglar. "Took 'em five months. No good. I had some relief the year I tried Finkelham's Extract, Balm of Gilead poultices, and Pott's Pain Pulverizer; but I think it was the buckeye I carried in my pocket what done the trick."

"Is yours worse in the morning or at night?" asked the citizen.

"Night," said the burglar; "just when I'm busiest. Say, take down that arm of yours—I guess you won't——Say! did you ever try Blickerstaff's Blood Builder?"

"I never did. Does yours come in paroxysms or is it a steady pain?"

The burglar sat down on the foot of the bed and rested his gun on his crossed knees.

"It jumps," said he. "It strikes me when I ain't looking for it. I had to give up second-story work because I got stuck sometimes half-way up. Tell you what—I don't believe the bloomin' doctors know what is good for it."

"Same here. I've spent a thousand dollars without getting any relief. Yours swell any?"

"Of mornings. And when it's goin' to rain—great Christopher!"

"Me, too," said the citizen. "I can tell when a streak of humidity the size of a tablecloth starts from Florida on its way to New York. And if I pass a theatre where there's an 'East Lynne' matinée going on, the moisture starts my left arm jumping like a toothache."

"It's undiluted—hades!" said the burglar.

"You're dead right," said the citizen.

The burglar looked down at his pistol and thrust it into his pocket with an awkward attempt at ease.

"Say, old man," he said, constrainedly, "ever try opodeldoc?"

"Slop!" said the citizen angrily. "Might as well rub on restaurant butter."

"Sure," concurred the burglar. "It's a salve suitable for little Minnie when the kitty scratches her finger. I'll tell you what! We're up against it. I only find one thing that eases her up. Hey? Little old sanitary, ameliorating, lest-we-forget Booze. Say—this job's off—'scuse me—get on your clothes and let's go out and have some. 'Scuse the liberty, but—ouch! There she goes again!"

"For a week," said the citizen, "I haven't been able to dress myself without help. I'm afraid Thomas is in bed, and——"

"Climb out," said the burglar, "I'll help you get into your duds."

The conventional returned as a tidal wave and flooded the citizen. He stroked his brown-and-gray beard.

"It's very unusual——" he began.

"Here's your shirt," said the burglar, "fall out. I know a man who said Omberry's Ointment fixed him in two weeks so he could use both hands in tying his four-in-hand."

As they were going out the door the citizen turned and started back.

" 'Liked to forgot my money," he explained; "laid it on the dresser last night."

The burglar caught him by the right sleeve.

"Come on," he said, bluffly. "I ask you. Leave it alone. I've got the price. Ever try witch hazel and oil of winter-green?"

The Whirligig of Life

~~~~~~~~~~~~~~~~~~~~~~~~~~~~~~~~~~~~

JUSTICE-OF-THE-PEACE Benaja Widdup sat in the door of his office smoking his elder-stem pipe. Halfway to the Zenith the Cumberland range rose blue-gray in the afternoon haze. A speckled hen swaggered down the main street of the "settlement," cackling foolishly.

Up the road came a sound of creaking axles, and then a slow cloud of dust, and then a bull-cart bearing Ransie Bilbro and his wife. The cart stopped at the Justice's door, and the two climbed down. Ransie was a narrow six feet of sallow brown skin and yellow hair. The imperturbability of the mountains hung upon him like a suit of armor. The woman was calicoed, angled, snuff-brushed, and weary with unknown desires. Through it all gleamed a faint protest of cheated youth unconscious of its loss.

The Justice of the Peace slipped his feet into his shoes, for the sake of dignity, and moved to let them enter.

"We-all," said the woman, in a voice like the wind blowing through pine boughs, "wants a divo'ce." She looked at Ransie to see if he noted any flaw or ambiguity or evasion or partiality or self-partisanship in her statement of their business.

"A divo'ce," repeated Ransie, with a solemn nod. "We-all can't git along together nohow. It's lonesome enough fur to live in the mount'ins when a man and a woman keers fur one another. But when she's a-spittin' like a wildcat or a-sullenin' like a hoot-owl in the cabin, a man ain't got no call to live with her."

"When he's a no-'count varmint," said the woman, without any especial warmth, "a-traipsin' along of scalawags and moonshiners and a-layin' on his back pizen 'ith co'n whiskey, and a-pesterin' folks with a pack o' hungry, triflin' houn's to feed!"

"When she keeps a-throwin' skillet lids," came Ransie's antiphony, "and slings b'ilin' water on the best coon-dog in the Cumberlands, and sets herself again' cookin' a man's victuals, and keeps him awake o' nights accusin' him of a sight of doin's!"

"When he's al'ays a-fightin' the revenuers, and gits a hard name in the mount'ins fur a mean man, who's gwine to be able fur to sleep o' nights?"

The Justice of the Peace stirred deliberately to his duties. He placed his one chair and a wooden stool for his petitioners. He opened his book of statutes on the table and scanned the index. Presently he wiped his spectacles and shifted his inkstand.

"The law and the statutes," said he, "air silent on the subjeck of divo'ce as fur as the jurisdiction of this co't air concerned. But, accordin' to equity and the Constitution and the golden rule, it's a bad barg'in that can't run both ways. If a justice of the peace can marry a couple, it's plain that he is bound to be able to divo'ce 'em. This here office will issue a decree of divo'ce and abide by the decision of the Supreme Co't to hold it good."

Ransie Bilbro drew a small tobacco-bag from his trousers pocket. Out of this he shook upon the table a five-dollar note. "Sold a b'arskin and two foxes fur that," he remarked. "It's all the money we got."

"The regular price of a divo'ce in this co't," said the Justice, "air five dollars." He stuffed the bill into the pocket of his homespun vest with a deceptive air of indifference. With much bodily toil and mental travail he wrote the decree upon half a sheet of foolscap, and then copied it upon the other. Ransie Bilbro and his wife listened to his reading of the document that was to give them freedom:

Know all men by these presents that Ransie Bilbro and his wife, Ariela Bilbro, this day personally appeared before me and promises that hereinafter they will neither love, honor, nor obey each other, neither for better nor worse, being of sound mind and body, and accept summons for divorce according to the peace and dignity of the State. Herein fail not, so help you God. Benaja Widdup, justice of the peace in and for the county of Piedmont, State of Tennessee.

The Justice was about to hand one of the documents to Ransie. The voice of Ariela delayed the transfer. Both men looked at her. Their dull masculinity was confronted by something sudden and unexpected in the woman.

"Judge, don't you give him that air paper yit. 'Tain't all settled, nohow. I got to have my rights first. I got to have my ali-money. 'Tain't no kind of a way to do fur a man to divo'ce his wife 'thout her havin' a cent fur to do with. I'm a-layin' off to be a-goin' up to brother Ed's up on Hogback Mount'in. I'm bound fur to hev a pa'r of shoes and some snuff and things besides. Ef Rance kin affo'd a divo'ce, let him pay me ali-money."

Ransie Bilbro was stricken to dumb perplexity. There had been no previous hint of alimony. Women were always bringing up startling and unlooked-for issues.

Justice Benaja Widdup felt that the point demanded judicial decision. The authorities were also silent on the subject of alimony. But the woman's feet were bare. The trail to Hogback Mountain was steep and flinty.

"Ariela Bilbro," he asked, in official tones, "how much did you 'low would be good and sufficient ali-money in the case befo' the co't?"

"I 'lowed," she answered, "fur the shoes and all, to say five dollars. That ain't much fur ali-money, but I reckon that'll git me up to brother Ed's."

"The amount," said the Justice, "air not onreasonable. Ransie Bilbro, you air ordered by the co't to pay the plaintiff the sum of five dollars befo' the decree of divo'ce air issued."

"I hain't no mo' money," breathed Ransie, heavily. "I done paid you all I had."

"Otherwise," said the Justice, looking severely over his spectacles, "you air in contempt of co't."

"I reckon if you gimme till to-morrow," pleaded the husband, "I mout be able to rake or scrape it up somewhars. I never looked for to be a-payin' no ali-money."

"The case air adjourned," said Benaja Widdup, "till to-morrow, when you-all will present yo'selves and obey the order of the co't. Followin' of which the decrees of divo'ce will be delivered." He sat down in the door and began to loosen a shoestring.

"We mout as well go down to Uncle Ziah's," decided Ransie, "and spend the night." He climbed into the cart on one side, and Ariela climbed in on the other. Obeying the flap of his rope, the little red bull slowly came around on a tack, and the cart crawled away in the nimbus arising from its wheels.

Justice-of-the-peace Benaja Widdup smoked his elder-stem pipe. Late in the afternoon he got his weekly paper, and read it until the twilight dimmed its lines. Then he lit the tallow candle on his table, and read until the moon rose, marking the time for supper. He lived in the double log cabin on the slope near the girdled poplar. Going home to supper he crossed a little branch darkened by a laurel thicket. The dark figure of a man stepped from the laurels and pointed a rifle at his breast. His hat was pulled down low, and something covered most of his face.

"I want yo' money," said the figure, "'thout any talk. I'm gettin' nervous, and my finger's a-wabblin' on this here trigger."

"I've only got f-f-five dollars," said the Justice, producing it from his vest pocket.

"Roll it up," came the order, "and stick it in the end of this here gun-bar'l."

The bill was crisp and new. Even fingers that were clumsy and trembling found little difficulty in making a spill of it and inserting it (this with less ease) into the muzzle of the rifle.

"Now I reckon you kin be goin' along," said the robber.
The Justice lingered not on his way.

The next day came the little red bull, drawing the cart to
the office door. Benaja Widdup had his shoes on, for he was
expecting the visit. In his presence Ransie Bilbro handed to
his wife a five-dollar bill. The official's eye sharply viewed it.
It seemed to curl up as though it had been rolled and inserted
into the end of a gun-barrel. But the Justice refrained from
comment. It is true that other bills might be inclined to curl.
He handed each one a decree of divorce. Each stood awk-
wardly silent, slowly folding the guarantee of freedom. The
woman cast a shy glance full of constraint at Ransie.

"I reckon you'll be goin' back up to the cabin," she said,
"along 'ith the bull-cart. There's bread in the tin box settin'
on the shelf. I put the bacon in the b'ilin'-pot to keep the
hounds from gettin' it. Don't forget to wind the clock to-
night."

"You air a-goin' to your brother Ed's?" asked Ransie, with
fine unconcern.

"I was 'lowin' to get along up thar afore night. I ain't
sayin' as they'll pester theyselves any to make me welcome,
but I hain't nowhar else fur to go. It's a right smart ways,
and I reckon I better be goin'. I'll be a-sayin' good-bye, Ranse
—that is, if you keer fur to say so."

"I don't know as anybody's a hound dog," said Ransie, in
a martyr's voice, "fur to not want to say good-bye—'less you
air so anxious to git away that you don't want me to say it."

Ariela was silent. She folded the five-dollar bill and her
decree carefully, and placed them in the bosom of her dress.
Benaja Widdup watched the money disappear with mournful
eyes behind his spectacles.

And then with his next words he achieved rank (as his
thoughts ran) with either the great crowd of the world's
sympathizers or the little crowd of its great financiers.

"Be kind o' lonesome in the old cabin to-night, Ransie," she
said.

Ransie Bilbro stared out at the Cumberlands, clear blue now in the sunlight. He did not look at Ariela.

"I 'low it might be lonesome," he said; "but when folks gits mad and wants a divo'ce, you can't make folks stay."

"There's others wanted a divo'ce," said Ariela, speaking to the wooden stool. "Besides, nobody don't want nobody to stay."

"Nobody never said they didn't."

"Nobody never said they did. I reckon I better start on now to brother Ed's."

"Nobody can't wind that old clock."

"Want me to go along 'ith you in the cart and wind it fur you, Ranse?"

The mountaineer's countenance was proof against emotion. But he reached out a big hand and enclosed Ariela's thin brown one. Her soul peeped out once through her impassive face, hallowing it.

"Them hounds sha'n't pester you no more," said Ransie. "I reckon I been mean and low down. You wind that clock, Ariela."

"My heart hit's in that cabin, Ranse," she whispered, "along 'ith you. I ain't a-goin' to git mad no more. Le's be startin', Ranse, so's we kin git home by sundown."

Justice-of-the-peace Benaja Widdup interposed as they started for the door, forgetting his presence.

"In the name of the State of Tennessee," he said, "I forbid you-all to be a-defyin' of its laws and statutes. This co't is mo' than willin' and full of joy to see the clouds of discord and misunderstandin' rollin' away from two lovin' hearts, but it air the duty of the co't to p'eserve the morals and integrity of the State. The co't reminds you that you air no longer man and wife, but air divo'ced by regular decree, and as such air not entitled to the benefits and 'purtenances of the matter monal estate."

Ariela caught Ransie's arm. Did those words mean that she must lose him now when they had just learned the lesson of life?

"But the co't air prepared," went on the Justice, "fur to

remove the disabilities set up by the decree of divo'ce. The co't air on hand to perform the solemn ceremony of marri'ge, thus fixin' things up and enablin' the parties in the case to resume the honor'ble and elevatin' state of mattermony which they desires. The fee fur performin' said ceremony will be, in this case, to wit, five dollars."

Ariela caught the gleam of promise in his words. Swiftly her hand went to her bosom. Freely as an alighting dove the bill fluttered to the Justice's table. Her sallow cheek colored as she stood hand in hand with Ransie and listened to the reuniting words.

Ransie helped her into the cart, and climbed in beside her. The little red bull turned once more, and they set out, hand-clasped, for the mountains.

Justice-of-the-peace Benaja Widdup sat in his door and took off his shoes. Once again he fingered the bill tucked down in his vest pocket. Once again he smoked his elder-stem pipe. Once again the speckled hen swaggered down the main street of the "settlement," cackling foolishly.

A Newspaper Story

AT 8 A.M. it lay on Giuseppi's news-stand, still damp from the presses. Giuseppi, with the cunning of his ilk, philandered on the opposite corner leaving his patrons to help themselves, no doubt on a theory related to the hypothesis of the watched pot.

This particular newspaper was, according to its custom and design, an educator, a guide, a monitor, a champion, and a household counsellor and *vade mecum*.

From its many excellencies might be selected three editorials. One was in simple and chaste but illuminating language directed to parents and teachers, deprecating corporal punishment for children.

Another was an accusive and significant warning addressed to a notorious labor leader who was on the point of instigating his clients to a troublesome strike.

The third was an eloquent demand that the police force be sustained and aided in everything that tended to increase its efficiency as public guardians and servants.

Besides these more important chidings and requisitions upon the store of good citizenship was a wise prescription or form of procedure laid out by the editor of the heart-to-heart column in the specific case of a young man who had complained of the obduracy of his lady love, teaching him how he might win her.

Again, there was, on the beauty page, a complete answer to a young lady inquirer who desired admonition toward the securing of bright eyes, rosy cheeks, and a beautiful countenance.

One other item requiring special cognizance was a brief "personal," running thus:

DEAR JACK:—Forgive me. You were right. Meet me at corner of Madison and —th at 8:30 this morning. We leave at noon.
                                                        PENITENT.

At 8 o'clock a young man with a haggard look and the feverish gleam of unrest in his eye dropped a penny and picked up the top paper as he passed Giuseppi's stand. A sleepless night had left him a late riser. There was an office to be reached by nine, and a shave and a hasty cup of coffee to be crowded into the interval.

He visited his barber shop and then hurried on his way. He pocketed his paper, meditating a belated perusal of it at the luncheon hour. At the next corner it fell from his pocket, carrying with it his pair of new gloves. Three blocks he walked, missed the gloves and turned back fuming.

Just on the half-hour he reached the corner where lay the gloves and paper. But he strangely ignored that which he had come to seek. He was holding two little hands as tightly as ever he could and looking into two penitent brown eyes, while joy rioted in his heart.

"Dear Jack," she said, "I knew you would be here on time."

"I wonder what she means by that," he was saying to himself; "but it's all right, it's all right."

A big wind puffed out of the west, picked up the paper from the sidewalk, opened it and sent it flying and whirling down a side street. Up that street was driving a skittish bay to a spider-wheel buggy the young man who had written to the heart-to-heart editor for a recipe that he might win her for whom he sighed.

The wind, with a prankish flurry, flapped the flying newspaper against the face of the skittish bay. There was a lengthened streak of bay mingled with the red of running gear that stretched itself out for four blocks. Then a water-hydrant played its part in the cosmogony, the buggy became match wood as fore-ordained, and the driver rested very quietly where he had been flung on the asphalt in front of a certain brownstone mansion.

They came out and had him inside very promptly. And there was one who made herself a pillow for his head, and cared for no curious eyes, bending over and saying, "Oh, it was you; it was you all the time, Bobby! Couldn't you see it? And if you die, why, so must I, and——"

But in all this wind we must hurry to keep in touch with our paper.

Policeman O'Brine arrested it as a character dangerous to traffic. Straightening its dishevelled leaves with his big, slow fingers, he stood a few feet from the family entrance of the Shandon Bells Café. One headline he spelled out ponderously. "The Papers to the Front in a Move to Help the Police."

But, whist! the voice of Danny, the head bartender, through the crack of the door: "Here's a nip for ye, Mike, ould man."

Behind the widespread, amicable columns of the press

Policeman O'Brine receives swiftly his nip of the real stuff. He moves away, stalwart, refreshed, fortified, to his duties. Might not the editor man view with pride the early, the spiritual, the literal fruit that had blessed his labors.

Policeman O'Brine folded the paper and poked it playfully under the arm of a small boy that was passing. That boy was named Johnny, and he took the paper home with him. His sister was named Gladys, and she had written to the beauty editor of the paper asking for the practicable touchstone of beauty. That was weeks ago, and she had ceased to look for an answer. Gladys was a pale girl, with dull eyes and a discontented expression. She was dressing to go up to the avenue to get some braid. Beneath her skirt she pinned two leaves of the paper Johnny had brought. When she walked the rustling sound was an exact imitation of the real thing.

On the street she met the Brown girl from the flat below and stopped to talk. The Brown girl turned green. Only silk at $5 a yard could make the sound that she heard when Gladys moved. The Brown girl, consumed by jealousy, said something spiteful and went her way, with pinched lips.

Gladys proceeded towards the avenue. Her eyes now sparkled like jagerfonteins. A rosy bloom visited her cheeks; a triumphant, subtle, vivifying smile transfigured her face. She was beautiful. Could the beauty editor have seen her then! There was something in her answer in the paper, I believe, about cultivating a kind feeling towards others in order to make plain features attractive.

The labor leader against whom the paper's solemn and weighty editorial injunction was laid was the father of Gladys and Johnny. He picked up the remains of the journal from which Gladys had ravished a cosmetic of silken sounds. The editorial did not come under his eye, but instead it was greeted by one of those ingenious and specious puzzle problems that enthrall alike the simpleton and the sage.

The labor leader tore off half of the page, provided himself with table, pencil, and paper and glued himself to the puzzle.

Three hours later, after waiting vainly for him at the appointed place, other more conservative leaders declared and ruled in favor of arbitration, and the strike with its attendant dangers was averted. Subsequent editions of the paper referred, in colored inks, to the clarion tone of its successful denunciation of the labor leader's intended designs.

The remaining leaves of the active journal also went loyally to the proving of its potency.

When Johnny returned from school he sought a secluded spot and removed the missing columns from the inside of his clothing, where they had been artfully distributed so as to successfully defend such areas as are generally attacked during scholastic castigations. Johnny attended a private school and had had trouble with his teacher. As has been said, there was an excellent editorial against corporal punishment in that morning's issue, and no doubt it had its effect.

After this can any one doubt the power of the press?

The Voice of the City

~~~~~~

TWENTY-FIVE years ago the school children used to chant their lessons. The manner of their delivery was a singsong recitative between the utterance of an Episcopal minister and the drone of a tired sawmill. I mean no disrespect. We must have lumber and sawdust.

I remember one beautiful and instructive little lyric that emanated from the physiology class. The most striking line of it was this:

"The shin-bone is the long-est bone in the human bod-y."

What an inestimable boon it would have been if all the corporeal and spiritual facts pertaining to man had thus been tunefully and logically inculcated in our youthful minds! But what we gained in anatomy, music, and philosophy was meagre.

The other day I became confused. I needed a ray of light. I turned back to those school days for aid. But in all the nasal harmonies we whined forth from those hard benches I could not recall one that treated of the voice of agglomerated mankind.

In other words, of the composite vocal message of massed humanity.

In other words, of the Voice of a Big City.

Now, the individual voice is not lacking. We can understand the song of the poet, the ripple of the brook, the meaning of the man who wants $5 until next Monday, the inscriptions on the tombs of the Pharaohs, the language of flowers, the "step lively" of the conductor, and the prelude of the milk cans at 4 A.M. Certain large-eared ones even assert that they are wise to the vibrations of the tympanum produced by concussion of the air emanating from Mr. H. James. But who can comprehend the meaning of the voice of the city?

I went out for to see.

First, I asked Aurelia. She wore white Swiss and a hat with flowers on it, and ribbons and ends of things fluttered here and there.

"Tell me," I said, stammeringly, for I have no voice of my own, "what does this big—er—enormous—er—whopping city say? It must have a voice of some kind. Does it ever speak to you? How do you interpret its meaning? It is a tremendous mass, but it must have a key."

"Like a Saratoga trunk?" asked Aurelia.

"No," said I. "Please do not refer to the lid. I have a fancy that every city has a voice. Each one has something to say to the one who can hear it. What does the big one say to you?"

"All cities," said Aurelia, judiciously, "say the same thing. When they get through saying it there is an echo from Philadelphia. So, they are unanimous."

"Here are 4,000,000 people," said I, scholastically, "compressed upon an island, which is mostly lamb surrounded by Wall Street water. The conjunction of so many units into so small a space must result in an identity—or, or rather a homogeneity—that finds its oral expression through a common channel. It is, as you might say, a consensus of translation, concentrating in a crystallized, general idea which reveals itself in what may be termed the Voice of the City. Can you tell me what it is?"

Aurelia smiled wonderfully. She sat on the high stoop. A spray of insolent ivy bobbed against her right ear. A ray of impudent moonlight flickered upon her nose. But I was adamant, nickel-plated.

"I must go and find out," I said, "what is the Voice of this City. Other cities have voices. It is an assignment. I must have it. New York," I continued, in a rising tone, "had better not hand me a cigar and say: 'Old man, I can't talk for publication.' No other city acts in that way. Chicago says, unhesitatingly, 'I will'; Philadelphia says, 'I should'; New Orleans says, 'I used to'; Louisville says, 'Don't care if I do'; St. Louis says, 'Excuse me'; Pittsburgh says, 'Smoke up.' Now, New York——"

Aurelia smiled.

"Very well," said I, "I must go elsewhere and find out."

I went into a palace, tile-floored, cherub-ceilinged, and square with the cop. I put my foot on the brass rail and said to Billy Magnus, the best bartender in the diocese:

"Billy, you've lived in New York a long time—what kind of a song-and-dance does this old town give you? What I mean is, doesn't the gab of it seem to kind of bunch up and slide over the bar to you in a sort of amalgamated tip that hits off the burg in a kind of an epigram with a dash of bitters and a slice of——"

"Excuse me a minute," said Billy, "somebody's punching the button at the side door."

He went away; came back with an empty tin bucket; again vanished with it full; returned and said to me:

"That was Mame. She rings twice. She likes a glass of beer

for supper. Her and the kid. If you ever saw that little skeesicks of mine brace up in his high chair and take his beer and—— But, say, what was yours? I get kind of excited when I hear them two rings—was it the baseball score or gin fizz you asked for?"

"Ginger ale," I answered.

I walked up to Broadway. I saw a cop on the corner. The cops take kids up, women across, and men in. I went up to him.

"If I'm not exceeding the spiel limit," I said, "let me ask you. You see New York during its vocative hours. It is the function of you and your brother cops to preserve the acoustics of the city. There must be a civic voice that is intelligible to you. At night during your lonely rounds you must have heard it. What is the epitome of its turmoil and shouting? What does the city say to you?"

"Friend," said the policeman, spinning his club, "it don't say nothing. I get my orders from the man higher up. Say, I guess you're all right. Stand here for a few minutes and keep an eye open for the roundsman."

The cop melted into the darkness of the side street. In ten minutes he had returned.

"Married last Tuesday," he said, half gruffly. "You know how they are. She comes to that corner at nine every night for a—comes to say 'hello!' I generally manage to be there. Say, what was it you asked me a bit ago—what's doing in the city? Oh, there's a roof-garden or two just opened, twelve blocks up."

I crossed a crow's-foot of street-car tracks, and skirted the edge of an umbrageous park. An artificial Diana, gilded, heroic, poised, wind-ruled, on the tower, shimmered in the clear light of her namesake in the sky. Along came my poet, hurrying, hatted, haired, emitting dactyls, spondees and dactylis. I seized him.

"Bill," said I (in the magazine he is Cleon), "give me a lift. I am on an assignment to find out the Voice of the City. You see, it's a special order. Ordinarily a symposium comprising the views of Henry Clews, John L. Sullivan, Edwin Markham, May Irwin and Charles Schwab would be about all. But this is a different matter. We want a broad, poetic, mystic vocalization of the city's soul and meaning. You are the very chap to give me a hint. Some years ago a man got at the Niagara Falls and gave us its pitch. The note was about two feet below the lowest G on the piano. Now, you can't put New York into a note unless it's better indorsed than that. But give me an idea of what it would say if it should speak. It is bound to be a mighty and far-reaching utterance. To arrive at it we must take the tremendous crash of the chords of the day's traffic, the laughter and music of the night, the solemn tones of Dr. Parkhurst, the rag-time, the weeping, the stealthy hum of cab-wheels, the shout of the press agent, the tinkle of fountains on the roof-gardens, the hullabaloo of the strawberry vender and the covers of *Everybody's Maga-zine,* the whispers of the lovers in the parks—all these sounds must go into your Voice—not combined, but mixed, and of the mixture an essence made; and of the essence an extract—an audible extract, of which one drop shall form the thing we seek."

"Do you remember," asked the poet, with a chuckle, "that California girl we met at Stiver's studio last week? Well, I'm on my way to see her. She repeated that poem of mine, 'The Tribute of Spring,' word for word. She's the smartest proposition in this town just at present. Say, how does this con-founded tie look? I spoiled four before I got one to set right."

"And the Voice that I asked you about?" I inquired.

"Oh, she doesn't sing," said Cleon. "But you ought to hear her recite my 'Angel of the Inshore Wind.'"

I passed on. I cornered a newsboy and he flashed at me prophetic pink papers that outstripped the news by two revo-lutions of the clock's longest hand.

"Son," I said, while I pretended to chase coins in my penny pocket, "doesn't it sometimes seem to you as if the city ought to be able to talk? All these ups and downs and funny business and queer things happening every day—what would it say, do you think, if it could speak?"

"Quit yer kiddin'," said the boy. "Wot paper yer want? I got no time to waste. It's Mag's birthday, and I want thirty cents to git her a present."

Here was no interpreter of the city's mouth-piece. I bought a paper, and consigned its undeclared treaties, its premeditated murders and unfought battles to an ash can.

Again I repaired to the park and sat in the moon shade. I thought and thought, and wondered why none could tell me what I asked for.

And then, as swift as light from a fixed star, the answer came to me. I arose and hurried—hurried as so many reasoners must, back around my circle. I knew the answer and I hugged it in my breast as I flew, fearing lest someone would stop me and demand my secret.

Aurelia was still on the stoop. The moon was higher and the ivy shadows were deeper. I sat at her side and we watched a little cloud tilt at the drifting moon and go asunder quite pale and discomfited.

And then, wonder of wonders and delight of delights! our hands somehow touched, and our fingers closed together and did not part.

After half an hour Aurelia said, with that smile of hers:

"Do you know, you haven't spoken a word since you came back!"

"That," said I, nodding wisely, "is the Voice of the City."

One Thousand Dollars

"ONE thousand dollars," repeated Lawyer Tolman, solemnly and severely, "and here is the money."

Young Gillian gave a decidedly amused laugh as he fingered the thin package of new fifty-dollar notes.

"It's such a confoundedly awkward amount," he explained, genially, to the lawyer. "If it had been ten thousand a fellow might wind up with a lot of fireworks and do himself credit. Even fifty dollars would have been less trouble."

"You heard the reading of your uncle's will," continued Lawyer Tolman, professionally dry in his tones. "I do not know if you paid much attention to its details. I must remind you of one. You are required to render to us an account of the manner of expenditure of this $1,000 as soon as you have disposed of it. The will stipulates that. I trust that you will so far comply with the late Mr. Gillian's wishes."

"You may depend upon it," said the young man, politely, "in spite of the extra expense it will entail. I may have to engage a secretary. I was never good at accounts."

Gillian went to his club. There he hunted out one whom he called Old Bryson.

Old Bryson was calm and forty and sequestered. He was in a corner reading a book, and when he saw Gillian approaching he sighed, laid down his book and took off his glasses.

"Old Bryson, wake up," said Gillian. "I've a funny story to tell you."

"I wish you would tell it to someone in the billiard room," said Old Bryson. "You know how I hate your stories."

"This is a better one than usual," said Gillian, rolling a

cigarette; "and I'm glad to tell it to you. It's too sad and funny to go with the rattling of billiard balls. I've just come from my late uncle's firm of legal corsairs. He leaves me an even thousand dollars. Now, what can a man possibly do with a thousand dollars?"

"I thought," said Old Bryson, showing as much interest as a bee shows in a vinegar cruet, "that the late Septimus Gillian was worth something like half a million."

"He was," assented Gillian, joyously, "and that's where the joke comes in. He's left his whole cargo of doubloons to a microbe. That is, part of it goes to the man who invents a new bacillus and the rest to establish a hospital for doing away with it again. There are one or two trifling bequests on the side. The butler and the housekeeper get a seal ring and $10 each. His nephew gets $1,000."

"You've always had plenty of money to spend," observed Old Bryson.

"Tons," said Gillian. "Uncle was the fairy godmother as far as an allowance was concerned."

"Any other heirs?" asked Old Bryson.

"None." Gillian frowned at his cigarette and kicked the upholstered leather of a divan uneasily. "There is a Miss Hayden, a ward of my uncle, who lived in his house. She's a quiet thing—musical—the daughter of somebody who was unlucky enough to be his friend. I forgot to say that she was in on the seal ring and $10 joke, too. I wish I had been. Then I could have had two bottles of *brut*, tipped the waiter with the ring, and had the whole business off my hands. Don't be superior and insulting, Old Bryson—tell me what a fellow can do with a thousand dollars."

Old Bryson rubbed his glasses and smiled. And when Old Bryson smiled, Gillian knew that he intended to be more offensive than ever.

"A thousand dollars," he said, "means much or little. One man may buy a happy home with it and laugh at Rockefeller. Another could send his wife South with it and save her life. A thousand dollars would buy pure milk for one hundred babies during June, July, and August and save fifty of their lives. You could count upon a half hour's diversion with it at faro in one of the fortified art galleries. It would furnish an education to an ambitious boy. I am told that a genuine Corot was secured for that amount in an auction room yesterday. You could move to a New Hampshire town and live respectably two years on it. You could rent Madison Square Garden for one evening with it, and lecture your audience, if you should have one, on the precariousness of the profession of heir presumptive."

"People might like you, Old Bryson," said Gillian, almost unruffled, "if you wouldn't moralize. I asked you to tell me what I could do with a thousand dollars."

"You?" said Bryson, with a gentle laugh. "Why, Bobby Gillian, there's only one logical thing you could do. You can go buy Miss Lotta Lauriere a diamond pendant with the money, and then take yourself off to Idaho and inflict your presence upon a ranch. I advise a sheep ranch, as I have a particular dislike for sheep."

"Thanks," said Gillian, rising. "I thought I could depend upon you, Old Bryson. You've hit on the very scheme. I wanted to chuck the money in a lump, for I've got to turn in an account for it, and I hate itemizing."

Gillian phoned for a cab and said to the driver:

"The stage entrance of the Columbine Theatre."

Miss Lotta Lauriere was assisting nature with a powder puff, almost ready for her call at a crowded matinée, when her dresser mentioned the name of Mr. Gillian.

"Let it in," said Miss Lauriere. "Now, what is it, Bobby? I'm going on in two minutes."

"Rabbit-foot your right ear a little," suggested Gillian, critically. "That's better. It won't take two minutes for me. What do you say to a little thing in the pendant line? I can stand three ciphers with a figure one in front of 'em."

"Oh, just as you say," carolled Miss Lauriere.

"My right glove, Adams. Say, Bobby, did you see that necklace Della Stacey had on the other night? Twenty-two hundred dollars it cost at Tiffany's. But, of course—pull my sash a little to the left, Adams."

"Miss Lauriere for the opening chorus!" cried the call boy without.

Gillian strolled out to where his cab was waiting.

"What would you do with a thousand dollars if you had it?" he asked the driver.

"Open a s'loon," said the cabby promptly and huskily. "I know a place I could take money in with both hands. It's a four-story brick on a corner. I've got it figured out. Second story—Chinks and chop suey; third floor—manicures and foreign missions; fourth floor—poolroom. If you was thinking of putting up the cap——"

"Oh, no," said Gillian, "I merely asked from curiosity. I take you by the hour. Drive till I tell you to stop."

Eight blocks down Broadway Gillian poked up the trap with his cane and got out. A blind man sat upon a stool on the sidewalk selling pencils. Gillian went out and stood before him.

"Excuse me," he said, "but would you mind telling me what you would do if you had a thousand dollars?"

"You got out of that cab that just drove up, didn't you?" asked the blind man.

"I did," said Gillian.

"I guess you are all right," said the pencil dealer, "to ride in a cab by daylight. Take a look at that, if you like."

He drew a small book from his coat pocket and held it out. Gillian opened it and saw that it was a bank deposit book. It showed a balance of $1,785 to the blind man's credit.

Gillian returned the book and got into the cab.

"I forgot something," he said. "You may drive to the law offices of Tolman & Sharp, at —— Broadway."

Lawyer Tolman looked at him hostilely and inquiringly through his gold-rimmed glasses.

"I beg your pardon," said Gillian, cheerfully, "but may I ask you a question? It is not an impertinent one, I hope. Was Miss Hayden left anything by my uncle's will besides the ring and the $10?"

"Nothing," said Mr. Tolman.

"I thank you very much, sir," said Gillian, and out he went to his cab. He gave the driver the address of his late uncle's home.

Miss Hayden was writing letters in the library. She was small and slender and clothed in black. But you would have noticed her eyes. Gillian drifted in with his air of regarding the world as inconsequent.

"I've just come from old Tolman's," he explained. "They've been going over the papers down there. They found a"— Gillian searched his memory for a legal term—"they found an amendment or a postscript or something to the will. It seemed that the old boy loosened up a little on second thought and willed you a thousand dollars. I was driving up this way and Tolman asked me to bring you the money. Here it is. You'd better count it to see if it's right." Gillian laid the money beside her hand on the desk.

Miss Hayden turned white. "Oh!" she said, and again "Oh!"

Gillian half turned and looked out of the window.

"I suppose, of course," he said, in a low voice, "that you know I love you."

"I am sorry," said Miss Hayden, taking up her money.

"There is no use?" asked Gillian, almost light-heartedly.

"I am sorry," she said again.

"May I write a note?" asked Gillian, with a smile. He seated himself at the big library table. She supplied him with paper and pen, and then went back to her secrétaire.

Gillian made out his account of his expenditure of the thousand dollars in these words:

"Paid by the black sheep, Robert Gillian, $1,000 on account of the eternal happiness, owed by Heaven to the best and dearest woman on earth."

Gillian slipped his writing into an envelope, bowed and went his way.

His cab stopped again at the offices of Tolman & Sharp.

"I have expended the thousand dollars," he said, cheerily, to Tolman of the gold glasses, "and I have come to render account of it, as I agreed. There is quite a feeling of summer in the air—do you not think so, Mr. Tolman?" He tossed a white envelope on the lawyer's table. "You will find there a memorandum, sir, of the *modus operandi* of the vanishing of the dollars."

Without touching the envelope, Mr. Tolman went to a door and called his partner, Sharp. Together they explored the caverns of an immense safe. Forth they dragged as trophy of their search a big envelope sealed with wax. This they forcibly invaded, and wagged their venerable heads together over its contents. Then Tolman became spokesman.

"Mr. Gillian," he said, formally, "there was a codicil to your uncle's will. It was intrusted to us privately, with instructions that it be not opened until you had furnished us with a full account of your handling of the $1,000 bequest in the will. As you have fulfilled the conditions, my partner and I have read the codicil. I do not wish to encumber your understanding with its legal phraseology, but I will acquaint you with the spirit of its contents.

"In the event that your disposition of the $1,000 demonstrates that you possess any of the qualifications that deserve reward, much benefit will accrue to you. Mr. Sharp and I are named as the judges, and I assure you that we will do our duty strictly according to justice—with liberality. We are not at all unfavorably disposed toward you, Mr. Gillian. But let us return to the letter of the codicil. If your disposal of the money in question has been prudent, wise, or unselfish, it is in our power to hand you over bonds to the value of $50,000, which have been placed in our hands for that purpose. But if—as our client, the late Mr. Gillian, explicitly provides—you have used this money as you have used money in the past—I quote the late Mr. Gillian—in reprehensible dissipation among disreputable associates—the $50,000 is to be paid to Miriam Hayden, ward of the late Mr. Gillian, without delay. Now, Mr. Gillian, Mr. Sharp and I will examine your account in regard to the $1,000. You submit it in writing, I believe. I hope you will repose confidence in our decision."

Mr. Tolman reached for the envelope. Gillian was a little the quicker in taking it up. He tore the account and its cover leisurely into strips and dropped them into his pocket.

"It's all right," he said, smilingly. "There isn't a bit of need to bother you with this. I don't suppose you'd understand these itemized bets, anyway. I lost the thousand dollars on the races. Good-day to you, gentlemen."

Tolman & Sharp shook their heads mournfully at each other when Gillian left, for they heard him whistling gayly in the hallway as he waited for the elevator.

The Trimmed Lamp

OF course there are two sides to the question. Let us look at the other. We often hear "shop-girls" spoken of. No such persons exist. There are girls who work in shops. They make their living that way. But why turn their occupation into an adjective? Let us be fair. We do not refer to the girls who live on Fifth Avenue as "marriage-girls."

Lou and Nancy were chums. They came to the big city to find work because there was not enough to eat at their homes to go around. Nancy was nineteen; Lou was twenty. Both were pretty, active country girls who had no ambition to go on the stage.

The little cherub that sits up aloft guided them to a cheap and respectable boarding-house. Both found positions and became wage earners. They remained chums. It is at the end of six months that I would beg you to step forward and be introduced to them. Meddlesome Reader: My Lady Friends, Miss Nancy and Miss Lou. While you are shaking hands please take notice—cautiously—of their attire. Yes, cautiously; for they are as quick to resent a stare as a lady in a box at the horse show is.

Lou is a piece-work ironer in a hand laundry. She is

clothed in a badly fitting purple dress, and her hat plume is four inches too long; but her ermine muff and scarf cost $25, and its fellow beasts will be ticketed in the windows at $7.98 before the season is over. Her cheeks are pink, and her light blue eyes bright. Contentment radiates from her.

Nancy you would call a shop-girl—because you have the habit. There is no type; but a perverse generation is always seeking a type; so this is what the type should be. She has the high-ratted pompadour and the exaggerated straight-front. Her skirt is shoddy, but has the correct flare. No furs protect her against the bitter spring air, but she wears her short broadcloth jacket as jauntily as though it were Persian lamb! On her face and in her eyes, remorseless type-seeker, is the typical shop-girl expression. It is a look of silent but contemptuous revolt against cheated womanhood; of sad prophecy of the vengeance to come. When she laughs her loudest the look is still there. The same look can be seen in the eyes of Russian peasants; and those of us left will see it some day on Gabriel's face when he comes to blow us up. It is a look that should wither and abash man; but he has been known to smirk at it and offer flowers—with a string tied to them.

Now lift your hat and come away, while you receive Lou's cheery "See you again," and the sardonic, sweet smile of Nancy that seems, somehow, to miss you and go fluttering like a white moth up over the housetops to the stars.

The two waited on the corner for Dan. Dan was Lou's steady company. Faithful? Well, he was on hand when Mary would have had to hire a dozen subpœna servers to find her lamb.

"Ain't you cold, Nancy?" said Lou. "Say, what a chump you are for working in that old store for $8 a week! I made $18.50 last week. Of course ironing isn't as swell work as selling lace behind a counter, but it pays. None of us ironers make less than $10. And I don't know that it's any less respectful work, either."

"You can have it," said Nancy, with uplifted nose. "I'll take my eight a week and hall bedroom. I like to be among nice things and swell people. And look what a chance I've got! Why, one of our glove girls married a Pittsburgh—a steel maker, or blacksmith or something—the other day, worth a million dollars. I'll catch a swell myself some time. I ain't bragging on my looks or anything; but I'll take my chances where there's big prizes offered. What show would a girl have in a laundry?"

"Why, that's where I met Dan," said Lou, triumphantly. "He came in for his Sunday shirt and collars and saw me at the first board, ironing. We all try to get to work at the first board. Ella Maginnis was sick that day, and I had her place. He said he noticed my arms first, how round and white they was. I had my sleeves rolled up. Some nice fellows come into laundries. You can tell 'em by their bringing their clothes in suit cases, and turning in the door sharp and sudden."

"How can you wear a waist like that, Lou?" said Nancy, gazing down at the offending article with sweet scorn in her heavy-lidded eyes. "It shows fierce taste."

"This waist!" said Lou, with wide-eyed indignation. "Why, I paid $16 for this waist. It's worth twenty-five. A woman left it to be laundered, and never called for it. The boss sold it to me. It's got yards and yards of hand embroidery on it. Better talk about that ugly, plain thing you've got on."

"This ugly, plain thing," said Nancy, calmly, "was copied from one that Mrs. Van Alstyne Fisher was wearing. The girls say her bill in the store last year was $12,000. I made mine, myself. It cost me $1.50. Ten feet away you couldn't tell it from hers."

"Oh, well," said Lou, good-naturedly, "if you want to starve and put on airs, go ahead. But I'll take my job and good wages; and after hours give me something as fancy and attractive to wear as I am able to buy."

But just then Dan came—a serious young man with a ready-made necktie, who had escaped the city's brand of frivolity—an electrician earning $30 per week who looked upon Lou with the sad eyes of Romeo, and thought her embroidered waist a web in which any fly should delight to be caught.

"My friend, Mr. Owens—shake hands with Miss Danforth," said Lou.

"I'm mighty glad to know you, Miss Danforth," said Dan, with outstretched hand. "I've heard Lou speak of you so often."

"Thanks," said Nancy, touching his fingers with the tips of her cool ones, "I've heard her mention you—a few times."

Lou giggled.

"Did you get that handshake from Mrs. Van Alstyne Fisher, Nance?" she asked.

"If I did, you can feel safe in copying it," said Nancy.

"Oh, I couldn't use it at all. It's too stylish for me. It's intended to set off diamond rings, that high shake is. Wait till I get a few and then I'll try it."

"Learn it first," said Nancy, wisely, "and you'll be more likely to get the rings."

"Now, to settle this argument," said Dan, with his ready, cheerful smile, "let me make you a proposition. As I can't take both of you up to Tiffany's and do the right thing, what do you say to a little vaudeville? I've got the tickets. How about looking at stage diamonds since we can't shake hands with the real sparklers?"

The faithful squire took his place close to the curb; Lou next, a little peacocky in her bright and pretty clothes; Nancy on the inside, slender, and soberly clothed as the sparrow, but with the true Van Alstyne Fisher walk—thus they set out for their evening's moderate diversion.

I do not suppose that many look upon a great department store as an educational institution. But the one in which Nancy worked was something like that to her. She was surrounded by beautiful things that breathed of taste and refinement. If you live in an atmosphere of luxury, luxury is yours whether your money pays for it, or another's.

The people she served were mostly women whose dress, manners, and position in the social world were quoted as criterions. From them Nancy began to take toll—the best from each according to her view.

From one she would copy a practise or gesture, from another an eloquent lifting of an eyebrow, from others, a manner of walking, of carrying a purse, of smiling, of greeting a friend, of addressing "inferiors in station." From her best beloved model, Mrs. Van Alstyne Fisher, she made requisition for that excellent thing, a soft, low voice as clear as silver and as perfect in articulation as the notes of a thrush. Suffused in the aura of this high social refinement and good breeding, it was impossible for her to escape a deeper effect of it. As good habits are said to be better than good principles, so, perhaps, good manners are better than good habits. The teachings of your parents may not keep alive your New England conscience; but if you sit on a straight-back chair and repeat the words "prisms and pilgrims" forty times the devil will flee from you. And when Nancy spoke in the Van Alstyne Fisher tones she felt the thrill of *noblesse oblige* to her very bones.

There was another source of learning in the great departmental school. Whenever you see three or four shop-girls gather in a bunch and jingle their wire bracelets as an accompaniment to apparently frivolous conversation, do not think that they are there for the purpose of criticizing the way Ethel does her back hair. The meeting may lack the dignity of the deliberative bodies of man; but it has all the importance of the occasion on which Eve and her first daughter first put their heads together to make Adam understand his proper place in the household. It is Woman's Conference for Common Defense and Exchange of Strategical Theories of Attack and Repulse upon and against the World, which is a Stage, and Man, its Audience who Persists in Throwing Bouquets Thereupon. Woman, the most helpless of the young of any animal—with the fawn's grace but without its fleetness; with the bird's beauty but without its power of flight; with the honey-bee's burden of sweetness but without its—— Oh, let's drop that simile—some of us may have been stung.

During this council of war they pass weapons one to another, and exchange stratagems that each has devised and formulated out of the tactics of life.

"I says to 'im," says Sadie, "ain't you the fresh thing! Who do you suppose I am, to be addressing such a remark to me? And what do you think he says back to me?"

The heads, brown, black, flaxen, red, and yellow bob together; the answer is given; and the parry to the thrust is decided upon, to be used by each thereafter in passages-at-arms with the common enemy, man.

Thus Nancy learned the art of defense; and to women successful defense means victory.

The curriculum of a department store is a wide one. Perhaps no other college could have fitted her as well for her life's ambition—the drawing of a matrimonial prize.

Her station in the store was a favored one. The music room was near enough for her to hear and become familiar with the works of the best composers—at least to acquire the familiarity that passed for appreciation in the social world in which she was vaguely trying to set a tentative and aspiring foot. She absorbed the educating influence of art wares, of costly and dainty fabrics, of adornments that are almost culture to women.

The other girls soon became aware of Nancy's ambition. "Here comes your millionaire, Nancy," they would call to her whenever any man who looked the rôle approached her counter. It got to be a habit of men, who were hanging about while their women folks were shopping, to stroll over to the handkerchief counter and dawdle over the cambric squares. Nancy's imitation high-bred air and genuine dainty beauty was what attracted. Many men thus came to display their graces before her. Some of them may have been millionaires; others were certainly no more than their sedulous apes. Nancy learned to discriminate. There was a window at the end of the handkerchief counter; and she could see the rows of vehicles waiting for the shoppers in the street below. She looked and perceived that automobiles differ as well as do their owners.

Once a fascinating gentleman bought four dozen handkerchiefs, and wooed her across the counter with a King Cophetua air. When he had gone one of the girls said:

"What's wrong, Nance, that you didn't warm up to that fellow? He looks the swell article, all right, to me."

"Him?" said Nancy, with her coolest, sweetest, most impersonal, Van Alstyne Fisher smile; "not for mine. I saw him drive up outside. A 12 H. P. machine and an Irish chauffeur! And you saw what kind of handkerchiefs he bought—silk! And he's got dactylis on him. Give me the real thing or nothing, if you please."

Two of the most "refined" women in the store—a forelady and a cashier—had a few "swell gentlemen friends" with whom they now and then dined. Once they included Nancy in an invitation. The dinner took place in a spectacular café whose tables are engaged for New Year's Eve in advance. There were two "gentlemen friends"—one without any hair on his head—high living ungrew it; and we can prove it—the other a young man whose worth and sophistication he pressed upon you in two convincing ways—he swore that all the wine was corked; and he wore diamond cuff buttons. This young man perceived irresistible excellencies in Nancy. His taste ran to shop-girls; and here was one that added the voice and manners of his high social world to the franker charms of her own caste. So, on the following day, he appeared in the store and made her a serious proposal of marriage over a box of hemstitched, grass-bleached Irish linens. Nancy declined. A brown pompadour ten feet away had been using her eyes and ears. When the rejected suitor had gone she heaped carboys of upbraidings and horror upon Nancy's head.

"What a terrible little fool you are! That fellow's a millionaire—he's a nephew of old Van Skittles himself. And he was talking on the level, too. Have you gone crazy, Nance?"

"Have I?" said Nancy. "I didn't take him, did I? He isn't a millionaire so hard that you could notice it, anyhow. His family only allows him $20,000 a year to spend. The bald-headed fellow was guying him about it the other night at supper."

The brown pompadour came nearer and narrowed her eyes.

"Say, what do you want?" she inquired, in a voice hoarse for lack of chewing-gum. "Ain't that enough for you? Do you want to be a Mormon, and marry Rockefeller and Glad-

stone Dowie and the King of Spain and the whole bunch?
Ain't $20,000 a year good enough for you?"

Nancy flushed a little under the level gaze of the black,
shallow eyes.

"It wasn't altogether the money, Carrie," she explained.
"His friend caught him in a rank lie the other night at dinner.
It was about some girl he said he hadn't been to the theater
with. Well, I can't stand a liar. Put everything together—I
don't like him; and that settles it. When I sell out it's not
going to be on any bargain day. I've got to have something
that sits up in a chair like a man, anyhow. Yes, I'm looking
out for a catch; but it's got to be able to do something more
than make a noise like a toy bank."

"The physiopathic ward for yours!" said the brown pompadour, walking away.

These high ideas, if not ideals—Nancy continued to culti-
vate on $8 per week. She bivouacked on the trail of the
great unknown "catch" eating her dry bread and tightening
her belt day by day. On her face was the faint, soldierly,
sweet, grim smile of the preordained manhunter. The store
was her forest; and many times she raised her rifle at game
that seemed broad-antlered and big; but always some deep
unerring instinct—perhaps of the huntress, perhaps of the
woman—made her hold her fire and take up the trail again.

Lou flourished in the laundry. Out of her $18.50 per week
she paid $6 for her room and board. The rest went mainly for
clothes. Her opportunities for bettering her taste and manners were few compared with Nancy's. In the steaming
laundry there was nothing but work, work and her thoughts
of the evening pleasures to come. Many costly and showy
fabrics passed under her iron; and it may be that her growing fondness for dress was thus transmitted to her through
the conducting metal.

When the day's work was over Dan awaited her outside,
her faithful shadow in whatever light she stood.

Sometimes he cast an honest and troubled glance at Lou's
clothes that increased in conspicuity rather than in style;

but this was no disloyalty; he deprecated the attention they called to her in the streets.

And Lou was no less faithful to her chum. There was a law that Nancy should go with them on whatsoever outings they might take. Dan bore the extra burden heartily and in good cheer. It might be said that Lou furnished the color, Nancy the tone, and Dan the weight of the distraction-seeking trio. The escort, in his neat but obviously ready-made suit, his ready-made tie and unfailing, genial, ready-made wit never startled or clashed. He was of that good kind that you are likely to forget while they are present, but remember distinctly after they are gone.

To Nancy's superior taste the flavor of these ready-made pleasures was sometimes a little bitter; but she was young; and youth is a gourmand, when it cannot be a gourmet.

"Dan is always wanting me to marry him right away," Lou told her once. "But why should I? I'm independent. I can do as I please with the money I earn; and he never would agree for me to keep on working afterward. And say, Nance, what do you want to stick to that old store for, and half starve and half dress yourself? I could get you a place in the laundry right now if you'd come. It seems to me that you could afford to be a little less stuck-up if you could make a good deal more money."

"I don't think I'm stuck-up, Lou," said Nancy, "but I'd rather live on half rations and stay where I am. I suppose I've got the habit. It's the chance that I want. I don't expect to be always behind a counter. I'm learning something new every day. I'm right up against refined and rich people all the time—even if I do only wait on them; and I'm not missing any pointers that I see passing around."

"Caught your millionaire yet?" asked Lou with her teasing laugh.

"I haven't selected one yet," answered Nancy. "I've been looking them over."

"Goodness! the idea of picking over 'em! Don't you ever let one get by you, Nancy—even if he's a few dollars shy.

But of course you're joking—millionaires don't think about working girls like us."

"It might be better for them if they did," said Nancy, with cool wisdom. "Some of us could teach them how to take care of their money."

"If one was to speak to me," laughed Lou, "I know I'd have a duck-fit."

"That's because you don't know any. The only difference between swells and other people is you have to watch 'em closer. Don't you think that red silk lining is just a little bit too bright for that coat, Lou?"

Lou looked at the plain, dull olive jacket of her friend.

"Well, no, I don't—but it may seem so beside that faded-looking thing you've got on."

"This jacket," said Nancy, complacently, "has exactly the cut and fit of one that Mrs. Van Alstyne Fisher was wearing the other day. The material cost me $3.98. I suppose hers cost about $100 more."

"Oh, well," said Lou, lightly, "it don't strike me as millionaire bait. Shouldn't wonder if I catch one before you do, anyway."

Truly it would have taken a philosopher to decide upon the values of the theories held by the two friends. Lou, lacking that certain pride and fastidiousness that keeps stores and desks filled with girls working for the barest living, thumped away gaily with her iron in the noisy and stifling laundry. Her wages supported her even beyond the point of comfort; so that her dress profited until sometimes she cast a sidelong glance of impatience at the neat but inelegant apparel of Dan—Dan the constant, the immutable, the undeviating.

As for Nancy, her case was one of tens of thousands. Silk and jewels and laces and ornaments and the perfume and music of the fine world of good-breeding and taste—these were made for woman; they are her equitable portion. Let her keep near them if they are a part of life to her, and if she will. She is no traitor to herself, as Esau was; for she keeps her birthright and the pottage she earns is often very scant.

In this atmosphere Nancy belonged; and she throve in it and ate her frugal meals and schemed over her cheap dresses with a determined and contented mind. She already knew woman; and she was studying man, the animal, both as to his habits and eligibility. Some day she would bring down the game that she wanted; but she promised herself it would be what seemed to her the biggest and the best, and nothing smaller.

Thus she kept her lamp trimmed and burning to receive the bridegroom when he should come.

But another lesson she learned, perhaps unconsciously. Her standard of values began to shift and change. Sometimes the dollar-mark grew blurred in her mind's eye, and shaped itself into letters that spelled such words as "truth" and "honor" and now and then just "kindness." Let us make a likeness of one who hunts the moose or elk in some mighty wood. He sees a little dell, mossy and embowered, where a rill trickles, babbling to him of rest and comfort. At these times the spear of Nimrod himself grows blunt.

So, Nancy wondered sometimes if Persian lamb was always quoted at its market value by the hearts that it covered.

One Thursday evening Nancy left the store and turned across Sixth Avenue westward to the laundry. She was expected to go with Lou and Dan to a musical comedy.

Dan was just coming out of the laundry when she arrived. There was a queer, strained look on his face.

"I thought I would drop around to see if they had heard from her," he said.

"Heard from who?" asked Nancy. "Isn't Lou there?"

"I thought you knew," said Dan. "She hasn't been here or at the house where she lived since Monday. She moved all her things from there. She told one of the girls in the laundry she might be going to Europe."

"Hasn't anybody seen her anywhere?" asked Nancy.

Dan looked at her with his jaws set grimly, and a steely gleam in his steady gray eyes.

"They told me in the laundry," he said, harshly, "that they saw her pass yesterday—in an automobile. With one of the millionaires, I suppose, that you and Lou were forever busying your brains about."

For the first time Nancy quailed before a man. She laid her hand that trembled slightly on Dan's sleeve.

"You've no right to say such a thing to me, Dan—as if I had anything to do with it."

"I didn't mean it that way," said Dan, softening. He fumbled in his vest pocket.

"I've got the tickets for the show to-night," he said, with a gallant show of lightness. "If you——"

Nancy admired pluck whenever she saw it.

"I'll go with you, Dan," she said.

Three months went by before Nancy saw Lou again.

At twilight one evening the shop-girl was hurrying home along the border of a little quiet park. She heard her name called, and wheeled about in time to catch Lou rushing into her arms.

After the first embrace they drew their heads back as serpents do, ready to attack or to charm, with a thousand questions trembling on their swift tongues. And then Nancy noticed that prosperity had descended upon Lou, manifesting itself in costly furs, flashing gems, and creations of the tailor's art.

"You little fool!" cried Lou, loudly and affectionately. "I see you are still working in that store, and as shabby as ever. And how about that big catch you were going to make—nothing doing yet, I suppose?"

And then Lou looked, and saw that something better than prosperity had descended upon Nancy—something that shone brighter than gems in her eyes and redder than a rose in her cheeks, and that danced like electricity anxious to be loosed from the tip of her tongue.

"Yes, I'm still in the store," said Nancy, "but I'm going to leave it next week. I've made my catch—the biggest catch in the world. You won't mind now Lou, will you?—I'm going to be married to Dan—to Dan!—he's my Dan now—why, Lou!"

Around the corner of the park strolled one of those new-crop, smooth-faced young policemen that are making the force more endurable—at least to the eye. He saw a woman with an expensive fur coat, and diamond-ringed hands crouching down against the iron fence of the park sobbing turbulently, while a slender, plainly dressed working girl leaned close, trying to console her. But the Gibsonian cop, being of the new order, passed on, pretending not to notice, for he was wise enough to know that these matters are beyond help so far as the power he represents is concerned, though he rap the pavement with his nightstick till the sound goes up to the furthermost stars.

A Madison Square Arabian Night

TO Carson Chalmers, in his apartment near the square, Phillips brought the evening mail. Besides the routine correspondence there were two items bearing the same foreign postmark.

One of the incoming parcels contained a photograph of a woman. The other contained an interminable letter, over which Chalmers hung, absorbed, for a long time. The letter was from another woman; and it contained poisoned barbs, sweetly dipped in honey, and feathered with innuendoes concerning the photographed woman.

Chalmers tore this letter into a thousand bits and began to wear out his expensive rug by striding back and forth upon it. Thus an animal from the jungle acts when it is caged, and thus a caged man acts when he is housed in a jungle of doubt.

By and by the restless mood was overcome. The rug was not an enchanted one. For sixteen feet he could travel along it; three thousand miles was beyond its power to aid.

Phillips appeared. He never entered; he invariably appeared, like a well-oiled genie.

"Will you dine here, sir, or out?" he asked.

"Here," said Chalmers, "and in half an hour." He listened glumly to the January blasts making an Æolian trombone of the empty street.

"Wait," he said to the disappearing genie. "As I came home across the end of the square I saw many men standing there in rows. There was one mounted upon something, talking. Why do those men stand in rows, and why are they there?"

"They are homeless men, sir," said Phillips. "The man standing on the box tries to get lodging for them for the night. People come around to listen and give him money. Then he sends as many as the money will pay for to some lodging-house. That is why they stand in rows; they get sent to bed in order as they come."

"By the time dinner is served," said Chalmers, "have one of those men here. He will dine with me."

"W-w-which——" began Phillips, stammering for the first time during his service.

"Choose one at random," said Chalmers. "You might see that he is reasonably sober—and a certain amount of cleanliness will not be held against him. That is all."

It was an unusual thing for Carson Chalmers to play the Caliph. But on that night he felt the inefficacy of conventional antidotes to melancholy. Something wanton and egregious, something high-flavored and Arabian, he must have to lighten his mood.

On the half hour Phillips had finished his duties as slave of the lamp. The waiters from the restaurant below had whisked aloft the delectable dinner. The dining table, laid for two, glowed cheerily in the glow of the pink-shaded candles.

And now Phillips, as though he ushered a cardinal—or held in charge a burglar—wafted in the shivering guest who had been haled from the line of mendicant lodgers.

It is a common thing to call such men wrecks; if the comparison be used here it is the specific one of a derelict come to grief through fire. Even yet some flickering combustion illuminated the drifting hulk. His face and hands had been recently washed—a rite insisted upon by Phillips as a memorial to the slaughtered conventions. In the candle-light he stood, a flaw in the decorous fittings of the apartment. His face was a sickly white, covered almost to the eyes with a stubble the shade of a red Irish setter's coat. Phillips's comb had failed to control the pale brown hair, long matted and conformed to the contour of a constantly worn hat. His eyes were full of hopeless, tricky defiance like that seen in a cur's that is cornered by his tormentors. His shabby coat was buttoned high, but a quarter inch of redeeming collar showed above it. His manner was singularly free from embarrassment when Chalmers rose from his chair across the round dining table.

"If you will oblige me," said the host, "I will be glad to have your company at dinner."

"My name is Plumer," said the highway guest, in harsh and aggressive tones. "If you're like me, you like to know the name of the party you're dining with."

"I was going on to say," continued Chalmers somewhat hastily, "that mine is Chalmers. Will you sit opposite?"

Plumer, of the ruffled plumes, bent his knee for Phillips to slide the chair beneath him. He had an air of having sat at attended boards before. Phillips set out the anchovies and olives.

"Good!" barked Plumer; "going to be in courses, is it? All right, my jovial ruler of Bagdad. I'm your Scheherazade all the way to the toothpicks. You're the first Caliph with a genuine Oriental flavor I've struck since frost. What luck! And I was forty-third in line. I finished counting, just as your welcome emissary arrived to bid me to the feast. I had about as much chance of getting a bed to-night as I have of being the next President. How will you have the sad story of my life, Mr. Al Raschid—a chapter with each course or the whole edition with the cigars and coffee?"

"The situation does not seem a novel one to you," said Chalmers with a smile.

"By the chin whiskers of the prophet—no!" answered the guest. "New York's as full of cheap Haroun al Raschids as Bagdad is of fleas. I've been held up for my story with a loaded meal pointed at my head twenty times. Catch anybody in New York giving you something for nothing! They spell curiosity and charity with the same set of building blocks. Lots of 'em will stake you to a dime and chop-suey; and a few of 'em will play Caliph to the tune of a top sirloin; but every one of 'em will stand over you till they screw your autobiography out of you with foot notes, appendix and unpublished fragments. Oh, I know what to do when I see victuals coming toward me in little old Bagdad-on-the-Subway. I strike the asphalt three times with my forehead and get ready to spiel yarns for my supper. I claim descent from the late Tommy Tucker, who was forced to hand out vocal harmony for his pre-digested wheaterina and spoopju."

"I do not ask your story," said Chalmers. "I tell you frankly that it was a sudden whim that prompted me to send for some stranger to dine with me. I assure you you will not suffer through any curiosity of mine."

"Oh, fudge!" exclaimed the guest, enthusiastically tackling his soup; "I don't mind it a bit. I'm a regular Oriental magazine with a red cover and the leaves cut when the Caliph walks abroad. In fact, we fellows in the bed line have a sort of union rate for things of this sort. Somebody's always stopping and wanting to know what brought us down so low in the world. For a sandwich and a glass of beer I tell 'em that drink did it. For corned beef and cabbage and a cup of coffee I give 'em the hard-hearted-landlord—six-months-in-the-hospital-lost-job story. A sirloin steak and a quarter for a bed gets the Wall Street tragedy of the swept-away fortune and the gradual descent. This is the first spread of this kind I've stumbled against. I haven't got a story to fit it. I'll tell you what, Mr. Chalmers, I'm going to tell you the truth for this, if you'll listen to it. It'll be harder for you to believe than the made-up ones."

An hour later the Arabian guest lay back with a sigh of

satisfaction while Phillips brought the coffee and cigars and cleared the table.

"Did you ever hear of Sherrard Plumer?" he asked, with a strange smile.

"I remember the name," said Chalmers. "He was a painter, I think, of a good deal of prominence a few years ago."

"Five years," said the guest. "Then I went down like a chunk of lead. I'm Sherrard Plumer! I sold the last portrait I painted for $2,000. After that I couldn't have found a sitter for a gratis picture."

"What was the trouble?" Chalmers could not resist asking.

"Funny thing," answered Plumer, grimly. "Never quite understood it myself. For a while I swam like a cork. I broke into the swell crowd and got commissions right and left. The newspapers called me a fashionable painter. Then the funny things began to happen. Whenever I finished a picture people would come to see it, and whisper and look queerly at one another.

"I soon found out what the trouble was. I had a knack of bringing out in the face of a portrait the hidden character of the original. I don't know how I did it—I painted what I saw—but I know it did me. Some of my sitters were fearfully enraged and refused their pictures. I painted the portrait of a very beautiful and popular society dame. When it was finished her husband looked at it with a peculiar expression on his face, and the next week he sued for divorce.

"I remember one case of a prominent banker who sat for me. While I had his portrait on exhibition in my studio an acquaintance of his came in to look at it. 'Bless me,' says he, 'does he really look like that?' I told him it was considered a faithful likeness. 'I never noticed that expression about his eyes before,' said he; 'I think I'll drop downtown and change my bank account.' He did drop down, but the bank account was gone and so was Mr. Banker.

"It wasn't long till they put me out of business. People don't want their secret meannesses shown up in a picture. They can smile and twist their own faces and deceive you, but the picture can't. I couldn't get an order for another picture, and I had to give up. I worked as a newspaper artist for a while, and then for a lithographer, but my work with them got me into the same trouble. If I drew from a photograph my drawing showed up characteristics and expressions that you couldn't find in the photo, but I guess they were in the original, all right. The customers raised lively rows, especially the women, and I never could hold a job long. So I began to rest my weary head upon the breast of Old Booze for comfort. And pretty soon I was in the free-bed line and doing oral fiction for hand-outs among the food bazaars. Does the truthful statement weary thee, O Caliph? I can turn on the Wall Street disaster stop if you prefer, but that requires a tear, and I'm afraid I can't hustle one up after that good dinner."

"No, no," said Chalmers, earnestly, "you interest me very much. Did all of your portraits reveal some unpleasant trait, or were there some that did not suffer from the ordeal of your peculiar brush?"

"Some? Yes," said Plumer. "Children generally, a good many women and a sufficient number of men. All people aren't bad, you know. When they were all right the pictures were all right. As I said, I don't explain it, but I'm telling you facts."

On Chalmer's writing-table lay the photograph that he had received that day in the foreign mail. Ten minutes later he had Plumer at work making a sketch from it in pastels. At the end of an hour the artist rose and stretched wearily. "It's done," he yawned. "You'll excuse me for being so long. I got interested in the job. Lordy! but I'm tired. No bed last night, you know. Guess it'll have to be good-night now, O Commander of the Faithful!"

Chalmers went as far as the door with him and slipped some bills into his hand.

"Oh! I'll take 'em," said Plumer. "All that's included in the fall. Thanks. And for the very good dinner. I shall sleep on feathers tonight and dream of Bagdad. I hope it won't turn out to be a dream in the morning. Farewell, most excellent Caliph!"

Again Chalmers paced restlessly upon his rug. But his beat lay as far from the table whereon lay the pastel sketch as the room would permit. Twice, thrice, he tried to approach it, but failed. He could see the dun and gold and brown of the colors, but there was a wall about it built by his fears that kept him at a distance. He sat down and tried to calm himself. He sprang up and rang for Phillips.

"There is a young artist in this building," he said—"a Mr. Reineman—do you know which is his apartment?"

"Top floor, front, sir," said Phillips.

"Go up and ask him to favor me with his presence here for a few minutes."

Reineman came at once. Chalmers introduced himself.

"Mr. Reineman," said he, "there is a little pastel sketch on yonder table. I would be glad if you will give me your opinion of it as to its artistic merits and as a picture."

The young artist advanced to the table and took up the sketch. Chalmers half turned away, leaning upon the back of a chair.

"How—do—you find it?" he asked, slowly.

"As a drawing," said the artist, "I can't praise it enough. It's the work of a master—bold and fine and true. It puzzles me a little; I haven't seen any pastel work near as good in years."

"The face, man—the subject—the original—what would you say of that?"

"The face," said Reineman, "is the face of one of God's own angels. May I ask who——"

"My wife!" shouted Chalmers, wheeling and pouncing upon the astonished artist, gripping his hand and pounding his back. "She is traveling in Europe. Take that sketch, boy, and paint the picture of your life from it and leave the price to me."

The Rubaiyat of a Scotch Highball

~~~~~~

THIS document is intended to strike somewhere between a temperance lecture and the "Bartender's Guide." Relative to the latter, drink shall swell the theme and be set forth in abundance. Agreeably to the former, not an elbow shall be crooked.

Bob Babbitt was "off the stuff." Which means—as you will discover by referring to the unabridged dictionary of Bohemia—that he had "cut out the booze," that he was "on the water wagon." The reason for Bob's sudden attitude of hostility toward the "demon rum"—as the white ribboners miscall whiskey (see the "Bartender's Guide"), should be of interest to reformers and saloon-keepers.

There is always hope for a man who, when sober, will not concede or acknowledge that he was ever drunk. But when a man will say (in the apt words of the phrase-distiller), "I had a beautiful skate on last night," you will have to put stuff in his coffee as well as pray for him.

One evening on his way home Babbitt dropped in at the Broadway bar that he liked best. Always there were three or four fellows there from the downtown offices whom he knew. And then there would be highballs and stories, and he would hurry home to dinner a little late but feeling good, and a little sorry for the poor Standard Oil Company. On this evening as he entered he heard some one say: "Babbitt was in last night as full as a boiled owl."

Babbitt walked to the bar, and saw in the mirror that his face was as white as chalk. For the first time he had looked

Truth in the eyes. Others had lied to him; he had dissembled with himself. He was a drunkard, and had not known it. What he had fondly imagined was a pleasant exhilaration had been maudlin intoxication. His fancied wit had been drivel, his gay humors nothing but the noisy vagaries of a sot. But, never again!

"A glass of seltzer," he said to the bartender.

A little silence fell upon the group of his cronies, who had been expecting him to join them.

"Going off the stuff, Bob?" one of them asked politely and with more formality than the highballs ever called forth.

"Yes," said Babbitt.

Someone of the group took up the unwashed thread of a story he had been telling; the bartender shoved over a dime and a nickel change from the quarter, ungarnished with his customary smile; and Babbitt walked out.

Now, Babbitt had a home and a wife—but that is another story. And I will tell you that story, which will show you a better habit and a worse story than you could find in the man who invented the phrase.

It began away up in Sullivan County, where so many rivers and so much trouble begins—or begin; how would you say that? It was July, and Jessie was a summer boarder at the Mountain Squint Hotel, and Bob, who was just out of college, saw her one day—and they were married in September. That's the tabloid novel—one swallow of water, and it's gone.

But those July days!

Let the exclamation point expound it, for I shall not. For particulars you might read up on "Romeo and Juliet," and Abraham Lincoln's thrilling sonnet about "You can fool some of the people," &c., and Darwin's works.

But one thing I must tell you about. Both of them were mad over Omar's Rubaiyat. They knew every verse of the old bluffer by heart—not consecutively, but picking 'em out here and there as you fork the mushrooms in a fifty-cent steak à la Bordelaise. Sullivan County is full of rocks and trees; and Jessie used to sit on them, and—please be good—used to sit on the rocks; and Bob had a way of standing behind her with his hands over her shoulders holding her hands, and his face close to hers, and they would repeat over and over their favorite verses of the old tent-maker. They saw only the poetry and philosophy of the lines then—indeed, they agreed that the Wine was only an image, and that what was meant to be celebrated was some divinity, or maybe Love or Life. However, at that time neither of them had tasted the stuff that goes with a sixty-cent *table d'hôte.*

Where was I? Oh, they married and came to New York. Bob showed his college diploma, and accepted a position filling inkstands in a lawyer's office at $15 a week. At the end of two years he had worked up to $50, and gotten his first taste of Bohemia—the kind that won't stand the borax and formaldehyde tests.

They had two furnished rooms and a little kitchen. To Jess, accustomed to the mild but beautiful savor of a country town, the dreggy Bohemia was sugar and spice. She hung fish seines on the walls of her rooms, and bought a rakish-looking sideboard, and learned to play the banjo. Twice or thrice a week they dined at French or Italian *tables d'hôte* in a cloud of smoke, and brag and unshorn hair. Jess learned to drink a cocktail in order to get the cherry. At home she smoked a cigarette after dinner. She learned to pronounce Chianti, and leave her olive stones for the waiter to pick up. Once she assayed to say la, la la! in a crowd but got only as far as the second one. They met one or two couples while dining out and became friendly with them. The sideboard was stocked with Scotch and rye and a liqueur. They had their new friends in to dinner and all were laughing at nothing by 1 A.M. Some plastering fell in the room below them, for which Bob had to pay $4.50. Thus they footed it merrily on the ragged frontiers of the country that has no boundary lines or government.

And soon Bob fell in with his cronies and learned to keep his foot on the little rail six inches above the floor for an hour or so every afternoon before he went home. Drink always rubbed him the right way, and he would reach his rooms as jolly as a sandboy. Jessie would meet him at the door, and generally they would dance some insane kind of a rigadoon about the floor by way of greeting. Once when Bob's feet became confused and he tumbled headlong over a footstool Jessie laughed so heartily and long that he had to throw all the couch pillows at her to make her hush.

In such wise life was speeding for them on the day when Bob Babbitt first felt the power that the giftie gi'ed him.

But let us get back to our lamb and mint sauce.

When Bob got home that evening he found Jessie in a long apron cutting up a lobster for the Newburg. Usually when Bob came in mellow from his hour at the bar his welcome was hilarious, though somewhat tinctured with Scotch smoke.

By screams and snatches of song and certain audible testimonials of domestic felicity was his advent proclaimed. When she heard his foot on the stairs the old maid in the hall room always stuffed cotton into her ears. At first Jessie had shrunk from the rudeness and flavor of these spiritual greetings, but as the fog of the false Bohemia gradually encompassed her she came to accept them as love's true and proper greeting.

Bob came in without a word, smiled, kissed her neatly but noiselessly, took up a paper and sat down. In the hall room the old maid held her two plugs of cotton poised, filled with anxiety.

Jessie dropped lobster and knife and ran to him with frightened eyes.

"What's the matter, Bob, are you ill?"

"Not at all, dear."

"Then what's the matter with you?"

"Nothing."

Hearken, brethren. When She-who-has-a-right-to-ask interrogates you concerning a change she finds in your mood answer her thus: Tell her that you, in a sudden rage, have murdered your grandmother; tell her that you have robbed orphans and that remorse has stricken you; tell her your fortune is swept away; that you are beset by enemies, by bunions, by any kind of malevolent fate; but do not, if peace and happiness are worth as much as a grain of mustard seed to you—do not answer her "Nothing."

Jessie went back to the lobster in silence. She cast looks of darkest suspicion at Bob. He had never acted that way before.

When dinner was on the table she set out the bottle of Scotch and the glasses. Bob declined. "Tell you the truth, Jess," he said. "I've cut out the drink. Help yourself, of course. If you don't mind I'll try some of the seltzer straight."

"You've stopped drinking?" she said, looking at him steadily and unsmilingly. "What for?"

"It wasn't doing me any good," said Bob. "Don't you approve of the idea?"

Jessie raised her eyebrows and one shoulder slightly.

"Entirely," she said with a sculptured smile. "I could not conscientiously advise any one to drink or smoke, or whistle on Sunday."

The meal was finished almost in silence. Bob tried to make talk, but his efforts lacked the stimulus of previous evenings. He felt miserable, and once or twice his eye wandered toward the bottle, but each time the scathing words of his bibulous friend sounded in his ear, and his mouth set with determination.

Jessie felt the change deeply. The essence of their lives seemed to have departed suddenly. The restless fever, the false gayety, the unnatural excitement of the shoddy Bohemia in which they lived had dropped away in the space of the popping of a cork. She stole curious and forlorn glances at the dejected Bob, who bore the guilty look of at least a wife-beater or a family tyrant.

After dinner the colored maid who came in daily to perform such chores cleared away the things. Jessie, with an unreadable countenance, brought back the bottle of Scotch and the glasses and a bowl of cracked ice and set them on the table.

"May I ask," she said, with some of the ice in her tones, "whether I am to be included in your sudden spasm of goodness? If not, I'll make one for myself. It's rather chilly this evening, for some reason."

"Oh, come now, Jess," said Bob, good-naturedly, "don't be too rough on me. Help yourself, by all means. There's no danger of your overdoing it. But I thought there was with me; and that's why I quit. Have yours, and then let's get out the banjo and try over that new quickstep."

"I've heard," said Jessie in the tones of the oracle, "that drinking alone is a pernicious habit. No, I don't think I feel like playing this evening. If we are going to reform we may as well abandon the evil habit of banjo-playing, too."

She took up a book and sat in her little willow rocker on the other side of the table. Neither of them spoke for half an hour.

And then Bob laid down his paper and got up with a strange, absent look on his face and went behind her chair and reached over her shoulders, taking her hands in his, and laid his face close to hers.

In a moment to Jessie the walls of the seine-hung room vanished, and she saw the Sullivan County hills and rills. Bob felt her hands quiver in his as he began the verse from Old Omar:

> "Come, fill the Cup, and in the Fire of Spring
> The Winter Garment of Repentance fling:
> The Bird of Time has but a little way
> To fly—and Lo! the Bird is on the Wing!"

And then he walked to the table and poured a stiff drink of Scotch into a glass.

But in that moment a mountain breeze had somehow found its way in and blown away the mist of the false Bohemia.

Jessie leaped and with one fierce sweep of her hand sent

the bottle and glasses crashing to the floor. The same motion of her arm carried it around Bob's neck, where it met its mate and fastened tight.

"Oh, my God, Bobbie—not that verse—I see now. I wasn't always such a fool, was I? The other one, boy—the one that says: 'Remould it to the Heart's Desire.' Say that one—'to the Heart's Desire."

"I know that one," said Bob. "It goes:

> "Ah! Love, could you and I with Him conspire
> To grasp this sorry Scheme of Things entire
> Would not we——"

"Let me finish it," said Jessie.

> "Would not we shatter it to bits—and then
> Remould it nearer to the heart's Desire!"

"It's shattered all right," said Bob, crunching some glass under his heel.

In some dungeon below the accurate ear of Mrs. Pickens, the landlady, located the smash.

"It's that wild Mr. Babbitt coming home soused again," she said. "And he's got such a nice little wife, too!"

Two Thanksgiving Day Gentlemen

THERE is one day that is ours. There is one day when all we Americans who are not self-made go back to the old home to eat saleratus biscuits and marvel how much nearer to the porch the old pump looks than it used to. Bless the day. President Roosevelt gives it to us. We hear some talk of the Puritans, but don't just remember who they were. Bet we can lick 'em, anyhow, if they try to land again. Plymouth Rocks? Well, that sounds more familiar. Lots of us have had to come down to hens since the Turkey Trust got its work in. But somebody in Washington is leaking out advance information to 'em about these Thanksgiving proclamations.

The big city east of the cranberry bogs has made Thanksgiving Day an institution. The last Thursday in November is the only day in the year on which it recognizes the part of America lying across the ferries. It is the one day that is purely American. Yes, a day of celebration, exclusively American.

And now for the story which is to prove to you that we have traditions on this side of the ocean that are becoming older at a much rapider rate than those of England are—thanks to our git-up and enterprise.

Stuffy Pete took his seat on the third bench to the right as you enter Union Square from the east, at the walk opposite the fountain. Every Thanksgiving Day for nine years he had taken his seat there promptly at 1 o'clock. For every time he had done so things had happened to him—Charles Dickensy things that swelled his waistcoat above his heart, and equally on the other side.

But to-day Stuffy Pete's appearance at the annual trysting

place seemed to have been rather the result of habit than of the yearly hunger which, as the philanthropists seem to think, afflicts the poor at such extended intervals.

Certainly Pete was not hungry. He had just come from a feast that had left him of his powers barely those of respiration and locomotion. His eyes were like two pale gooseberries firmly imbedded in a swollen and gravy-smeared mask of putty. His breath came in short wheezes; a senatorial roll of adipose tissue denied a fashionable set to his upturned coat collar. Buttons that had been sewed upon his clothes by kind Salvation fingers a week before flew like pop-corn, strewing the earth around him. Ragged he was, with a split shirt front open to the wishbone; but the November breeze, carrying fine snowflakes, brought him only a grateful coolness. For Stuffy Pete was overcharged with the caloric produced by a super-bountiful dinner, beginning with oysters and ending with plum pudding, and including (it seemed to him) all the roast turkey and baked potatoes and chicken salad and squash pie and ice cream in the world. Wherefore he sat, gorged, and gazed upon the world with after-dinner contempt.

The meal had been an unexpected one. He was passing a red brick mansion near the beginning of Fifth Avenue, in which lived two old ladies of ancient family and a reverence for traditions. They even denied the existence of New York, and believed that Thanksgiving Day was declared solely for Washington Square. One of their traditional habits was to station a servant at the postern gate with orders to admit the first hungry wayfarer that came along after the hour of noon had struck, and banquet him to a finish. Stuffy Pete happened to pass by on his way to the park, and the seneschals gathered him in and upheld the custom of the castle.

After Stuffy Pete had gazed straight before him for ten minutes he was conscious of a desire for a more varied field of vision. With a tremendous effort he moved his head slowly to the left. And then his eyes bulged out fearfully, and his breath ceased, and the rough-shod ends of his short legs wriggled and rustled on the gravel.

For the Old Gentleman was coming across Fourth Avenue toward his bench.

Every Thanksgiving Day for nine years the Old Gentleman had come there and found Stuffy Pete on his bench. That was a thing that the Old Gentleman was trying to make a tradition of. Every Thanksgiving Day for nine years he had found Stuffy there, and had led him to a restaurant and watched him eat a big dinner. They do those things in England unconsciously. But this is a young country, and nine years is not so bad. The Old Gentleman was a stanch American patriot, and considered himself a pioneer in American tradition. In order to become picturesque we must keep on doing one thing for a long time without ever letting it get away from us. Something like collecting the weekly dimes in industrial insurance. Or cleaning the streets.

The Old Gentleman moved, straight and stately, toward the Institution that he was rearing. Truly, the annual feeding of Stuffy Pete was nothing national in its character, such as the Magna Charta or jam for breakfast was in England. But it was a step. It was almost feudal. It showed, at least, that a Custom was not impossible to New Y—ahem!—America.

The Old Gentleman was thin and tall and sixty. He was dressed all in black, and wore the old-fashioned kind of glasses that won't stay on your nose. His hair was whiter and thinner than it had been last year, and he seemed to make more use of his big, knobby cane with the crooked handle.

As his established benefactor came up Stuffy wheezed and shuddered like some woman's over-fat pug when a street dog bristles up at him. He would have flown, but all the skill of Santos-Dumont could not have separated him from his bench. Well had the myrmidons of the two old ladies done their work.

"Good morning," said the Old Gentleman. "I am glad to perceive that the vicissitudes of another year have spared you to move in health about the beautiful world. For that blessing alone this day of thanksgiving is well proclaimed to each of us. If you will come with me, my man, I will provide you with a dinner that should make your physical being accord with the mental."

That is what the Old Gentleman said every time. Every Thanksgiving Day for nine years. The words themselves almost formed an Institution. Nothing could be compared with them except the Declaration of Independence. Always before they had been music in Stuffy's ears. But now he looked up at the Old Gentleman's face with tearful agony in his own. The fine snow almost sizzled when it fell upon his perspiring brow. But the Old Gentleman shivered a little and turned his back to the wind.

Stuffy had always wondered why the Old Gentleman spoke his speech rather sadly. He did not know that it was because he was wishing every time that he had a son to succeed him. A son who would come there after he was gone—a son who would stand proud and strong before some subsequent Stuffy, and say: "In memory of my father." Then it would be an Institution.

But the Old Gentleman had no relatives. He lived in rented rooms in one of the decayed old family brownstone mansions in one of the quiet streets east of the park. In the winter he raised fuchsias in a little conservatory the size of a steamer trunk. In the spring he walked in the Easter parade. In the summer he lived at a farmhouse in the New Jersey hills, and sat in a wicker armchair, speaking of a butterfly, the ornithoptera amphrisius, that he hoped to find some day. In the autumn he fed Stuffy a dinner. These were the Old Gentleman's occupations.

Stuffy Pete looked up at him for a half minute, stewing and helpless in his own self-pity. The Old Gentleman's eyes were bright with the giving-pleasure. His face was getting more lined each year, but his little black necktie was in as jaunty a bow as ever, and his linen was beautiful and white, and his gray mustache was curled gracefully at the ends. And then Stuffy made a noise that sounded like peas bubbling in a pot. Speech was intended; and as the Old Gentleman had heard the sounds nine times before, he rightly construed them into Stuffy's old formula of acceptance.

"Thankee, sir. I'll go with ye, and much obliged. I'm very hungry, sir."

The coma of repletion had not prevented from entering Stuffy's mind the conviction that he was the basis of an Institution. His Thanksgiving appetite was not his own; it belonged by all the sacred rights of established custom, if not by the actual Statute of Limitations, to this kind old gentleman who had pre-empted it. True, America is free; but in order to establish tradition some one must be a repetend—a repeating decimal. The heroes are not all heroes of steel and gold. See one here that wielded only weapons of iron, badly silvered, and tin.

The Old Gentleman led his annual protégé southward to the restaurant, and to the table where the feast had always occurred. They were recognized.

"Here comes de old guy," said a waiter, "dat blows dat same bum to a meal every Thanksgiving."

The Old Gentleman sat across the table glowing like a smoked pearl at his corner-stone of future ancient Tradition. The waiters heaped the table with holiday food—and Stuffy, with a sigh that was mistaken for hunger's expression, raised knife and fork and carved for himself a crown of imperishable bay.

No more valiant hero ever fought his way through the ranks of an enemy. Turkey, chops, soups, vegetables, pies, disappeared before him as fast as they could be served. Gorged nearly to the uttermost when he entered the restaurant, the smell of food had almost caused him to lose his honor as a gentleman, but he rallied like a true knight. He saw the look of beneficent happiness on the Old Gentleman's face—a happier look than even the fuchsias and the ornithoptera amphrisius had ever brought to it—and he had not the heart to see it wane.

In an hour Stuffy leaned back with a battle won.

"Thankee kindly, sir," he puffed like a leaky steam pipe; "thankee kindly for a hearty meal."

Then he arose heavily with glazed eyes and started toward the kitchen. A waiter turned him about like a top, and pointed him toward the door. The Old Gentleman carefully counted out $1.30 in silver change, leaving three nickels for the waiter.

They parted as they did each year at the door, the Old Gentleman going south, Stuffy north.

Around the first corner Stuffy turned, and stood for one minute. Then he seemed to puff out his rags as an owl puffs out his feathers, and fell to the sidewalk like a sunstricken horse.

When the ambulance came the young surgeon and the driver cursed softly at his weight. There was no smell of whiskey to justify a transfer to the patrol wagon, so Stuffy and his two dinners went to the hospital. There they stretched him on a bed and began to test him for strange diseases, with the hope of getting a chance at some problem with the bare steel.

And lo! an hour later another ambulance brought the Old Gentleman. And they laid him on another bed and spoke of appendicitis, for he looked good for the bill.

But pretty soon one of the young doctors met one of the young nurses whose eyes he liked, and stopped to chat with her about the cases.

"That nice old gentleman over there, now," he said, "you wouldn't think that was a case of almost starvation. Proud old family, I guess. He told me he hadn't eaten a thing for three days."

The Buyer From Cactus City

~~~~~~~~~~~~~~~~~~~~~~~~~~~~~~~~~~~

IT is well that hay fever and colds do not obtain in the healthful vicinity of Cactus City, Texas, for the dry goods emporium of Navarro & Platt, situated there, is not to be sneezed at.

Twenty thousand people in Cactus City scatter their silver coin with liberal hands for the things that their hearts desire. The bulk of this semi-precious metal goes to Navarro & Platt. Their huge brick building covers enough ground to graze a dozen head of sheep. You can buy of them a rattle-snake-skin necktie, an automobile, or an eighty-five dollar, latest style, lady's tan coat in twenty different shades. Navarro & Platt first introduced pennies west of the Colorado River. They had been ranchmen with business heads, who saw that the world did not necessarily have to cease its revolutions after free grass went out.

Every spring, Navarro, senior partner, fifty-five, half-Spanish, cosmopolitan, able, polished, had "gone on" to New York to buy goods. This year he shied at taking up the long trail. He was undoubtedly growing older; and he looked at his watch several times a day before the hour came for his siesta.

"John," he said, to his junior partner, "you shall go on this year to buy the goods."

Platt looked tired.

"I'm told," said he, "that New York is a plumb dead town; but I'll go. I can take a whirl in San Antone for a few days on my way and have some fun."

Two weeks later a man in a Texas full dress suit—black

frock coat, broad-brimmed soft white hat, and lay-down collar ¾ inch high, with black, wrought-iron necktie—entered the wholesale cloak and suit establishment of Zizzbaum & Son, on lower Broadway.

Old Zizzbaum had the eye of an osprey, the memory of an elephant, and a mind that unfolded from him in three movements like the puzzle of the carpenter's rule. He rolled to the front like a brunette polar bear, and shook Platt's hand.

"And how is the good Mr. Navarro in Texas?" he said. "The trip was too long for him this year, so? We welcome Mr. Platt instead."

"A bull's eye," said Platt, "and I'd give forty acres of un-irrigated Pecos County land to know how you did it."

"I knew," grinned Zizzbaum, "just as I know that the rainfall in El Paso for the year was 28.5 inches, or an increase of 15 inches, and that therefore Navarro & Platt will buy a $15,000 stock of suits this spring instead of $10,000, as in a dry year. But that will be tomorrow. There is first a cigar in my private office that will remove from your mouth the taste of the ones you smuggled across the Rio Grande and like—because they are smuggled."

It was late in the afternoon and business for the day had ended. Zizzbaum left Platt with a half-smoked cigar, and came out of the private office to Son, who was arranging his diamond scarfpin before a mirror, ready to leave.

"Abey," he said, "you will have to take Mr. Platt around to-night and show him things. They are customers for ten years. Mr. Navarro and I we played chess every moment of spare time when he came. That is good, but Mr. Platt is a young man and this is his first visit to New York. He should amuse easily."

"All right," said Abey, screwing the guard tightly on his pin. "I'll take him on. After he's seen the Flatiron and the head waiter at the Hotel Astor and heard the phonograph play 'Under the Old Apple Tree' it'll be half-past ten, and Mr. Texas will be ready to roll up in his blanket. I've got a supper engagement at 11:30, but he'll be all to the Mrs. Winslow before then."

The next morning at 10 Platt walked into the store ready to do business. He had a bunch of hyacinths pinned on his lapel. Zizzbaum himself waited on him. Navarro & Platt were good customers, and never failed to take their discount for cash.

"And what did you think of our little town?" asked Zizzbaum, with the fatuous smile of the Manhattanite.

"I shouldn't care to live in it," said the Texan. "Your son and I knocked around quite a little last night. You've got good water, but Cactus City is better lit up."

"We've got a few lights on Broadway, don't you think, Mr. Platt?"

"And a good many shadows," said Platt. "I think I like your horses best. I haven't seen a crowbait since I've been in town."

Zizzbaum led him up stairs to show the samples of suits.

"Ask Miss Asher to come," he said to a clerk.

Miss Asher came, and Platt, of Navarro & Platt, felt for the first time the wonderful bright light of romance and glory descend upon him. He stood still as a granite cliff above the cañon of the Colorado, with his wide-open eyes fixed upon her. She noticed his look and flushed a little, which was contrary to her custom.

Miss Asher was the crack model of Zizzbaum & Son. She was of the blond type known as "medium," and her measurements even went the required 38-25-42 standard a little better. She had been at Zizzbaum's two years, and knew her business. Her eye was bright, but cool; and had she chosen to match her gaze against the optic of the famed basilisk, that fabulous monster's gaze would have wavered and softened first. Incidentally, she knew buyers.

"Now, Mr. Platt," said Zizzbaum, "I want you to see these princess gowns in the light shades. They will be the thing in your climate. This first, if you please, Miss Asher."

Swiftly in and out of the dressing-room the prize model flew, each time wearing a new costume and looking more stunning with every change. She posed with absolute self-possession before the stricken buyer, who stood, tongue-tied and motionless, while Zizzbaum orated oilily of the styles. On the model's face was her faint, impersonal professional smile that seemed to cover something like weariness or contempt.

When the display was over Platt seemed to hesitate. Zizzbaum was a little anxious, thinking that his customer might be inclined to try elsewhere. But Platt was only looking over in his mind the best building sites in Cactus City, trying to select one on which to build a house for his wife-to-be—who was just then in the dressing-room taking off an evening gown of lavender and tulle.

"Take your time, Mr. Platt," said Zizzbaum. "Think it over to-night. You won't find anybody else to meet our prices on goods like these. I'm afraid you're having a dull time in New York, Mr. Platt. A young man like you—of course, you miss the society of the ladies. Wouldn't you like a nice young lady to take out to dinner this evening? Miss Asher, now, is a very nice young lady; she will make it agreeable for you."

"Why, she doesn't know me," said Platt, wonderingly. "She doesn't know anything about me. Would she go? I'm not acquainted with her."

"Would she go?" repeated Zizzbaum, with uplifted eyebrows. "Sure, she would go. I will introduce you. Sure, she would go."

He called Miss Asher loudly.

She came, calm and slightly contemptuous, in her white shirt waist and plain black skirt.

"Mr. Platt would like the pleasure of your company to dinner this evening," said Zizzbaum walking away.

"Sure," said Miss Asher, looking at the ceiling. "I'd be much pleased. Nine-eleven West Twentieth Street. What time?"

"Say seven o'clock."

"All right, but please don't come ahead of time. I room with a school teacher, and she doesn't allow any gentleman to call in the room. There isn't any parlor, so you'll have to wait in the hall. I'll be ready."

At half-past seven Platt and Miss Asher sat at a table in a

Broadway restaurant. She was dressed in a plain, filmy black. Platt didn't know that it was all a part of her day's work.

With the unobtrusive aid of a good waiter he managed to order a respectable dinner, minus the usual Broadway preliminaries.

Miss Asher flashed upon him a dazzling smile.

"Mayn't I have something to drink?" she asked.

"Why, certainly," said Platt. "Anything you want."

"A dry Martini," she said to the waiter.

When it was brought and set before her Platt reached over and took it away.

"What is this?" he asked.

"A cocktail, of course."

"I thought it was some kind of tea you ordered. This is liquor. You can't drink this. What is your first name?"

"To my intimate friends," said Miss Asher, freezingly, "it is 'Helen.' "

"Listen, Helen," said Platt, leaning over the table. "For many years every time the spring flowers blossomed out on the prairies I got to thinking of somebody that I'd never seen or heard of. I knew it was you the minute I saw you yesterday. I'm going back home to-morrow, and you're going with me. I know it, for I saw it in your eyes when you first looked at me. You needn't kick, for you've got to fall into line. Here's a little trick I picked out for you on my way over."

He flicked a two-carat diamond solitaire ring across the table. Miss Asher flipped it back to him with her fork.

"Don't get fresh," she said, severely.

"I'm worth a hundred thousand dollars," said Platt. I'll build you the finest house in west Texas."

"You can't buy me, Mr. Buyer," said Miss Asher, "if you had a hundred million. I didn't think I'd have to call you down. You didn't look like the others to me at first, but I see you're all alike."

"All who?" asked Platt.

"All you buyers. You think because we girls have to go out to dinner with you or lose our jobs that you're privileged to say what you please. Well, forget it. I thought you were different from the others, but I see I was mistaken."

Platt struck his fingers on the table with a gesture of sudden, illuminating satisfaction.

"I've got it!" he exclaimed, almost hilariously—"the Nicholson place, over on the north side. There's a big grove of live oaks and a natural lake. The old house can be pulled down and the new one set further back."

"Put out your pipe," said Miss Asher. "I'm sorry to wake you up, but you fellows might as well get wise, once for all, to where you stand. I'm supposed to go to dinner with you and help jolly you along so you'll trade with old Zizzy, but don't expect to find me in any of the suits you buy."

"Do you mean to tell me," said Platt, "that you go out this way with customers, and they all—they all talk to you like I have?"

"They all make plays," said Miss Asher. "But I must say that you've got 'em beat in one respect. They generally talk diamonds, while you've actually dug one up."

"How long have you been working, Helen?"

"Got my name pat, haven't you? I've been supporting myself for eight years. I was a cash girl and a wrapper and then a shop girl until I was grown, and then I got to be a suit model. Mr. Texas Man, don't you think a little wine would make this dinner a little less dry?"

"You're not going to drink wine any more, dear. It's awful to think how—— I'll come to the store to-morrow and get you. I want you to pick out an automobile before we leave. That's all we need to buy here."

"Oh, cut that out. If you knew how sick I am of hearing such talk."

After the dinner they walked down Broadway and came upon Diana's little wooded park. The trees caught Platt's eye at once, and he must turn along under the winding walk beneath them. The lights shone upon two bright tears in the model's eyes.

"I don't like that," said Platt. "What's the matter?"

"Don't you mind, said Miss Asher. "Well, it's because—

well, I didn't think you were that kind when I first saw you. But you are all alike. And now will you take me home, or will I have to call a cop?"

Platt took her to the door of her boarding-house. They stood for a minute in the vestibule. She looked at him with such scorn in her eyes that even his heart of oak began to waver. His arm was halfway around her waist, when she struck him a stinging blow on the face with her open hand.

As he stepped back a ring fell from somewhere and bounded on the tiled floor. Platt groped for it and found it.

"Now, take your useless diamond and go, Mr. Buyer," she said.

"This was the other one—the wedding ring," said the Texan, holding the smooth gold band on the palm of his hand.

Miss Asher's eyes blazed upon him in the half darkness.

"Was that what you meant?—did you——"

Somebody opened the door from inside the house.

"Good-night," said Platt. "I'll see you at the store to-morrow."

Miss Asher ran up to her room and shook the school teacher until she sat up in bed ready to scream "Fire!"

"Where is it?" she cried.

"That's what I want to know." said the model. "You've studied geography, Emma, and you ought to know. Where is a town called Cac—Cac—Carac—Caracas City, I think they called it?"

"How dare you wake me up for that?" said the school teacher. "Caracas is in Venezuela, of course."

"What's it like?"

"Why, it's principally earthquakes and Negroes and monkeys and malarial fever and volcanoes."

"I don't care," said Miss Asher, blithely; "I'm going there to-morrow."

The Badge of Policeman O'Roon

IT cannot be denied that men and women have looked upon one another for the first time and become instantly enamored. It is a risky process, this love at first sight, before she has seen him in Bradstreet or he has seen her in curl papers. But these things do happen; and one instance must form a theme for this story—though not, thank Heaven, to the overshadowing of more vital and important subjects, such as drink, policemen, horses, and earldoms.

During a certain war a troop calling itself the Gentle Riders rode into history and one or two ambuscades. The Gentle Riders were recruited from the aristocracy of the wild men of the West and the wild men of the aristocracy of the East. In khaki there is little telling them one from another, so they became good friends and comrades all around.

Ellsworth Remsen, whose old Knickerbocker descent atoned for his modest rating at only ten millions, ate his canned beef gayly by the campfires of the Gentle Riders. The war was a great lark to him, so that he scarcely regretted polo and planked shad.

One of the troopers was a well-set-up, affable, cool young man, who called himself O'Roon. To this young man Remsen took an especial liking. The two rode side by side during the famous mooted up-hill charge that was disputed so hotly at the time by the Spaniards and afterward by the Democrats.

After the war Remsen came back to his polo and shad. One day a well-set-up, affable, cool young man disturbed him at his club, and he and O'Roon were soon pounding each other and exchanging opprobrious epithets after the manner of long-lost friends. O'Roon looked seedy and out of luck and perfectly contented. But it seemed that his content was only apparent.

"Get me a job, Remsen," he said. "I've just handed a barber my last shilling."

"No trouble at all," said Remsen. "I know a lot of men who have banks and stores and things downtown. Any particular line you fancy?"

"Yes," said O'Roon, with a look of interest. "I took a walk in your Central Park this morning. I'd like to be one of those bobbies on horseback. That would be about the ticket. Besides, it's the only thing I could do. I can ride a little and the fresh air suits me. Think you could land that for me?"

Remsen was sure that he could. And in a very short time he did. And they who were not above looking at mounted policemen might have seen a well-set-up, affable, cool young man on a prancing chestnut steed attending to his duties along the driveways of the park.

And now at the extreme risk of wearying old gentlemen who carry leather fob chains, and elderly ladies who—but no! grandmother herself yet thrills at foolish, immortal Romeo —there must be a hint of love at first sight.

It came just as Remsen was strolling into Fifth Avenue from his club a few doors away.

A motor car was creeping along foot by foot, impeded by a freshet of vehicles that filled the street. In the car was a chauffeur and an old gentleman with snowy side whiskers and a Scotch plaid cap which could not be worn while automobiling except by a personage. Not even a wine agent would dare do it. But these two were of no consequence—except, perhaps, for the guiding of the machine and the paying for it. At the old gentleman's side sat a young lady more beautiful than pomegranate blossoms, more exquisite than the first quarter moon viewed at twilight through the tops of oleanders. Remsen saw her and knew his fate. He could have flung himself under the very wheels that conveyed her, but he knew that would be the last means of attracting the attention of those who ride in motor cars. Slowly the auto passed, and, if we place the poets above the autoists, carried the heart of

Remsen with it. Here was a large city of millions, and many women who at a certain distance appear to resemble pomegranate blossoms. Yet he hoped to see her again; for each one fancies that his romance has its own tutelary guardian and divinity.

Luckily for Remsen's peace of mind there came a diversion in the guise of a reunion of the Gentle Riders of the city. There were not many of them—perhaps a score—and there was wassail and things to eat, and speeches and the Spaniard was bearded again in recapitulation. And when daylight threatened them the survivors prepared to depart. But some remained upon the battlefield. One of these was Trooper O'Roon, who was not seasoned to potent liquids. His legs declined to fulfil the obligations they had sworn to the police department.

"I'm stewed, Remsen," said O'Roon to his friend. "Why do they build hotels that go round and round like catherine wheels? They'll take away my shield and break me. I can think and talk con-con-consec-sec-secutively, but I s-s-stammer with my feet. I've got to go on duty in three hours. The jig is up, Remsen. The jig is up, I tell you."

"Look at me," said Remsen, who was his smiling self, pointing to his own face; "whom do you see here?"

"Goo' fellow," said O'Roon, dizzily. "Goo' old Remsen."

"Not so," said Remsen. "You see Mounted Policeman O'Roon. Look at your face—no; you can't do that without a glass—but look at mine, and think of yours. How much alike are we? As two French *table d'hôte* dinners. With your badge, on your horse, in your uniform, will I charm nurse-maids and prevent the grass from growing under people's feet in the Park this day. I will have your badge and your honor, besides having the jolliest lark I've been blessed with since we licked Spain."

Promptly on time the counterfeit presentment of Mounted Policeman O'Roon single-footed into the Park on his chestnut steed. In a uniform two men who are unlike will look alike; two who somewhat resemble each other in feature and figure will appear as twin brothers. So Remsen trotted down the bridle paths, enjoying himself hugely, so few real pleasures do ten-millionaires have.

Along the driveway in the early morning spun a victoria drawn by a pair of fiery bays. There was something foreign about the affair, for the Park is rarely used in the morning, except by unimportant people who love to be healthy, poor, and wise. In the vehicle sat an old gentleman with snowy side-whiskers and a Scotch plaid cap which could not be worn while driving except by a personage. At his side sat the lady of Remsen's heart—the lady who looked like pomegranate blossoms and the gibbous moon.

Remsen met them coming. At the instant of their passing her eyes looked into his, and but for the ever coward's heart of a true lover he could have sworn that she flushed a faint pink. He trotted on for twenty yards, and then wheeled his horse at the sound of runaway hoofs. The bays had bolted.

Remsen sent his chestnut after the victoria like a shot. There was work cut out for the impersonator of Policeman O'Roon. The chestnut ranged alongside the off bay thirty seconds after the chase began, rolled his eye back at Remsen, and said in the only manner open to policemen's horses:

"Well, you duffer, are you going to do your share? You're not O'Roon, but it seems to me if you'd lean to the right you could reach the reins of that foolish slow-running bay—ah! you're all right; O'Roon couldn't have done it more neatly!"

The runaway team was tugged to an inglorious halt by Remsen's tough muscles. The driver released his hands from the wrapped reins, jumped from his seat and stood at the heads of the team. The chestnut, approving his new rider, danced and pranced, reviling equinely the subdued bays. Remsen, lingering, was dimly conscious of a vague, impossible, unnecessary old gentleman in a Scotch cap who talked incessantly about something. And he was acutely conscious of a pair of violet eyes that would have drawn Saint Pyrites from his iron pillar—or whatever the allusion is—and of the lady's smile and look—a little frightened, but a look that, with the ever coward heart of a true lover, he could not yet construe.

They were asking his name and bestowing upon him well-bred thanks for his heroic deed, and the Scotch cap was especially babbling and insistent. But the eloquent appeal was in the eyes of the lady.

A little thrill of satisfaction ran through Remsen, because he had a name to give which, without undue pride, was worthy of being spoken in high places, and a small fortune which, with due pride, he could leave at his end without disgrace.

He opened his lips to speak and closed them again.

Who was he? Mounted Policeman O'Roon. The badge and the honor of his comrade were in his hands. If Ellsworth Remsen, ten-millionaire and Knickerbocker, had just rescued pomegranate blossoms and Scotch cap from possible death, where was Policeman O'Roon? Off his beat, exposed, disgraced, discharged. Love had come, but before that there had been something that demanded precedence—the fellowship of men on battlefields fighting an alien foe.

Remsen touched his cap, looked between the chestnut's ears, and took refuge in vernacularity.

"Don't mention it," he said, stolidly. "We policemen are paid to do these things. It's our duty."

And he rode away—rode away cursing *noblesse oblige*, but knowing he could never have done anything else.

At the end of the day Remsen sent the chestnut to his stable and went to O'Roon's room. The policeman was again a well-set-up, affable, cool young man who sat by the window smoking cigars.

"I wish you and the rest of the police force and all badges, horses, brass buttons, and men who can't drink two glasses of *brut* without getting upset were at the devil," said Remsen, feelingly.

O'Roon smiled with evident satisfaction.

"Good old Remsen," he said, affably. "I know all about it. They trailed me down and cornered me here two hours ago. There was a little row at home, you know, and I cut sticks just to show them. I don't believe I told you that my Governor was the Earl of Ardsley. Funny you should bob against them in the Park. If you damaged that horse of mine I'll never forgive you. I'm going to buy him and take him back with me. Oh, yes, and I think my sister—Lady Angela, you know—wants particularly for you to come up to the hotel with me this evening. Didn't lose my badge, did you, Remsen? I've got to turn that in at Headquarters when I resign."

The Last Leaf

~~~~~~

IN a little district west of Washington Square the streets have run crazy and broken themselves into small strips called "places." These "places" make strange angles and curves. One street crosses itself a time or two. An artist once discovered a valuable possibility in this street. Suppose a collector with a bill for paints, paper and canvas should, in traversing this route, suddenly meet himself coming back, without a cent having been paid on account!

So, to quaint old Greenwich Village the art people soon came prowling, hunting for north windows and eighteenth-century gables and Dutch attics and low rents. Then they imported some pewter mugs and a chafing dish or two from Sixth Avenue, and became a "colony."

At the top of a squatty, three-story brick Sue and Johnsy had their studio. "Johnsy" was familiar for Joanna. One was from Maine; the other from California. They had met at the *table d'hôte* of an Eighth Street "Delmonico's," and found their tastes in art, chicory salad and bishop sleeves so congenial that the joint studio resulted.

That was in May. In November a cold, unseen stranger, whom the doctors called Pneumonia, stalked about the colony, touching one here and there with his icy fingers. Over on the east side this ravager strode boldly, smiting his victims by scores, but his feet trod slowly through the maze of the narrow and moss-grown "places."

Mr. Pneumonia was not what you would call a chivalric old gentleman. A mite of a little woman with blood thinned by California zephyrs was hardly fair game for the red-fisted, short-breathed old duffer. But Johnsy he smote; and she lay, scarcely moving, on her painted iron bedstead, looking through the small Dutch window-panes at the blank side of the next brick house.

One morning the busy doctor invited Sue into the hallway with a shaggy, gray eyebrow.

"She has one chance in—let us say, ten," he said, as he shook down the mercury in his clinical thermometer. "And that chance is for her to want to live. This way people have of lining-up on the side of the undertaker makes the entire pharmacopœia look silly. Your little lady has made up her mind that she's not going to get well. Has she anything on her mind?"

"She—she wanted to paint the Bay of Naples some day," said Sue.

"Paint?—bosh! Has she anything on her mind worth thinking about twice—a man, for instance?"

"A man?" said Sue, with a jew's-harp twang in her voice. "Is a man worth—but, no, doctor; there is nothing of the kind."

"Well, it is the weakness, then," said the doctor. "I will do all that science, so far as it may filter through my efforts, can accomplish. But whenever my patient begins to count the carriages in her funeral procession I subtract 50 per cent. from the curative power of medicines. If you will get her to ask one question about the new winter styles in cloak sleeves I will promise you a one-in-five chance for her, instead of one in ten."

After the doctor had gone Sue went into the workroom and cried a Japanese napkin to a pulp. Then she swaggered into Johnsy's room with her drawing board, whistling ragtime.

Johnsy lay, scarcely making a ripple under the bedclothes, with her face toward the window. Sue stopped whistling, thinking she was asleep.

She arranged her board and began a pen-and-ink drawing to illustrate a magazine story. Young artists must pave their way to Art by drawing pictures for magazine stories that young authors write to pave their way to Literature.

As Sue was sketching a pair of elegant horseshow riding trousers and a monocle on the figure of the hero, an Idaho cowboy, she heard a low sound, several times repeated. She went quickly to the bedside.

Johnsy's eyes were open wide. She was looking out the window and counting—counting backward.

"Twelve," she said, and a little later "eleven"; and then "ten," and "nine"; and then "eight" and "seven," almost together.

Sue looked solicitously out of the window. What was there to count? There was only a bare, dreary yard to be seen, and the blank side of the brick house twenty feet away. An old, old ivy vine, gnarled and decayed at the roots, climbed half way up the brick wall. The cold breath of autumn had stricken its leaves from the vine until its skeleton branches clung, almost bare, to the crumbling bricks.

"What is it, dear?" asked Sue.

"Six," said Johnsy, in almost a whisper. "They're falling faster now. Three days ago there were almost a hundred. It made my head ache to count them. But now it's easy. There goes another one. There are only five left now."

"Five what, dear? Tell your Sudie."

"Leaves. On the ivy vine. When the last one falls I must go, too. I've known that for three days. Didn't the doctor tell you?"

"Oh, I never heard of such nonsense," complained Sue, with magnificent scorn. "What have old ivy leaves to do with your getting well? And you used to love that vine, so, you naughty girl. Don't be a goosey. Why, the doctor told me this morning that your chances for getting well real soon were—let's see exactly what he said—he said the chances were ten to one! Why, that's almost as good a chance as we have in New York when we ride on the street cars or walk past a new building. Try to take some broth now, and let Sudie go back to her drawing, so she can sell the editor man with it, and buy port wine for her sick child, and pork chops for her greedy self."

"You needn't get any more wine," said Johnsy, keeping her eyes fixed out the window. "There goes another. No, I don't want any broth. That leaves just four. I want to see the last one fall before it gets dark. Then I'll go, too."

"Johnsy, dear," said Sue, bending over her, "will you promise me to keep your eyes closed, and not look out the window until I am done working? I must hand those drawings in by to-morrow. I need the light, or I would draw the shade down."

"Couldn't you draw in the other room?" asked Johnsy, coldly.

"I'd rather be here by you," said Sue. "Besides, I don't want you to keep looking at those silly ivy leaves."

"Tell me as soon as you have finished," said Johnsy, closing her eyes, and lying white and still as a fallen statue, "because I want to see the last one fall. I'm tired of waiting. I'm tired of thinking. I want to turn loose my hold on everything, and go sailing down, down, just like one of those poor, tired leaves."

"Try to sleep," said Sue. "I must call Behrman up to be my model for the old hermit miner. I'll not be gone a minute. Don't try to move 'til I come back."

Old Behrman was a painter who lived on the ground floor beneath them. He was past sixty and had a Michael Angelo's Moses beard curling down from the head of a satyr along the body of an imp. Behrman was a failure in art. Forty years he had wielded the brush without getting near enough to touch the hem of his Mistress's robe. He had been always about to paint a masterpiece, but had never yet begun it. For several years he had painted nothing except now and then a daub in the line of commerce or advertising. He earned a little by serving as a model to those young artists in the colony who could not pay the price of a professional. He drank gin to excess, and still talked of his coming master-piece. For the rest he was a fierce little old man, who scoffed terribly at softness in any one, and who regarded himself as especial mastiff-in-waiting to protect the two young artists in the studio above.

Sue found Behrman smelling strongly of juniper berries in his dimly lighted den below. In one corner was a blank canvas on an easel that had been waiting there for twenty-five years to receive the first line of the masterpiece. She told him of Johnsy's fancy, and how she feared she would, indeed, light and fragile as a leaf herself, float away, when her slight hold upon the world grew weaker.

Old Behrman, with his red eyes plainly streaming, shouted his contempt and derision for such idiotic imaginings.

"Vass!" he cried. "Is dere people in de world mit der foolishness to die because leafs dey drop off from a con-founded vine? I haf not heard of such a thing. No, I will not bose as a model for your fool hermit-dunderhead. Vy do you allow dot silly pusiness to come in der brain of her? Ach, dot poor leetle Miss Yohnsy."

"She is very ill and weak," said Sue, "and the fever has left her mind morbid and full of strange fancies. Very well, Mr. Behrman, if you do not care to pose for me, you needn't. But I think you are a horrid old—old flibbertigibbet."

"You are just like a woman!" yelled Behrman. "Who said I will not bose? Go on. I come mit you. For half an hour I haf peen trying to say dot I am ready to bose. Gott! dis is not any blace in which one so goot as Miss Yohnsy shall lie sick. Some day I vill baint a masterpiece, and ve shall all go away. Gott! yes."

Johnsy was sleeping when they went upstairs. Sue pulled the shade down to the window-sill, and motioned Behrman into the other room. In there they peered out the window fearfully at the ivy vine. Then they looked at each other for a moment without speaking. A persistent, cold rain was fall-ing, mingled with snow. Behrman, in his old blue shirt, took his seat as the hermit miner on an upturned kettle for a rock.

When Sue awoke from an hour's sleep the next morning she found Johnsy with dull, wide-open eyes staring at the drawn green shade.

"Put it up; I want to see," she ordered, in a whisper.

Wearily Sue obeyed.

But, lo! after the beating rain and fierce gusts of wind that had endured through the livelong night, there yet stood out against the brick wall one ivy leaf. It was the last on the vine. Still dark green near its stem, but with its serrated edges tinted with the yellow of dissolution and decay, it hung bravely from a branch some twenty feet above the ground.

"It is the last one," said Johnsy. "I thought it would surely fall during the night. I heard the wind. It will fall to-day, and I shall die at the same time."

"Dear, dear!" said Sue, leaning her worn face down to the pillow, "think of me, if you won't think of yourself. What would I do?"

But Johnsy did not answer. The lonesomest thing in all the world is a soul when it is making ready to go on its mysterious, far journey. The fancy seemed to possess her more strongly as one by one the ties that bound her to friendship and to earth were loosed.

The day wore away, and even through the twilight they could see the lone ivy leaf clinging to its stem against the wall. And then, with the coming of the night the north wind was again loosed, while the rain still beat against the windows and pattered down from the low Dutch eaves.

When it was light enough Johnsy, the merciless, commanded that the shade be raised.

The ivy leaf was still there.

Johnsy lay for a long time looking at it. And then she called to Sue, who was stirring her chicken broth over the gas stove.

"I've been a bad girl, Sudie," said Johnsy. "Something has made that last leaf stay there to show me how wicked I was. It is a sin to want to die. You may bring me a little broth now, and some milk with a little port in it, and—no; bring me a hand-mirror first, and then pack some pillows about me, and I will sit up and watch you cook."

An hour later she said:

"Sudie, some day I hope to paint the Bay of Naples."

The doctor came in the afternoon, and Sue had an excuse to go into the hallway as he left.

"Even chances," said the doctor, taking Sue's thin, shaking hand in his. "With good nursing you'll win. And now I must see another case I have downstairs. Behrman, his name is—some kind of an artist, I believe. Pneumonia, too. He is an old, weak man, and the attack is acute. There is no hope for him; but he goes to the hospital to-day to be made more comfortable."

The next day the doctor said to Sue: "She's out of danger. You've won. Nutrition and care now—that's all."

And that afternoon Sue came to the bed where Johnsy lay, contentedly knitting a very blue and very useless woollen shoulder scarf, and put one arm around her, pillows and all.

"I have something to tell you, white mouse," she said. "Mr. Behrman died of pneumonia to-day in the hospital. He was ill only two days. The janitor found him on the morning of the first day in his room downstairs helpless with pain. His shoes and clothing were wet through and icy cold. They couldn't imagine where he had been on such a dreadful night. And then they found a lantern, still lighted, and a ladder that had been dragged from its place, and some scattered brushes, and a palette with green and yellow colors mixed on it, and—look out the window, dear, at the last ivy leaf on the wall. Didn't you wonder why it never fluttered or moved when the wind blew? Ah, darling, it's Behrman's masterpiece—he painted it there the night that the last leaf fell."

The Tale of a Tainted Tenner

MONEY talks, but you may think that the conversation of a little old ten-dollar bill in New York would be nothing more than a whisper. Oh, very well! Pass up this *sotto voce* autobiography of an X if you like. If you are one of the kind that prefers to listen to John D.'s checkbook roar at you through a megaphone as it passes by, all right. But don't forget that small change can say a word to the point now and then. The next time you tip your grocer's clerk a silver quarter to give you extra weight of his boss's goods read the four words above the lady's head. How are they for repartee?

I am a ten-dollar Treasury note, series of 1901. You may have seen one in a friend's hand. On my face, in the centre, is a picture of the bison Americanus, miscalled a buffalo by fifty or sixty millions of Americans. The heads of Capt. Lewis and Capt. Clark adorn the ends. On my back is the graceful figure of Liberty or Ceres or Maxine Elliott standing in the centre of the stage on a conservatory plant. My references is —or are—Section 3,588, Revised Statutes. Ten cold, hard dollars—I don't say whether silver, gold, lead or iron—Uncle Sam will hand you over his counter if you want to cash me in.

I beg you will excuse any conversational breaks that I make—thanks, I knew you would—got that sneaking little respect and agreeable feeling toward even an X, haven't you? You see, a tainted bill doesn't have much chance to acquire a correct form of expression. I never knew a really cultured and educated person that could afford to hold a ten-spot any longer than it would take to do an Arthur Duffy to the nearest That's All! sign or delicatessen store.

For a six-year-old, I've had a lively and gorgeous circulation. I guess I've paid as many debts as the man who dies. I've been owned by a good many kinds of people. But a little old ragged, damp, dingy five-dollar silver certificate gave me a jar one day. I was next to it in the fat and bad-smelling purse of a butcher.

"Hey, you Sitting Bull," says I, "don't scrouge so. Anyhow, don't you think it's about time you went in on a customs payment and got reissued? For a series of 1899 you're a sight."

"Oh, don't get crackly just because you're a Buffalo bill," says the fiver. "You'd be limp, too, if you'd been stuffed down in a thick cotton-and-lisle-thread under an elastic all day, and the thermometer not a degree under 85 in the store."

"I never heard of a pocketbook like that," says I. "Who carried you?"

"A shopgirl," says the five-spot.

"What's that?" I had to ask.

"You'll never know till their millennium comes," says the fiver.

Just then a two-dollar bill behind me with a George Washington head, spoke up to the fiver:

"Aw, cut out yer kicks. Ain't lisle thread good enough for yer? If you was under all cotton like I'd been to-day, and choked up with factory dust till the lady with the cornucopia on me sneezed half a dozen times, you'd have some reason to complain."

That was the next day after I arrived in New York. I came in a $500 package of tens to a Brooklyn bank from one of its Pennsylvania correspondents—and I haven't made the acquaintance of any of the five and two spots' friends' pocketbooks yet. Silk for mine, every time.

I was lucky money. I kept on the move. Sometimes I changed hands twenty times a day. I saw the inside of every business; I fought for my owner's every pleasure. It seemed that on Saturday nights I never missed being slapped down on a bar. Tens were always slapped down, while ones and twos were slid over to the bartenders folded. I got in the habit of looking for mine, and I managed to soak in a little straight or some spilled Martini or Manhattan whenever I could. Once I got tied up in a great greasy roll of bills in a pushcart peddler's jeans. I thought I never would get in circulation again, for the future department store owner lived on eight cents' worth of dog meat and onions a day. But this peddler got into trouble one day on account of having his cart too near a crossing, and I was rescued. I always will feel grateful to the cop that got me. He changed me at a cigar store near the Bowery that was running a crap game in the back room. So it was the Captain of the precinct, after all, that did me the best turn, when he got his. He blew me for wine and the next evening in a Broadway restaurant; and I really felt as glad to get back again as an Astor does when he sees the lights of Charing Cross.

A tainted ten certainly does get action on Broadway. I was alimony once, and got folded in a little dogskin purse among a lot of dimes. They were bragging about the busy times there were in Ossining whenever three girls got hold of one of them during the ice cream season. But it's Slow Moving Vehicles Keep to the Right for the little Bok tips when you think of the way we bison plasters refuse to stick to anything during the rush lobster hour.

The first I ever heard of tainted money was one night when a good thing with a Van to his name threw me over with some other bills to buy a stack of blues.

About midnight a big, easy-going man with a fat face like a monk's and the eye of a janitor with his wages raised took me and a lot of other notes and rolled us into what is termed a "wad" among the money tainters.

"Ticket me for five hundred," said he to the banker, "and look out for everything, Charlie. I'm going out for a stroll in the glen before the moonlight fades from the brow of the cliff. If anybody finds the roof in their way there's $60,000 wrapped in a comic supplement in the upper left-hand corner of the safe. Be bold; everywhere be bold, but be not bowled over. 'Night.'"

I found myself between two $20 gold certificates. One of 'em says to me:

"Well, old shorthorn, you're in luck to-night. You'll see something of life. Old Jack's going to make the Tenderloin look like a hamburg steak."

"Explain," says I. "I'm used to joints, but I don't care for filet mignon with the kind of sauce you serve."

" 'Xcuse me," said the twenty. "Old Jack is the proprietor of this gambling house. He's going on a whiz to-night because he offered $50,000 to a church and it refused to accept it because they said his money was tainted."

"What is a church?" I asked.

"Oh, I forgot," says the twenty, "that I was talking to a tenner. Of course you don't know. You're too much to put into the contribution basket, and not enough to buy anything at a bazaar. A church is—a large building in which penwipers and tidies are sold at $20 each."

I don't care much about chinning with gold certificates. There's a streak of yellow in 'em. All is not gold that quitters.

Old Jack certainly was a gilt-edged sport. When it came his time to loosen up he never referred the waiter to an actuary.

By and by it got around that he was smiting the rock in the wilderness; and all along Broadway things with cold noses and hot gullets fell in on our trail. The third Jungle Book was there waiting for somebody to put covers on it. Old Jack's money may have had a taint to it, but all the same he had orders for his Camembert piling up on him every minute. First his friends rallied round him; and then the fellows that his friends knew by sight; and then a few of his enemies buried the hatchet; and finally he was buying souvenirs for so many Neapolitan fisher maidens and butterfly octettes that the head waiters were 'phoning all over town for Julian Mitchell to please come around and get them into some kind of order.

At last we floated into an uptown café that I knew by heart. When the hod-carriers' union in jackets and aprons saw us coming the chief goal kicker called out: "Six—eleven—forty-two—nineteen—twelve" to his men, and they put on nose guards till it was clear whether we meant Port Arthur or Portsmouth. But old Jack wasn't working for the furniture and glass factories that night. He sat down quiet and sang "Ramble" in a half-hearted way. His feelings had been hurt, so the twenty told me, because his offer to the church had been refused.

But the wassail went on; and Brady himself couldn't have hammered the thirst mob into a better imitation of the real penchant for the stuff that you screw out of a bottle with a napkin.

Old Jack paid the twenty above me for a round, leaving me on the outside of his roll. He laid the roll on the table and sent for the proprietor.

"Mike," says he, "here's money that the good people have refused. Will it buy of your wares in the name of the devil? They say it's tainted."

"It will," says Mike, "and I'll put it in the drawer next to the bills that was paid to the parson's daughter for kisses at the church fair to build a new parsonage for the parson's daughter to live in."

At 1 o'clock when the hod-carriers were making ready to close up the front and keep the inside open, a woman slips in the door of the restaurant and comes up to Old Jack's table. You've seen the kind—black shawl, creepy hair, ragged skirt, white face, eyes a cross between Gabriel's and a sick kitten's—the kind of woman that's always on the lookout for an automobile or the mendicancy squad—and she stands there without a word and looks at the money.

Old Jack gets up, peels me off the roll and hands me to her with a bow.

"Madam," says he, just like actors I've heard, "here is a tainted bill. I am a gambler. This bill came to me to-night from a gentleman's son. Where he got it I do not know. If you will do me the favor to accept it, it is yours."

The woman took me with a trembling hand.

"Sir," said she, "I counted thousands of this issue of bills into packages when they were virgin from the presses. I was a clerk in the Treasury Department. There was an official to whom I owed my position. You say they are tainted now. If you only knew—but I won't say any more. Thank you with all my heart, sir—thank you—thank you."

Where do you suppose that woman carried me almost at a run? To a bakery. Away from Old Jack and a sizzling good time to a bakery. And I got changed, and she does a Sheridan-twenty-miles-away with a dozen rolls and a section of jelly cake as big as a turbine water-wheel. Of course I lost sight of her then, for I was snowed up in the bakery, wondering whether I'd get changed at the drug store the next day in an alum deal or paid over to the cement works.

A week afterward I butted up against one of the one-dollar bills the baker had given the woman for change.

"Hello, E35039669," says I, "weren't you in the change for me in a bakery last Saturday night?"

"Yep," says the solitaire in his free and easy style.

"How did the deal turn out?" I asked.

"She blew E17051431 for milk and round steak," says the one-spot. "She kept me till the rent man came. It was a bum room with a sick kid in it. But you ought to have seen him go for the bread and tincture of formaldehyde. Half-starved, I guess. Then she prayed some. Don't get stuck up, tenner. We one-spots hear ten prayers, when you hear one. She said something about 'who giveth to the poor.' Oh, let's cut out the slum talk. I'm certainly tired of the company that keeps me. I wish I was big enough to move in society with you tainted bills."

"Shut up," says I, "there's no such thing. I know the rest of it. There's a 'lendeth to the Lord' somewhere in it. Now look on my back and read what you see there."

"This note is a legal tender at its face value for all debts public and private."

"This talk about tainted money makes me tired," says I.

A Municipal Report

~~~~~~

The cities are full of pride,
Challenging each to each—
This from her mountainside,
That from her burthened beach.
                              R. KIPLING

Fancy a novel about Chicago or Buffalo, let us say, or
Nashville, Tennessee! There are just three big cities in the
United States that are "story cities"—New York, of course,
New Orleans, and, best of the lot, San Francisco.—FRANK
NORRIS.

EAST is east, and west is San Francisco, according to
Californians. Californians are a race of people; they are not
merely inhabitants of a State. They are the Southerners of
the West. Now, Chicagoans are no less loyal to their city;
but when you ask them why, they stammer and speak of lake
fish and the new Odd Fellows Building. But Californians go
into detail.

Of course they have, in the climate, an argument that is
good for half an hour while you are thinking of your coal
bills and heavy underwear. But as soon as they come to mistake your silence for conviction, madness comes upon them,
and they picture the city of the Golden Gate as the Bagdad
of the New World. So far, as a matter of opinion, no refuta-
tion is necessary. But dear cousins all (from Adam and Eve
descended), it is a rash one who will lay his finger on the
map and say "In this town there can be no romance—what
could happen here?" Yes, it is a bold and a rash deed to

challenge in one sentence history, romance, and Rand and McNally.

NASHVILLE.—A city, port of delivery, and the capital of the State of Tennessee, is on the Cumberland River and on the N. C. & St. L. and the L. & N. railroads. This city is regarded as the most important educational centre in the South.

I stepped off the train at 8 P. M. Having searched thesaurus in vain for adjectives, I must, as a substitution, hie me to comparison in the form of a recipe.

Take of London fog 30 parts; malaria 10 parts; gas leaks 20 parts; dewdrops gathered in a brick yard at sunrise, 25 parts; odor of honeysuckle 15 parts. Mix.

The mixture will give you an approximate conception of a Nashville drizzle. It is not so fragrant as a moth-ball nor as thick as peasoup; but 'tis enough—'twill serve.

I went to a hotel in a tumbril. It required strong self-suppression for me to keep from climbing to the top of it and giving an imitation of Sidney Carton. The vehicle was drawn by beasts of a bygone era and driven by something dark and emancipated.

I was sleepy and tired, so when I got to the hotel I hurriedly paid it the fifty cents it demanded (with approximate lagniappe, I assure you). I knew its habits; and I did not want to hear it prate about its old "marster" or anything that happened "befo' de wah."

The hotel was one of the kind described as "renovated." That means $20,000 worth of new marble pillars, tiling, electric lights and brass cuspidors in the lobby, and a new L. & N. time table and a lithograph of Lookout Mountain in each one of the great rooms above. The management was without reproach, the attention full of exquisite Southern courtesy, the service as slow as the progress of a snail and as good-humored as Rip Van Winkle. The food was worth traveling a thousand miles for. There is no other hotel in the world where you can get such chicken livers *en brochette*.

At dinner I asked a Negro waiter if there was anything doing in town. He pondered gravely for a minute, and then replied: "Well, boss, I don't really reckon there's anything at all doin' after sundown."

Sundown had been accomplished: it had been drowned in the drizzle long before. So that spectacle was denied me. But I went forth upon the streets in the drizzle to see what might be there.

It is built on undulating grounds; and the streets are lighted by electricity at a cost of $32,470 per annum.

As I left the hotel there was a race riot. Down upon me charged a company of freedmen, or Arabs, or Zulus, armed with—no, I saw with relief that they were not rifles, but whips. And I saw dimly a caravan of black, clumsy vehicles; and at the reassuring shouts, "Kyar you anywhere in the town, boss, fuh fifty cents," I reasoned that I was merely a "fare" instead of a victim.

I walked through long streets, all leading uphill. I wondered how those streets ever came down again. Perhaps they didn't until they were "graded." On a few of the "main streets" I saw lights in stores here and there; saw street cars go by conveying worthy burghers hither and yon; saw people pass engaged in the art of conversation, and heard a burst of semi-lively laughter issuing from a soda-water and ice-cream parlor. The streets other than "main" seemed to have enticed upon their borders houses consecrated to peace and domesticity. In many of them lights shone behind discreetly drawn window shades, in a few pianos tinkled orderly and irreproachable music. There was, indeed, little "doing." I wished I had come before sundown. So I returned to my hotel.

In November, 1864, the Confederate General Hood advanced against Nashville, where he shut up a National force under General Thomas. The latter then sallied forth and defeated the Confederates in a terrible conflict.

All my life I have heard of, admired, and witnessed the

fine marksmanship of the South in its peaceful conflicts in the tobacco-chewing regions. But in my hotel a surprise awaited me. There were twelve bright, new, imposing, capacious brass cuspidors in the great lobby, tall enough to be called urns and so wide-mouthed that the crack pitcher of a lady baseball team should have been able to throw a ball into one of them at five paces distant. But, although a terrible battle had raged and was still raging, the enemy had not suffered. Bright, new, imposing, capacious, untouched, they stood. But, shades of Jefferson Brick! the tile floor—the beautiful tile floor! I could not avoid thinking of the battle of Nashville, and trying to draw, as is my foolish habit, some deductions about hereditary marksmanship.

Here I first saw Major (by misplaced courtesy) Wentworth Caswell. I knew him for a type the moment my eyes suffered from the sight of him. A rat has no geographical habitat. My old friend, A. Tennyson, said, as he so well said almost everything:

> Prophet, curse me the blabbing lip,
> And curse me the British vermin, the rat.

Let us regard the word "British" as interchangeable *ad lib*. A rat is a rat.

This man was hunting about the hotel lobby like a starved dog that had forgotten where he had buried a bone. He had a face of great acreage, red, pulpy, and with a kind of sleepy massiveness like that of Buddha. He possessed one single virtue—he was very smoothly shaven. The mark of the beast is not indelible upon a man until he goes about with a stubble. I think that if he had not used his razor that day I would have repulsed his advances, and the criminal calendar of the world would have been spared the addition of one murder.

I happened to be standing within five feet of a cuspidor when Major Caswell opened fire upon it. I had been observant enough to perceive that the attacking force was using Gatlings instead of squirrel rifles, so I sidestepped so promptly that the major seized the opportunity to apologize to a noncombatant. He had the blabbing lip. In four minutes he had become my friend and had dragged me to the bar.

I desire to interpolate here that I am a Southerner. But I am not one by profession or trade. I eschew the string tie, the slouch hat, the Prince Albert, the number of bales of cotton destroyed by Sherman, and plug chewing. When the orchestra plays "Dixie" I do not cheer. I slide a little lower on the leather-cornered seat and, well, order another Würzburger and wish that Longstreet had—but what's the use?

Major Caswell banged the bar with his fist, and the first gun at Fort Sumter re-echoed. When he fired the last one at Appomattox I began to hope. But then he began on family trees, and demonstrated that Adam was only a third cousin of a collateral branch of the Caswell family. Genealogy disposed of, he took up, to my distaste, his private family matters. He spoke of his wife, traced her descent back to Eve, and profanely denied any possible rumor that she may have had relations in the land of Nod.

By this time I began to suspect that he was trying to obscure by noise the fact that he had ordered the drinks, on the chance that I would be bewildered into paying for them. But when they were down he crashed a silver dollar loudly upon the bar. Then, of course, another serving was obligatory. And when I had paid for that I took leave of him brusquely; for I wanted no more of him. But before I had obtained my release he had prated loudly of an income that his wife received, and showed a handful of silver money.

When I got my key at the desk the clerk said to me courteously: "If that man Caswell has annoyed you, and if you would like to make a complaint, we will have him ejected. He is a nuisance, a loafer, and without any known means of support, although he seems to have some money most the time. But we don't seem to be able to hit upon any means of throwing him out legally."

"Why, no," said I, after some reflection; "I don't see my way clear to making a complaint. But I would like to place myself on record as asserting that I do not care for his company. Your town," I continued, "seems to be a quiet one.

What manner of entertainment, adventure, or excitement, have you to offer to the stranger within your gates?"

"Well, sir," said the clerk, "there will be a show here next Thursday. It is—I'll look it up and have the announcement sent up to your room with the ice water. Good-night."

After I went up to my room I looked out the window. It was only about ten o'clock, but I looked upon a silent town. The drizzle continued, spangled with dim lights, as far apart as currants in a cake sold at the Ladies' Exchange.

"A quiet place," I said to myself, as my first shoe struck the ceiling of the occupant of the room beneath mine. "Nothing of the life here that gives color and good variety to the cities in the East and West. Just a good, ordinary, hum-drum, business town."

Nashville occupies a foremost place among the manufacturing centres of the country. It is the fifth boot and shoe market in the United States, the largest candy and cracker manufacturing city in the South, and does an enormous wholesale drygoods, grocery, and drug business.

I must tell you how I came to be in Nashville, and I assure you the digression brings as much tedium to me as it does to you. I was traveling elsewhere on my own business, but I had a commission from a Northern literary magazine to stop over there and establish a personal connection between the publication and one of its contributors, Azalea Adair.

Adair (there was no clue to the personality except the handwriting) had sent in some essays (lost art!) and poems that had made the editors swear approvingly over their one o'clock luncheon. So they had commissioned me to round up said Adair and corner by contract his or her output at two cents a word before some other publisher offered her ten or twenty.

At nine o'clock the next morning, after my chicken livers *en brochette* (try them if you can find that hotel), I strayed out into the drizzle, which was still on for an unlimited run. At the first corner I came upon Uncle Cæsar. He was a stalwart Negro, older than the pyramids, with gray wool and a face that reminded me of Brutus, and a second afterwards of the late King Cettiwayo. He wore the most remarkable coat that I ever had seen or expect to see. It reached to his ankles and had once been a Confederate gray in colors. But rain and sun and age had so variegated it that Joseph's coat, beside it, would have faded to a pale monochrome. I must linger with that coat, for it has to do with the story—the story that is so long in coming, because you can hardly expect anything to happen in Nashville.

Once it must have been the military coat of an officer. The cape of it had vanished, but all adown its front it had been frogged and tasseled magnificently. But now the frogs and tassels were gone. In their stead had been patiently stitched (I surmised by some surviving "black mammy") new frogs made of cunningly twisted common hempen twine. This twine was frayed and disheveled. It must have been added to the coat as a substitute for vanished splendors, with tasteless but painstaking devotion, for it followed faithfully the curves of the long-missing frogs. And, to complete the comedy and pathos of the garment, all its buttons were gone save one. The second button from the top alone remained. The coat was fastened by other twine strings tied through the button-holes and other holes rudely pierced in the opposite side. There was never such a weird garment so fantastically be-decked and of so many mottled hues. The lone button was the size of a half-dollar, made of yellow horn and sewed on with coarse twine.

This Negro stood by a carriage so old that Ham himself might have started a hack line with it after he left the ark with the two animals hitched to it. As I approached he threw open the door, drew out a feather duster, waved it without using it, and said in deep, rumbling tones:

"Step right in, suh; ain't a speck of dust in it—jus' got back from a funeral, suh."

I inferred that on such gala occasions carriages were given an extra cleaning. I looked up and down the street and per-ceived that there was little choice among the vehicles for hire that lined the curb. I looked in my memorandum book for the address of Azalea Adair.

"I want to go to 861 Jessamine Street," I said, and was about to step into the hack. But for an instant the thick, long, gorilla-like arm of the Negro barred me. On his massive and saturnine face a look of sudden suspicion and enmity flashed for a moment. Then, with quickly returning conviction, he asked, blandishingly: "What are you gwine there for, boss?"

"What is that to you?" I asked, a little sharply.

"Nothin', suh, jus' nothin'. Only it's a lonesome kind of part of town and few folks ever has business out there. Step right in. The seats is clean—jes' got back from a funeral, suh."

A mile and a half it must have been to our journey's end. I could hear nothing but the fearful rattle of the ancient hack over the uneven brick paving; I could smell nothing but the drizzle, now further flavored with coal smoke and something like a mixture of tar and oleander blossoms. All I could see through the streaming windows were two rows of dim houses.

The city has an area of 10 square miles; 181 miles of streets, of which 137 miles are paved; a system of waterworks that cost $2,000,000, with 77 miles of mains.

Eight-sixty-one Jessamine Street was a decayed mansion. Thirty yards back from the street it stood, outmerged in a splendid grove of trees and untrimmed shrubbery. A row of box bushes overflowed and almost hid the paling fence from sight; the gate was kept closed by a rope noose that encircled the gate post and the first paling of the gate. But when you got inside you saw that 861 was a shell, a shadow, a ghost of former grandeur and excellence. But in the story, I have not yet got inside.

When the hack had ceased from rattling and the weary quadrupeds came to a rest I handed my jehu his fifty cents with an additional quarter, feeling a glow of conscious generosity as I did so. He refused it.

"It's two dollars, suh," he said.

"How's that?" I asked. "I plainly heard you call out at the hotel. 'Fifty cents to any part of the town.'"

"It's two dollars, suh," he repeated obstinately. "It's a long ways from the hotel."

"It is within the city limits and well within them," I argued. "Don't think that you have picked up a greenhorn Yankee. Do you see those hills over there?" I went on, pointing toward the east (I could not see them, myself, for the drizzle); "well, I was born and raised on their other side. You old fool nigger, can't you tell people from other people when you see 'em?"

The grim face of King Cettiwayo softened. "Is you from the South, suh? I reckon it was them shoes of yourn' fooled me. They is somethin' sharp in the toes for a Southern gen'l'man to wear."

"Then the charge is fifty cents, I suppose?" said I, inexorably.

His former expression, a mingling of cupidity and hostility, returned, remained ten seconds, and vanished.

"Boss," he said, "fifty cents is right; but I *needs* two dollars, suh; I'm *obleeged* to have two dollars. I ain't *demandin'* it now, suh; after I knows whar you's from; I'm jus sayin' that I *has* to have two dollars to-night and business is mighty po'."

Peace and confidence settled upon his heavy features. He had been luckier than he had hoped. Instead of having picked up a greenhorn, ignorant of rates, he had come upon an inheritance.

"You confounded old rascal," I said, reaching down to my pocket, "you ought to be turned over to the police."

For the first time I saw him smile. He knew; *he knew;* HE kNEW.

I gave him two one-dollar bills. As I handed them over I noticed that one of them had seen parlous times. Its upper right-hand corner was missing, and it had been torn through in the middle, but joined again. A strip of blue tissue paper, pasted over the split, preserved its negotiability.

Enough of the African bandit for the present: I left him happy, lifted the rope, and opened the creaky gate.

The house, as I said, was a shell. A paint brush had not touched it in twenty years. I could not see why a strong wind should not have bowled it over like a house of cards until I looked again at the trees that hugged it close—the trees that saw the battle of Nashville and still drew their protecting branches around it against storm and enemy and cold.

Azalea Adair, fifty years old, white-haired, a descendant of the cavaliers, as thin and frail as the house she lived in, robed in the cheapest and cleanest dress I ever saw, with an air as simple as a queen's, received me.

The reception room seemed a mile square, because there was nothing in it except some rows of books, on unpainted white-pine bookshelves, a cracked marble-topped table, a rag rug, a hairless horsehair sofa, and two or three chairs. Yes, there was a picture on the wall, a colored crayon drawing of a cluster of pansies. I looked around for the portrait of Andrew Jackson and the pine-cone hanging basket but they were not there.

Azalea Adair and I had conversation, a little of which will be repeated to you. She was a product of the old South, gently nurtured in the sheltered life. Her learning was not broad, but was deep and of splendid originality in its somewhat narrow scope. She had been educated at home, and her knowledge of the world was derived from inference and by inspiration. Of such is the precious, small group of essayists made. While she talked to me I kept brushing my fingers, trying, unconsciously, to rid them guiltily of the absent dust from the half-calf backs of Lamb, Chaucer, Hazlitt, Marcus Aurelius, Montaigne, and Hood. She was exquisite, she was a valuable discovery. Nearly everybody nowadays knows too much—oh, so much too much—of real life.

I could perceive clearly that Azalea Adair was very poor. A house and a dress she had, not much else, I fancied. So, divided between my duty to the magazine and my loyalty to the poets and essayists who fought Thomas in the valley of the Cumberland, I listened to her voice which was like a harpsichord's, and found that I could not speak of contracts. In the presence of the nine Muses and the three Graces one hesitated to lower the topic to two cents. There would have to be another colloquy after I had regained my commercialism. But I spoke of my mission, and three o'clock of the next afternoon was set for the discussion of the business proposition.

"Your town," I said, as I began to make ready to depart (which is the time for smooth generalities), "seems to be a quiet, sedate place. A home town, I should say, where few things out of the ordinary ever happen."

It carries on an extensive trade in stoves and hollow ware with the West and South, and its flouring mills have a daily capacity of more than 2,000 barrels.

Azalea Adair seemed to reflect.

"I have never thought of it that way," she said, with a kind of sincere intensity that seemed to belong to her. "Isn't it in the still, quiet places that things do happen? I fancy that when God began to create the earth on the first Monday morning one could have leaned out one's window and heard the drops of mud splashing from His trowel as He built up the everlasting hills. What did the noisiest project in the world—I mean the building of the tower of Babel—result in finally? A page and a half of Esperanto in the *North American Review.*"

"Of course," said I, platitudinously, "human nature is the same everywhere; but there is more color—er—more drama and movement and—er—romance in some cities than in others."

"On the surface," said Azalea Adair. "I have traveled many times around the world in a golden airship wafted on two wings—print and dreams. I have seen (on one of my imaginary tours) the Sultan of Turkey bowstring with his own hands one of his wives who had uncovered her face in public. I have seen a man in Nashville tear up his theatre tickets because his wife was going out with her face covered—with rice powder. In San Francisco's Chinatown I saw the slave girl Sing Yee dipped slowly, inch by inch, in boiling almond oil to make her swear she would never see her American lover again. She gave in when the boiling oil had reached three inches above her knee. At a euchre party in East Nashville the other night I saw Kitty Morgan cut dead by seven of her schoolmates and lifelong friends because she had married a house painter. The boiling oil was sizzling as high as her heart; but I wish you could have seen the fine little smile that she carried from table to table. Oh, yes, it is a humdrum town. Just a few miles of red brick houses and mud and stores and lumber yards."

Some one had knocked hollowly at the back of the house. Azalea Adair breathed a soft apology and went to investigate the sound. She came back in three minutes with brightened eyes, a faint flush on her cheeks, and ten years lifted from her shoulders.

"You must have a cup of tea before you go," she said, "and a sugar cake."

She reached and shook a little iron bell. In shuffled a small Negro girl about twelve, barefoot, not very tidy, glowering at me with thumb in mouth and bulging eyes.

Azalea Adair opened a tiny, worn purse and drew out a dollar bill, a dollar bill with the upper right-hand corner missing, torn in two pieces and pasted together again with a strip of blue tissue paper. It was one of those bills I had given the piratical Negro—there was no doubt of it.

"Go up to Mr. Baker's store on the corner, Impy," she said, handing the girl the dollar bill, "and get a quarter of a pound of tea—the kind he always sends me—and ten cents' worth of sugar cakes. Now, hurry. The supply of tea in the house happens to be exhausted," she explained to me.

Impy left by the back way. Before the scrape of her hard, bare feet had died away on the back porch, a wild shriek—I was sure it was hers—filled the hollow house. Then the deep, gruff tones of an angry man's voice mingled with the girl's further squeals and unintelligible words.

Azalea Adair rose without surprise or emotion and disappeared. For two minutes I heard the hoarse rumble of the man's voice; then something like an oath and a slight scuffle, and she returned calmly to her chair.

"This is a roomy house," she said, "and I have a tenant for part of it. I am sorry to have to rescind my invitation to tea. It is impossible to get the kind I always use at the store. Perhaps to-morrow Mr. Baker will be able to supply me."

I was sure that Impy had not had time to leave the house. I inquired concerning street-car lines and took my leave. After I was well on my way I remembered that I had not learned Azalea Adair's name. But to-morrow would do.

The same day I started in on the course of iniquity that this uneventful city forced upon me. I was in the town only two days, but in that time I managed to lie shamelessly by telegraph, and to be an accomplice—after the fact, if that is the correct legal term—to a murder.

As I rounded the corner nearest my hotel the Afrite coachman of the polychromatic, nonpareil coat seized me, swung open the dungeony door of his peripatetic sarcophagus, flirted his feather duster and began his ritual: "Step right in, boss. Carriage is clean—jus' got back from a funeral. Fifty cents to any——"

And then he knew me and grinned broadly. " 'Scuse me, boss; you is de gen'l'man what rid out with me dis mawnin'. Thank you kindly, suh."

"I am going out to 861 again to-morrow afternoon at three," said I, "and if you will be here, I'll let you drive me. So you know Miss Adair?" I concluded, thinking of my dollar bill.

"I belonged to her father, Judge Adair, suh," he replied.

"I judge that she is pretty poor," I said. "She hasn't much money to speak of, has she?"

For an instant I looked again at the fierce countenance of King Cettiwayo, and then he changed back to an extortionate old Negro hack driver.

"She ain't gwine to starve, suh," he said, slowly. "She has reso'ces, suh; she has reso'ces."

"I shall pay you fifty cents for the trip," said I.

"Dat is puffeckly correct, suh," he answered, humbly. "I jus' *had* to have dat two dollars dis mawnin' boss."

I went to the hotel and lied by electricity. I wired the magazine: "A. Adair holds out for eight cents a word."

The answer that came back was: "Give it to her quick, you duffer."

Just before dinner "Major" Wentworth Caswell bore down upon me with the greetings of a long-lost friend. I have seen few men whom I have so instantaneously hated, and of whom it was so difficult to be rid. I was standing at the bar when he invaded me; therefore I could not wave the white ribbon in his face. I would have paid gladly for the drinks, hoping thereby, to escape another; but he was one of those despicable, roaring, advertising bibbers who must have brass bands and fireworks attend upon every cent that they waste in their follies.

With an air of producing millions he drew two one-dollar bills from a pocket and dashed one of them upon the bar. I looked once more at the dollar bill with the upper right-hand corner missing, torn through the middle, and patched with a strip of blue tissue paper. It was my dollar again. It could have been no other.

I went up to my room. The drizzle and the monotony of a dreary, eventless Southern town had made me tired and listless. I remember that just before I went to bed I mentally disposed of the mysterious dollar bill (which might have formed the clue to a tremendously fine detective story of San Francisco) by saying to myself sleepily: "Seems as if a lot of people here own stock in the Hack-Drivers' Trust. Pays dividends promptly, too. Wonder if——" Then I fell asleep.

King Cettiwayo was at his post the next day, and rattled my bones over the stones out to 861. He was to wait and rattle me back again when I was ready.

Azalea Adair looked paler and cleaner and frailer than she had looked on the day before. After she had signed the contract at eight cents per word she grew still paler and began to slip out of her chair. Without much trouble I managed to get her up on the antediluvian horsehair sofa and then I ran

out to the sidewalk and yelled to the coffee-colored Pirate
to bring a doctor. With a wisdom that I had not suspected
in him, he abandoned his team and struck off up the street
afoot, realizing the value of speed. In ten minutes he returned with a grave, gray-haired, and capable man of medicine. In a few words (worth much less than eight cents each)
I explained to him my presence in the hollow house of mystery. He bowed with stately understanding, and turned to the
old Negro.

"Uncle Cæsar," he said, calmly, "run up to my house and
ask Miss Lucy to give you a cream pitcher full of fresh milk
and half a tumbler of port wine. And hurry back. Don't drive—
run. I want you to get back sometime this week."

It occurred to me that Dr. Merriman also felt a distrust
as to the speeding powers of the land-pirate's steeds. After
Uncle Cæsar was gone, lumberingly, but swiftly, up the
street, the doctor looked me over with great politeness and as
much careful calculation until he had decided that I might
do.

"It is only a case of insufficient nutrition," he said. "In
other words, the result of poverty, pride, and starvation.
Mrs. Caswell has many devoted friends who would be glad
to aid her, but she will accept nothing except from that old
Negro, Uncle Cæsar, who was once owned by her family."

"Mrs. Caswell!" said I, in surprise. And then I looked at
the contract and saw that she had signed it "Azalea Adair
Caswell."

"I thought she was Miss Adair," I said.

"Married to a drunken, worthless loafer, sir," said the
doctor. "It is said that he robs her even of the small sums
that her old servant contributes toward her support."

When the milk and wine had been brought the doctor
soon revived Azalea Adair. She sat up and talked of the
beauty of the autumn leaves that were then in season and
their height of color. She referred lightly to her fainting
seizure as the outcome of an old palpitation of the heart.
Impy fanned her as she lay on the sofa. The doctor was due
elsewhere, and I followed him to the door. I told him that it

was within my power and intentions to make a reasonable advance of money to Azalea Adair on future contributions to the magazine, and he seemed pleased.

"By the way," he said, "perhaps you would like to know that you have had royalty for a coachman. Old Cæsar's grandfather was a king in the Congo. Cæsar himself has royal ways, as you may have observed."

As the doctor was moving off I heard Uncle Cæsar's voice inside: "Did he git bofe of dem two dollars from you, Mis' Zalea?"

"Yes, Cæsar," I heard Azalea Adair answer, weakly. And then I went in and concluded business negotiations with our contributor. I assumed the responsibility of advancing fifty dollars, putting it as a necessary formality in binding our bargain. And then Uncle Cæsar drove me back to the hotel.

Here ends all of the story as far as I can testify as a witness. The rest must be only bare statements of facts.

At about six o'clock I went out for a stroll. Uncle Cæsar was at his corner. He threw open the door of his carriage, flourished his duster, and began his depressing formula: "Step right in, suh. Fifty cents to anywhere in the city—hack's puffickly clean, suh—jus' got back from a funeral——"

And then he recognized me. I think his eyesight was getting bad. His coat had taken on a few more faded shades of color, the twine strings were more frayed and ragged, the last remaining button—the button of yellow horn—was gone. A motley descendant of kings was Uncle Cæsar!

About two hours later I saw an excited crowd besieging the front of the drug store. In a desert where nothing happens this was manna; so I wedged my way inside. On an extemporized couch of empty boxes and chairs was stretched the mortal corporeality of Major Wentworth Caswell. A doctor was testing him for the mortal ingredient. His decision was that it was conspicuous by its absence.

The erstwhile Major had been found dead on a dark street and brought by curious and ennuied citizens to the drug store. The late human being had been engaged in terrific battle—the details showed that. Loafer and reprobate though he had been, he had been also a warrior. But he had lost. His hands were yet clinched so tightly that his fingers could not be opened. The gentle citizens who had known him stood about and searched their vocabularies to find some good words, if it were possible, to speak of him. One kind-looking man said, after much thought: "When 'Cas' was about fo'teen he was one of the best spellers in the school."

While I stood there the fingers of the right hand of "the man that was," which hung down the side of a white pine box, relaxed, and dropped something at my feet. I covered it with one foot quietly, and a little later on I picked it up and pocketed it. I reasoned that in his last struggle his hand must have seized that object unwittingly and held it in a death grip.

At the hotel that night the main topic of conversation, with the possible exceptions of politics and prohibition, was the demise of Major Caswell. I heard one man say to a group of listeners:

"In my opinion, gentlemen, Caswell was murdered by some of these no-account niggers for his money. He had fifty dollars this afternoon which he showed to several gentlemen in the hotel. When he was found the money was not on his person."

I left the city the next morning at nine, and as the train was crossing the bridge over the Cumberland River I took out of my pocket a yellow horn overcoat button the size of a fifty-cent piece, with frayed ends of coarse twine hanging from it, and cast it out of the window into the slow, muddy waters below.

I wonder what's doing in Buffalo!

Compliments of the Season

～～～～～～～～～～～～～～～～～～

THERE are no more Christmas stories to write. Fiction is exhausted; and newspaper items, the next best, are manufactured by clever young journalists who have married early and have an engagingly pessimistic view of life. Therefore, for seasonable diversion, we are reduced to two very questionable sources—facts and philosophy. We will begin with—whichever you choose to call it.

Children are pestilential little animals with which we have to cope under a bewildering variety of conditions. Especially when childish sorrows overwhelm them are we put to our wits' ends. We exhaust our paltry store of consolation; and then beat them, sobbing, to sleep. Then we grovel in the dust of a million years, and ask God why. Thus we crawl out of the rattrap. As for the children, no one understands them except old maids, hunchbacks, and shepherd dogs.

Now come the facts in the case of the Rag-Doll, the Tatterdemalion, and the Twenty-fifth of December.

On the tenth of that month the Child of the Millionaire lost her rag-doll. There were many servants in the Millionaire's palace on the Hudson, and these ransacked the house and grounds, but without finding the lost treasure. The Child was a girl of five, and one of those perverse little beasts that often wound the sensibilities of wealthy parents by fixing their affections upon some vulgar, inexpensive toy instead of upon diamond-studded automobiles and pony phaetons.

The Child grieved sorely and truly, a thing inexplicable to the Millionaire, to whom the rag-doll market was about as interesting as Bay State Gas; and to the Lady, the Child's mother, who was all form—that is, nearly all, as you shall see.

The Child cried inconsolably, and grew hollow-eyed, knock-kneed, spindling, and cory-kilverty in many other respects. The Millionaire smiled and tapped his coffers confidently. The pick of the output of the French and German toymakers was rushed by special delivery to the mansion; but Rachel refused to be comforted. She was weeping for her rag child, and was for a high protective tariff against all foreign foolishness. Then doctors with the finest bedside manners and stopwatches were called in. One by one they chattered futilely about peptomanganate of iron and sea voyages and hypophosphites until their stopwatches showed that Bill Rendered was under the wire for show or place. Then, as men, they advised that the rag-doll be found as soon as possible and restored to its mourning parent. The Child sniffed at therapeutics, chewed a thumb, and wailed for her Betsy. And all this time cablegrams were coming from Santa Claus saying that he would soon be here and enjoining us to show a true Christian spirit and let up on the poolrooms and tontine policies and platoon systems long enough to give him a welcome. Everywhere the spirit of Christmas was diffusing itself. The banks were refusing loans, the pawnbrokers had doubled their gang of helpers, people bumped your shins on the streets with red sleds, Thomas and Jeremiah bubbled before you on the bars while you waited on one foot, holly-wreaths of hospitality were hung in windows of the stores, they who had 'em were getting out their furs. You hardly knew which was the best bet in balls—three, high, moth, or snow. It was no time at which to lose the rag-doll of your heart.

If Doctor Watson's investigating friend had been called in to solve this mysterious disappearance he might have observed on the Millionaire's wall a copy of "The Vampire." That would have quickly suggested, by induction, "A rag and a bone and a hank of hair." "Flip," a Scotch terrier, next to the rag-doll in the Child's heart, frisked through the halls. The hank of hair! Aha! X, the unfound quantity, represented the rag-doll. But, the bone? Well, when dogs find bones they—— Done! it were an easy and a fruitful task to examine Flip's forefeet. Look, Watson! Earth—dried earth between the toes. Of course, the dog—but Sherlock was not there. Therefore it devolves. But topography and architecture must intervene.

The Millionaire's palace occupied a lordly space. In front of it was a lawn close-mowed as a South Ireland man's face two days after a shave. At one side of it, and fronting on another street, was a pleasaunce trimmed to a leaf, and the garage and stables. The Scotch pup had ravished the rag-doll from the nursery, dragged it to a corner of the lawn, dug a hole, and buried it after the manner of careless undertakers. There you have the mystery solved, and no checks to write for the hypodermical wizard or fi'-pun notes to toss to the sergeant. Then let's get down to the heart of the thing, tiresome readers—the Christmas heart of the thing.

Fuzzy was drunk—not riotously or helplessly or loquaciously, as you or I might get, but decently, appropriately, and inoffensively, as becomes a gentleman down on his luck.

Fuzzy was a soldier of misfortune. The road, the haystack, the park bench, the kitchen door, the bitter round of eleemosynary beds-with-shower-bath-attachment, the petty pickings and ignobly garnered largesse of great cities—these formed the chapters of his history.

Fuzzy walked toward the river, down the street that bounded one side of the Millionaire's house and grounds. He saw a leg of Betsy, the lost rag-doll, protruding, like the clue to a Lilliputian murder mystery, from its untimely grave in a corner of the fence. He dragged forth the maltreated infant, tucked it under his arm, and went on his way crooning a road song of his brethren that no doll that has been brought up to the sheltered life should hear. Well for Betsy that she had no ears. And well that she had no eyes save unseeing circles of black; for the faces of Fuzzy and the Scotch terrier were those of brothers, and the heart of no rag-doll could withstand twice to become the prey of such fearsome monsters.

Though you may not know it, Grogan's saloon stands

near the river and near the foot of the street down which
Fuzzy traveled. In Grogan's, Christmas cheer was already
rampant.

Fuzzy entered with his doll. He fancied that as a mummer
at the feast of Saturn he might earn a few drops from the
wassail cup.

He set Betsy on the bar and addressed her loudly and
humorously, seasoning his speech with exaggerated compliments and endearments as one entertaining his lady friend.
The loafers and bibbers around caught the farce of it, and
roared. The bartender gave Fuzzy a drink. Oh, many of us
carry rag-dolls.

"One for the lady?" suggested Fuzzy, impudently, and
tucked another contribution to Art beneath his waistcoat.

He began to see possibilities in Betsy. His first-night had
been a success. Visions of a vaudeville circuit about town
dawned upon him.

In a group near the stove sat "Pigeon" McCarthy, Black
Riley, and "One-ear" Mike, well and unfavorably known in
the tough shoe-string district that blackened the left bank
of the river. They passed a newspaper back and forth among
themselves. The item that each solid and blunt forefinger
pointed out was an advertisement headed "One Hundred
Dollars Reward." To earn it one must return the rag-doll lost,
strayed, or stolen from the Millionaire's mansion. It seemed
that grief still ravaged, unchecked, in the bosom of the too
faithful Child. Flip, the terrier, capered and shook his absurd
whisker before her, powerless to distract. She wailed for her
Betsy in the faces of walking, talking, mamaing, and eye-
closing French Mabelles and Violettes. The advertisement was
a last resort.

Black Riley came from behind the stove and approached
Fuzzy in his one-sided parabolic way.

The Christmas mummer, flushed with success, had tucked
Betsy under his arm, and was about to depart to the filling
of impromptu dates elsewhere.

"Say, 'Bo," said Black Riley to him, "where did you cop
out dat doll?"

"This doll?" asked Fuzzy, touching Betsy with his fore-finger to be sure that she was the one referred to. "Why, this doll was presented to me by the Emperor of Beloochistan. I have seven hundred others in my country home in Newport. This doll——"

"Cheese the funny business," said Riley. "You swiped it or picked it up at de house on de hill where—but never mind dat. You want to take fifty cents for de rags, and take it quick. Me brother's kid at home might be wantin' to play wid it. Hey- what?"

He produced the coin.

Fuzzy laughed a gurgling, insolent, alcoholic laugh in his face. Go to the office of Sarah Bernhardt's manager and pro-pose to him that she be released from a night's performance to entertain the Tackytown Lyceum and Literary Coterie. You will hear the duplicate of Fuzzy's laugh.

Black Riley gauged Fuzzy quickly with his blueberry eye as a wrestler does. His hand was itching to play the Roman and wrest the rag Sabine from the extemporaneous merry-andrew who was entertaining an angel unaware. But he re-frained. Fuzzy was fat and solid and big. Three inches of well-nourished corporeity, defended from the winter winds by dingy linen, intervened between his vest and trousers. Countless small, circular wrinkles running around his coat-sleeves and knees guaranteed the quality of his bone and muscle. His small, blue eyes, bathed in the moisture of altruism and wooziness, looked upon you kindly, yet without abashment. He was whiskerly, whiskly, fleshily formidable. So, Black Riley temporized.

"Wot'll you take for it, den?" he asked.

"Money," said Fuzzy, with husky firmness, "cannot buy her."

He was intoxicated with the artist's first sweet cup of at-tainment. To set a faded-blue, earth-stained rag-doll on a bar, to hold mimic converse with it, and to find his heart leaping with the sense of plaudits earned and his throat scorching with free libations poured in his honor—could base coin buy him from such achievements? You will perceive that Fuzzy had the temperament.

Fuzzy walked out with the gait of a trained sea-lion in search of other cafés to conquer.

Though the dusk of twilight was hardly yet apparent, lights were beginning to spangle the city like popcorn bursting in a deep skillet. Christmas Eve, impatiently expected, was peeping over the brink of the hour. Millions had prepared for its celebration. Towns would be painted red. You, yourself, have heard the horns and dodged the capers of the Saturnalians.

"Pigeon" McCarthy, Black Riley, and "One-ear" Mike held a hasty converse outside Grogan's. They were narrow-chested, pallid striplings, not fighters in the open, but more dangerous in their ways of warfare than the most terrible of Turks. Fuzzy, in a pitched battle, could have eaten the three of them. In a go-as-you-please encounter he was already doomed.

They overtook him just as he and Betsy were entering Costigan's Casino. They deflected him, and shoved the newspaper under his nose. Fuzzy could read—and more.

"Boys," said he, "you are certainly damn true friends. Give me a week to think it over."

The soul of the real artist is quenched with difficulty.

The boys carefully pointed out to him that advertisements were soulless, and that the deficiencies of the day might not be supplied by the morrow.

"A cool hundred," said Fuzzy, thoughtfully and mushily.

"Boys," said he, "you are true friends. I'll go up and claim the reward. The show business is not what it used to be."

Night was falling more surely. The three tagged at his sides to the foot of the rise on which stood the Millionaire's house. There Fuzzy turned upon them acrimoniously.

"You are a pack of putty-faced beagle-hounds," he roared. "Go away."

They went away—a little way.

In "Pigeon" McCarthy's pocket was a section of one-inch gas-pipes eight inches long. In one end of it and in the middle of it was a lead slug. One-half of it was packed tight with solder. Black Riley carried a slung-shot, being a conventional thug. "One-ear" Mike relied upon a pair of brass knucks—an heirloom in the family.

"Why fetch and carry," said Black Riley, "when some one will do it for ye? Let him bring it out to us. Hey—what?"

"We can chuck him in the river," said "Pigeon" McCarthy, "with a stone tied to his feet."

"Youse guys make me tired," said "One-ear" Mike sadly. "Ain't progress ever appealed to none of yez? Sprinkle a little gasoline on 'im, and drop 'im on the Drive—well?"

Fuzzy entered the Millionaire's gate and zigzagged toward the softly glowing entrance of the mansion. The three goblins came up to the gate and lingered—one on each side of it, one beyond the roadway. They fingered their cold metal and leather, confident.

Fuzzy rang the door-bell, smiling foolishly and dreamily. An atavistic instinct prompted him to reach for the button of his right glove. But he wore no gloves; so his left hand dropped, embarrassed.

The particular menial whose duty it was to open doors to silks and laces shied at first sight of Fuzzy. But a second glance took in his passport, his card of admission, his surety of welcome—the lost rag-doll of the daughter of the house dangling under his arm.

Fuzzy was admitted into a great hall, dim with the glow from unseen lights. The hireling went away and returned with a maid and the Child. The doll was restored to the mourning one. She clasped her lost darling to her breast; and then, with the inordinate selfishness and candor of childhood, stamped her foot and whined hatred and fear of the odious being who had rescued her from the depths of sorrow and despair. Fuzzy wriggled himself into an ingratiatory attitude and essayed the idiotic smile and blattering small talk that is supposed to charm the budding intellect of the young. The Child bawled, and was dragged away, hugging her Betsy close.

There came the Secretary, pale, poised, polished, gliding in pumps, and worshipping pomp and ceremony. He counted out into Fuzzy's hand ten ten-dollar bills; then dropped his eye upon the door, transferred it to James, its custodian, indicated the obnoxious earner of the reward with the other, and allowed his pumps to waft him away to secretarial regions.

James gathered Fuzzy with his own commanding optic and swept him as far as the front door.

When the money touched Fuzzy's dingy palm his first instinct was to take to his heels; but a second thought restrained him from that blunder of etiquette. It was his; it had been given him. It—and, oh, what an elysium it opened to the gaze of his mind's eye! He had tumbled to the foot of the ladder; he was hungry, homeless, friendless, ragged, cold, drifting; and he held in his hand the key to a paradise of the mud-honey that he craved. The fairy doll had waved a wand with her rag-stuffed hand; and now wherever he might go the enchanted palaces with shining foot-rests and magic red fluids in gleaming glassware would be open to him.

He followed James to the door.

He paused there as the flunky drew open the great mahogany portal for him to pass into the vestibule.

Beyond the wrought-iron gates in the dark highway Black Riley and his two pals casually strolled, fingering under their coats the inevitably fatal weapons that were to make the reward of the rag-doll theirs.

Fuzzy stopped at the Millionaire's door and bethought himself. Like little sprigs of mistletoe on a dead tree, certain living green thoughts and memories began to decorate his confused mind. He was quite drunk, mind you, and the present was beginning to fade. Those wreaths and festoons of holly with their scarlet berries making the great hall gay— where had he seen such things before? Somewhere he had known polished floors and odors of fresh flowers in winter, and—some one was singing a song in the house that he thought he had heard before. Some one singing and playing a harp. Of course, it was Christmas—Fuzzy thought he must have been pretty drunk to have overlooked that.

And then he went out of the present, and there came back

to him out of some impossible, vanished, and irrevocable past a little, pure-white, transient, forgotten ghost—the spirit of *noblesse oblige*. Upon a gentleman certain things devolve.

James opened the outer door. A stream of light went down the graveled walk to the iron gate. Black Riley, McCarthy, and "One-ear" Mike saw, and carelessly drew their sinister cordon closer about the gate.

With a more imperious gesture than James's master had ever used or could ever use, Fuzzy compelled the menial to close the door. Upon a gentleman certain things devolve. Especially at the Christmas season.

"It is cust—customary," he said to James, the flustered, "when a gentleman calls on Christmas Eve to pass the compliments of the season with the lady of the house. You und'stand? I shall not move shtep till I pass compl'ments season with lady the house. Und'stand?"

There was an argument. James lost. Fuzzy raised his voice and sent it through the house unpleasantly. I did not say he was a gentleman. He was simply a tramp being visited by a ghost.

A sterling silver bell rang. James went back to answer it, leaving Fuzzy in the hall. James explained somewhere to some one.

Then he came and conducted Fuzzy to the library.

The Lady entered a moment later. She was more beautiful and holy than any picture that Fuzzy had seen. She smiled, and said something about a doll. Fuzzy didn't understand that; he remembered nothing about a doll.

A footman brought in two small glasses of sparkling wine on a stamped sterling-silver waiter. The Lady took one. The other was handed to Fuzzy.

As his fingers closed on the slender glass stem his disabilities dropped from him for one brief moment. He straightened himself; and Time, so disobliging to most of us, turned backward to accommodate Fuzzy.

Forgotten Christmas ghosts whiter than the false beards of the most opulent Kris Kringle were rising in the fumes of Grogan's whisky. What had the Millionaire's mansion to do with a long wainscoted Virginia hall, where the riders were grouped around a silver punch-bowl drinking the ancient toast of the House? And why should the patter of the cab horses' hoofs on the frozen street be in any wise related to the sound of the saddled hunters stamping under the shelter of the west veranda? And what had Fuzzy to do with any of it?

The Lady, looking at him over her glass, let her condescending smile fade away like a false dawn. Her eyes turned serious. She saw something beneath the rags and Scotch terrier whiskers that she did not understand. But it did not matter.

Fuzzy lifted his glass and smiled vacantly.

"P-pardon, lady," he said, "but couldn't leave without exchangin' comp'ments sheason with lady th' house. 'Gainst princ'ples gen'leman do sho."

And then he began the ancient salutation that was a tradition in the House when men wore lace ruffles and powder.

"The blessings of another year——"

Fuzzy's memory failed him. The Lady prompted:

"—Be upon this hearth."

"—The guest——" stammered Fuzzy.

"—And upon her who——" continued the Lady, with a leading smile.

"Oh, cut it out," said Fuzzy, ill-manneredly. "I can't remember. Drink hearty."

Fuzzy had shot his arrow. They drank. The Lady smiled again the smile of her caste. James enveloped Fuzzy and reconducted him toward the front door. The harp music still softly drifted through the house.

Outside, Black Riley breathed on his cold hands and hugged the gate.

"I wonder," said the Lady to herself, musing, "who—but there were so many who came. I wonder whether memory is a curse or a blessing to them after they have fallen so low."

Fuzzy and his escort were nearly at the door. The Lady called: "James!"

James stalked back obsequiously, leaving Fuzzy waiting unsteadily, with his brief spark of the divine fire gone.

Outside, Black Riley stamped his cold feet and got a firmer grip on his section of gas-pipe.

"You will conduct this gentleman," said the Lady, "downstairs. Then tell Louis to get out the Mercedes and take him to whatever place he wishes to go."

American Literature

Edited by:

Carl Bode—Professor of English, University of Maryland
Leon Howard—Professor of English, University of California at Los Angeles
Louis B. Wright—Director, Folger Shakespeare Library

Volume I—The 17th and 18th Centuries   W • 1090/90¢

Including works of the Colonial and Revolutionary periods, selections by Bradstreet, Taylor, Edwards, Franklin, Bryant, Irving, Cooper, and many others.

Volume II—The First Part of the 19th Century   W • 1091/90¢

Selections fom the works of Poe, Hawthorne, Emerson, Thoreau, Dana, Parkman, Melville, Longfellow, Stowe, Whittier, Simms, and the works of minor writers.

Volume III—The Last Part of the 19th Century   W • 1092/90¢

Civil War verse, and selections by Timrod, Lanier, Jackson, Howells, Whitman, Dickinson, Harte, Ward, Twain, Crane, and others.

Each volume contains critical introductory essays preceding each section as well as biographical information and up-to-date annotated bibliographies for each author.   *Three volume boxed set—$2.70 (#59351)*

Other Distinguished Anthologies of American Literature

THE NEW POCKET ANTHOLOGY OF AMERICAN VERSE. Edited by Oscar Williams. A noted collection spanning the last 300 years, with special emphasis on the writers of the twentieth century.   W • 0908/75¢

A POCKET BOOK OF MODERN AMERICAN SHORT STORIES. Edited by Phillip Van Doren Stern. Stories written during the twenties and thirties by such renowned writers as Hemingway, Fitzgerald, Caldwell, Faulkner, Steinbeck, and Lardner.   W • 0530/60¢

MIDCENTURY. Edited by Orville Prescott. Twenty American short stories written since the end of World War II by such authors as E. B. White, Jean Stafford, Shirley Jackson, and John P. Marquand.
       W • 0265/45¢

THIS IS AMERICA. Edited by Max J. Herzberg. An exciting and diversified collection of stories, lyrics, essays, biographies, papers, orations, and sayings revealing the spirit of America from the Mayflower Compact to FDR.   50083/50¢

LIVING DOCUMENTS IN AMERICAN HISTORY. Edited by John Anthony Scott. A unique collection of over 60 of the most significant political, literary, and folk documents from earliest colonial times to the Civil War—with introductions, bibliography, and songs.   W • 1040/90¢

If your bookseller does not have the titles you want, you may order them by sending retail price, plus 10¢ per book for postage and handling, to: Mail Service Department, Washington Square Press, Inc., 1 West 39th Street, New York, New York 10018. Please enclose check or money order—*do not send cash.* WSP 3/7